DIRT ROAD MAIN STREET

A Novel

CYNTHIA L. CLARK

outskirts press

Outskirts Press, Inc.
http://www.outskirtspress.com

ISBN: 978-1-9772-3450-6

Outskirts Press and the "OP" logo are trademarks belonging to Outskirts Press, Inc.

PRINTED IN THE UNITED STATES OF AMERICA

For the many roads traveled in search of a memory.

He captured my soul in an instant.
I couldn't believe my eyes.
My heart knew right from the start.
But it caught me by surprise.

I always knew there was one for me.
And he was standing there.
But fate had played a trick on us.
He had little time to spare.

But it didn't seem to matter
Passion flared and there's no doubt
It sparked a fire so intense
It could never be put out.

He took my heart and he kept it.
You could say I gave it away.
I never wanted it back again.
But I wanted him to stay.

I knew he was somewhere out there.
I felt it in my soul.
Unless somehow, I could see him again
I never could be whole.

Then one day he found me,
After so many empty years.
That fire had left a tiny spark
Not extinguished by the tears.

Cynthia L. Clark "It Was You, You Are Him"

INTRODUCTION

I was listening to some classic rock-and-roll songs when I heard "Chevy Van" by Sammy Johns from 1973. It's a song about a young man who gives a free-spirited girl a ride in his van. After a brief romantic interlude and at the end of the road, he leaves her on the main street of a tiny town knowing he will never see her again.

As I listened to the lyrics of the song, I asked myself, *what would happen if they did meet again?* And thus, the story of *Dirt Road Main Street* was brought to life, and I was able to elaborate on the simple circumstances in the song and to write the answer to my own rhetorical question.

As in my debut novel, *Boulder Girl, Remember Me When the Moon Hangs Low*, there is an eclectic collection of songs that accompanies Holly Harris and Ben "Tano" Montano throughout the novel, especially since Tano's character is a member of a rock band. I have listed the songs, which range from country to rock to classical, by chapter at the end of the novel and I encourage you to listen to them and to share a memory with Holly and Tano.

CHAPTER 1

"Could I get a large coffee to go?"

A tall, handsome young man with dark curly hair, about thirty years old sat alone at the lunch counter at the Four Corners Diner. He had just finished the Apache breakfast at the diner in southern Colorado.

The middle-aged server, Rosie, nodded. She was taken by the chiseled features of his face, two distinct dimples on his cheeks, the dark moustache that fringed his upper lip, the wavy black hair that curled at the back of his neck. When she approached him with the coffee, she looked directly into his light golden-brown eyes. She sighed wistfully and let her thoughts wander. *Back in the day, I woulda grabbed ahold of that sweet thing and had my way with him.*

"Where ya headed there, young man?"

He looked up at Rosie's bloated face which was masked by heavy makeup. He reached into his faded jeans and pulled out a small wad of cash and handed it to Rosie. "I'm headed into Oklahoma. I got a gig in north Texas. Amarillo. In a couple of days."

"A gig? Are you some kind of a rock star or something?" Rosie blatantly batted her eyes at him.

"Naw. Not a rock star. I play bass guitar with a couple of other guys. Maybe you heard of us. Badge. We do some country and some rock, play some covers, classic rock, some blues, some original stuff, too. I'm meeting up with the band on Wednesday."

"Hey, ya got an album? A CD or something?" Rosie continued to flirt with him but clearly to no avail.

"Yeah, we made a CD a while back. Let me go out to my van and see if I got any out there. But you can catch us on YouTube, too."

Rosie watched as he walked out the door to his custom painted blue and white Chevy van. His shoulders were broad and muscular, and his abs were tight. *Football player. Nice ass. I like a man with a fine ass.*

The inside of the van was warming from the early morning sun. He fished around in the console and glove box and found what he was looking for and strolled back to the diner. Rosie stood by the window watching him.

"Here ya go. Give it a listen. It's okay. Not the greatest recording but it'll give you an idea of what we play."

Rosie took the *Dusty Highway* CD from him and held it to her big bosomed chest. "Thank you, stranger. I'll give it a listen. Hey, maybe you could sign your autograph on this?" Rosie handed him a paper napkin and took a pen from her shirt pocket.

"Sure. My friends call me Tano. I'm Benjamin Cody Montano."

"Pleased to make your acquaintance, Benjamin Cody Montano. You stop on back here if you come through Springfield again. Drive safe now."

"Sure thing." Tano grabbed the coffee and winked at Rosie. She blushed slightly but it was invisible under the pancake makeup on her face.

Tano called Boulder, Colorado, his home, but he was rarely there. He was part owner of a trendy rustic tequila bar called Tumbleweed. He had traveled with his band for most of the past year as their popularity began to spread across the west. He returned to Boulder to visit his family for the past week, in between Badge gigs. His mother's health had not been good for the past few months and he needed to see for himself how she was. He was encouraged by her recovery and had a positive vibe when he left.

Tano could have flown and met the band. But he had another reason for making the road trip. He knew that on his way to Amarillo he could take a detour route through Oklahoma. There was a tiny town, Sage, that was his destination. There was a girl there. Well, he hoped she was there. It had been five years since he left her there on a dirt road main street in that tiny town. And in the years that followed, he thought about her often, until he was tired of just thinking about her. He wanted to see her, hear her, touch her again. He knew it was a long shot. A girl like that wouldn't stay in a small town for long.

On this August Sunday morning, as he pulled away from the diner and out onto the highway, his thoughts turned to her again. His windshield was a movie screen as he watched the memories of her unfold. Holly. Her name was Holly.

CHAPTER 2

FIVE YEARS EARLIER

"Hey, dude. Why don't you take these amps in your van? You only got a couple of guitars. We're full up over here." The short, pudgy lead guitarist from Badge, Randy Larson, gestured to Tano as they proceeded to load up. They just finished a show in San Angelo, Texas. The next stop would be Garden City, Kansas, in two days.

"Yeah, sure," Tano mumbled. Randy dragged the equipment over to Tano's van and loaded it in the back. There was still room for more gear, but it was already tucked away in the back of Randy's pickup under the topper.

"Here, slide Rocky's fiddle in there, too. Okay, that's it. See ya in Garden City on Thursday. Rocky, Jack and me are headin' out now. You?"

"I think I'll head out in the morning. Gonna check out the Super 8 up the road." Tano followed them out onto the road and turned at the next stop light. Normally they traveled caravan style. But Tano needed some time alone to get away from the weed, away from the booze, away from the women, away from the noise of the guys, just to think.

He was tired, but the vibration of the concert still rang in his ears. The last song of the set, a Zac Brown Band ballad, "Free," played over and over in his head. He instinctively moved his fingers on his left hand as if they were still resting on the neck of the guitar. Fortunately, it was one of his favorite songs.

He checked into a room, threw his monogrammed leather bag on a chair, and fell into bed. As he often did to fall asleep, he hummed a Spanish tune to himself that his mother had taught him as a child. But "Free" still played in his head.

Tano woke when the sun peeked through a crack in the heavy dark brown curtain. He turned on the TV for some noise, showered and threw his gear into his bag. He had noticed that there was a little diner across the road from the Super 8 when he pulled in the night before. When he walked across the street, he couldn't help but notice a beautiful red-haired girl standing near the front door of the diner.

She was in her twenties, copper wavy hair to her waist, average height, but the holey faded jeans revealed long tan legs. She looked steadily toward the road as if she was waiting for someone. She turned and smiled slightly at Tano when he passed by her, but quickly looked away.

Tano sat in a booth near the front window where he could still see the girl. Every few minutes she pulled her phone out of her jean jacket pocket and looked at it. She wore several silver and turquoise bracelets that she shook on her left arm from time to time. Probably for something to do while she waited. Tano finished the eggs, bacon, home fries, and whole wheat toast that he ordered.

A waitress brought a coffee refill. She noticed that he saw the girl. "That poor little gal was here all night waitin' for some jerk. Pretty little thing drank a whole pot of coffee and a Coca-Cola. I told her no bus would be swingin' by here until noon."

"She must be wired with all of that caffeine. Thanks." He left a tip on the table and walked up to the hostess and paid for his meal.

The girl was still standing there when he opened the door of the diner. He started to walk toward his van, but on an impulse, he turned and walked back toward her. Something made him want to speak to her. Something told him that he would regret it if he didn't.

"Hey, uh, you need a lift somewhere or something?"

"A guy—a friend—was supposed to give me a ride back home last night after the Badge concert. I've been calling him. I don't know where he is. I think he got high and ditched me. He's a dumbass anyway." She looked toward the road.

"Where's home?"

"Oklahoma. In the Panhandle."

"I'm headed to Garden City, Kansas, and driving through Oklahoma. Want a ride?" The girl looked at him with serious light blue eyes. He could see slight apprehension as she spun the offer in her mind. "I'm sure that your mama told you never to ride with strangers. So I'm Tano. We aren't strangers anymore." Tano smiled at her and reached out to shake her hand.

She took her sunglasses off and looked at him with tired baby blue eyes which widened with recognition as she shook his hand. "Tano? Tano from Badge?" Tano nodded. She studied his face for a few moments and softly said, "Okay, for a few miles." She took her phone out of her pocket and held it in her hand for security and walked with him to his van.

"You just let me know when you want to get out." He hoped that it wouldn't be soon. He was drawn to her and wanted to get to know her.

"You know, I've never hitched before. And the only reason I am is that I love your music. So I guess you're okay. My name is Holly." Tano smiled at her weak logic. She leaned her head back on the head rest and closed her eyes. After only a few miles, she nodded off a few times but shook herself awake, not wanting to be unaware of the stranger who drove her.

Tano reached over and lightly touched her leg and said, "Dream of rock and roll." But she didn't hear him. She was already asleep.

CHAPTER 3

Holly continued to doze as Tano drove through Texas. He listened to country music quietly and glanced at her periodically. She continued to hold her phone in her hand. The big fabric purse she carried had fallen off her lap and onto the floor. For some reason, her sitting in the seat next to him felt natural and good. After about an hour, she began to stir and yawn. She looked around and tried to remember where she was.

"Where are we now? How long have I been asleep?"

"An hour or so. Well, sleepy head, we are near a little town called Aspermont. Pretty much in the center of Texas with a way to go before the Oklahoma Panhandle. Are you hungry or anything? It's almost noon."

"Could you stop somewhere so I can use the restroom? I had a gallon of coffee back there."

"Sure." They continued to ride in silence while Holly looked out at the Texas prairie. The sun shining on her through the windshield warmed her skin and Tano could smell the light perfume she wore. Or maybe it was her hair. Lilies of the valley—like the fragrance worn by a girl he once dated in high school.

"I really appreciate the lift. I was getting tired of waiting to leave back there." Her mood seemed to have improved with the nap and she appeared more beautiful. Her cheeks were rosy, and her long hair drifted down her arms in gold and copper ringlets. She gestured while she spoke and the bracelets on her arm jingled. She began to squirm in her seat. Tano knew that he needed to stop soon. A billboard pointed to a Phillips 66 station three miles up the road. Tano pulled into the station. As soon as the van stopped, Holly jumped out and went inside. Tano took his time and filled his tank. Soon Holly emerged with her jean jacket tied around her waist.

"Come in with me. Let's get some snacks for the road." Tano suggested.

Holly grabbed her bag and went inside with him. She picked up a bag of red licorice.

"I always travel with red licorice," she said to Tano.

"Well, then let's get some. How about some Cheetos? Apples? What suits your fancy?"

"Anything. I always eat light." Tano grabbed a couple of apples that looked fresh, a small bag of Cheetos and a couple of bottles of water. "Here, I'll get the licorice—if you let me have some."

"Thanks, I'll share."

Soon they were back on the road, and Holly opened up.

She told Tano that she was born and raised in Sage, Oklahoma, and that she was twenty-two. She had two brothers and a sister. Her father was a farm machinery mechanic. Her mother raised goats, made cheese, yogurt and jam, and wrote cookbooks. They both worked on the small farm that they owned. She graduated from high school a year early and attended a community college for two years then transferred to the University of Colorado in Colorado Springs and just graduated with a degree in economics and a minor in dance.

"I always wanted to be a dancer. I loved ballet and I advanced as far as I could but because of where we live, dance instructors would come and go. Besides, what would anyone do with a degree in dance? I just graduated a couple of months ago and I've been taking a little time to chill and figure it out."

"So, is that guy—the one who left you in San Angelo—your boyfriend?"

"No, he would like to be. There's no chemistry there and I don't just hook up." Holly quickly changed the subject. "Tell me about you. Other than you play bass guitar with Badge." She smiled at him and touched his arm for a moment.

Tano told her that he was born and raised in Boulder with three brothers and a sister. He played football in high school and at CU as a running back. After he graduated with a degree in business administration, he partnered up with his college roommate and bought the Tumbleweed Bar about three years before.

"It's on the Pearl Street Mall which is the trendy place to hang when you're in Boulder. We carry select brands of tequila, local brews and gourmet fusion pizza. But my band, well, Badge, came together in college. The typical garage band, playing around when we could. But all four of us wanted to take it all the way and so we travel. And now I'm here with you heading to another gig. I don't know what will come of it, but now's the time to give it a shot in case one of us decides to settle down."

"Well, I'm a fan. I first heard your music on the *Dusty Highway* CD that my college roommate played. I liked it so much she burned me a copy. Oh, jeez—you probably don't like knowing that."

Tano laughed. "I know that happens. But your roommate made you a fan and so it's all good."

"Do you have a girlfriend in Boulder? Or somewhere else?"

"Sort of. There's a girl that I see when I'm home there. Rochelle. But we're not exclusive. Really just good friends. I'm gone a lot and I don't expect her to just sit around and wait for me to come back every so often. And she doesn't."

Holly was quiet and looked out the window at the passing scenery, which was a redundant blur of sage brush and cactus. Tano was aware of the sudden silence.

"What about you? Got a boyfriend? A fiancé?"

"No, not now. I had a boyfriend in college. It was serious, I thought. But marriage to him would have been a mistake, trapped me, confined me. He was into himself more than he was into me. He moved on and got engaged to someone else. I have a couple of friends I hang with, and I'm good. I'm only twenty-two. No regrets."

Silence again and then Holly softly asked, "Tano, could you turn on some Badge music? When I hear that music again, I'll always think of this ride with you. It's not often that a girl from Oklahoma gets to hitch with a guitarist from a rock band."

"Sure." He found a Badge playlist on his phone. Whenever he listened to Badge tracks, his critical ear would hear mistakes or a stanza that could be improved instead of just enjoying the music. But today, his thoughts were on Holly and not the tunes. He liked her already.

As Tano watched the road ahead, he saw a gigantic white fluffy thunderhead building height in the distance. It looked like a monstrous thunderstorm was looming directly in the path ahead of them. He would keep an eye on it but wondered if he should detour to Lubbock.

"Do you need to be home today? There is a big storm up ahead. See it? I don't know if I should turn off and head to Lubbock or stay the course and see which way it moves, but I don't want to cause you to be late somewhere."

"I guess I would stay the course if I was driving. I don't want to be the reason you alter your plans."

"I'm good. Maybe you want to catch a bus in Lubbock. Maybe you're ready to go your own way. Maybe…"

Holly interrupted him. "I'm good for now. I'll tell you where I want you to let me out. I appreciate the ride so much. No one will believe that I was with you for a few hours today. But I don't want to impose."

"I enjoy the company, a new face. A pretty face." Tano smiled at her. Holly took her sunglasses off and smiled back. Tano could see her eyes. So clear and crystal blue.

Just as Tano thought, about twenty-five minutes later, a pounding rain began to fall. His windshield wipers could barely keep up with the deluge. A sign on the side of the road pointed to a roadside rest stop two miles up the road. Tano's van limped along the drenched highway while he struggled to see the road through the blur of rain on his windshield.

"There it is. We have to stop here for now." Rain noisily pounded the top and hood of the van. Lightning surged all around them with immediate crashing booms of thunder. The rain developed into small slushy hail and soon to balls of ice that plummeted and then bounced off the van. "This has to move over us soon."

Tano could see that Holly was stressed by the proximity of the lightning bolts and noise of the thunder as she flinched with each flash and crash. "Come here." Tano reached his arms out to Holly. "It's okay."

Holly immediately leaned into Tano with the console between them. Tano pulled her into his seat, onto his lap, with her long legs stretched out over the console onto the passenger side and just held her close. He discovered that it was her hair that carried the scent of the lilies of the valley. He felt her jolt slightly every time the thunder crashed. He was wrong—the storm was so big and wide and moving so slowly that it remained hanging over them. He turned her face toward his and looked into her eyes. And then he kissed her. Her lips were soft and warm. The kiss, which began as a gentle gesture, became more intense and deeper than either of them expected. Holly was genuinely into him. At least for that moment. It would have to be up to her if things went any further. He didn't want to see himself as a guy who picked up a hitchhiker just for a lay.

He soon found out where she wanted to go with the kiss. She unbuttoned the light green gauzy shirt that she wore exposing perfect little breasts in a rose-colored bra. She tried to straddle his lap, but the steering wheel was in the way.

"Let's get into the back." She stepped over the console and into the back seat. Tano followed and hastily moved things to make room for them. Holly laid on her back with Tano on top of her. He looked at her face and into her eyes. "Do you want this?"

"Yes, yes, I do," she said breathlessly. He felt her heart pounding in her chest. She was liquid and warm and ready with no need for foreplay. Clothes were unbuttoned, unzipped and tossed aside. As the rain and hail continued to wash over the van, Tano and Holly were passionately entwined as one accompanied by flashes of lightning and wild thunder until the finish.

\

CHAPTER 4

The Chevy van was a sauna from the humidity which encased it and the throbbing heat inside. Tano raised his head a few inches from Holly's face. Her eyes were closed and there was a slight smile on her lips. She opened her eyes and Tano gazed directly into them for few seconds. He noticed that one of her crystal blue eyes had a small unique speck of brown in it that couldn't be noticed from a distance. Holly looked away and rested her arm across her damp forehead. The hair near her face fell across the back seat in wet ringlets. Tano sat up and saw a little puddle of sweat in the hollow of her stomach. His hair and chest were dripping wet. He opened the window a few inches. The rain was still falling but gently now.

Holly sat up, rolled the window down beside her. She turned her face into the slight breeze that flowed in from the opening, closed her eyes and drew in a deep breath.

"Come here." Tano gestured to Holly. She scooted close to him and leaned into his shoulder. He put his arm around her. She was quiet and he wasn't sure what she was thinking. "Are you good?"

"Oh, yes," Holly responded in a voice that was almost a whisper. They sat in silence, still undressed, and listened to the light drip drop of the rain on the windshield of the van. "Tano?" she paused. "Tano?" Another pause as she collected her thoughts. "What just happened here—I wanted it. Everything about it felt right. I've never done anything like that before."

"Holly, it's good. I wanted it, too." Tano kept his response short. He could see that she was stressing about what he thought about her and he wanted to put her mind at ease. He pulled her closer to him and planted a light kiss on her cheek. After a minute or two, Holly began to gather her clothes from the floor of the backseat and slip them on. Tano slid on his jeans and buttoned his shirt.

"Do you think there's a restroom around here?" The windows of the van were completely fogged over. Tano opened the door, put one foot out and looked around.

"Yeah, over there. There's a bathroom."

Holly reached over the front seat and grabbed her fabric bag, slipped on her sandals, hopped out and trotted to the restroom. Although the rain continued to lightly fall, the roads were still covered in water, primed for hydroplaning. Tano decided that they wouldn't leave yet. While he waited for Holly, he reached into the back of the van, opened a guitar case, and took out his Fender acoustic guitar and began to strum the strings. His thoughts about Holly were confusing him. On the one hand, he had dozens, maybe a hundred one-night stands before. There was never a shortage of women when you play the guitar. When he was done with those women, he was done. Never another thought about them. But he already knew that Holly, for whatever reason, even though he barely knew her, was someone he wouldn't forget. Maybe their encounter at the diner was meant to be. She was gentle, down to earth, genuinely loving, and sensitive, too. But he felt a sudden twinge of regret knowing that soon they would arrive in Oklahoma, or sooner if she wanted to, she would be gone, and it was unlikely he would ever see her again.

Holly hopped back into the van. Fresh air whooshed into the steamy van when she opened the door. Her sandaled feet were spattered with mud from the parking lot. Her cheeks were rosy, her hair still in ringlets. The fresh air boosted her spirits. The doubt that she had about her uncharacteristically forward behavior disappeared, although she would always wonder about it.

"You have your guitar! Are you going to play?" Holly's voice sounded almost childlike.

"Yep, a little serenade. Unplugged. While we wait out this storm." He began to strum randomly at first until he chose a song in his mind. Appropriately, "Purple Rain," a Prince song that Badge played at the concert in San Angelo. The acoustic guitar couldn't match the electric intensity of the concert version, but when Tano looked at Holly's face, he knew it didn't matter. She touched her fingers to her lips and smiled at him. For a second, it looked like she was tearing up, but she blinked the tears away.

When he finished the song, she grinned widely at him, clapped, and then leaned forward and hugged him around his neck. "Thank you, Tano," she gushed. "I wish I had remembered to pick up my phone to record it. I've never heard 'Purple Rain' sound so pure."

Pointing to the back of the van, Holly asked, "Tano? Is that a violin back there?"

"Yes. It's Rocky's fiddle."

"Do you think he would mind if I took a look at it?"

"No. He isn't going to know anyway." He leaned over the back seat, opened the violin case, and handed the violin and bow to Holly. She turned in the seat to make room for her elbow and began to delicately slide the bow across the strings—at first just developing a feel for it, listening to detect if it was in tune.

"This Realist violin is first-class quality. Acoustic and electric in one instrument. Very nice." Then she began to play it. A delicate, melancholy classical tune with such great precision and skill that Tano's mouth fell open slightly.

"That was beautiful. I don't know what to say. Holly, you said you were a dancer, but I had no idea about the violin."

"Well, the one constant in my little town was the piano and violin teacher, Mrs. Dixon. So when I wasn't dancing, or helping my mom milk the goats, I played the violin to pass the time. I hope I didn't embarrass myself, playing a classical tune to a rocker. Maybe it was silly. But I thought I owed you one."

"I appreciate all music. What was that piece you played? The melody was so sad."

"It was Chopin. Nocturne in C-sharp Minor. I memorized it once for a recital and never forgot it." Holly laid the violin in her lap and held the bow.

Tano began to lightly strum the guitar to continue the impromptu give and take of the mini concert that evolved. Holly immediately recognized the beginning chords. "Free," the Zac Brown song that Badge played last at the concert. Holly spontaneously put the violin to her chin and began to play accompaniment to the song. She knew it so well, having played along with a Zac Brown CD at home one day when there was nothing to do but practice the violin or dance.

The unity of the two instruments was in perfect harmony, as if they had rehearsed it together many times. Like their love making had been. Once again, neither thought to pull their phone out to record the one-time experience. But they would never forget it. To them both, it was surreal. How did a day that began with so much disappointment become as magical as this one? Holly's heart began to feel heavy. Those stunning moments with Tano were fleeting. They would separate, probably forever, in a matter of hours when they ventured through Oklahoma. Holly sadly noticed that the rain had stopped. Tano saw it, too.

CHAPTER 5

"Holly? I guess we should head out."

It was late afternoon and the sun peaked between gray clouds drifting overhead. The rainwater was transformed into a mist above the road. Tano touched Holly lightly with his fingertips on her bare leg exposed by the tear in her faded blue jeans.

Holly laid her hand on his knee and said, "Yes. I suppose it is time to go." They put the instruments away and returned to the front seat. They were quiet as they drove away from the rest stop. To Holly, that little spot in the van in a thunderstorm in Texas had been a like a cocoon that encircled them for a few hours, in complete isolation from the rest of the world, leaving them alone to create some magic for themselves.

Tano, who was never one to be aware of his feelings in any depth, consciously felt a little sense of loss. Loss of those special moments with Holly that could never be duplicated and were burned into his memory. What was it about that girl? He couldn't put it into the right words.

Holly attempted to shake away the sadness that began to overtake her. She made a conscious decision to make some more memories and not let her sad thoughts ruin the rest of the ride. The drive wasn't over. There was still time. Maybe there would be some more magic.

Holly pulled her phone out and sent a text to someone. "I just texted that guy who was supposed to give me a ride and let him know I was on my way home. Not that he cares, but in case he did." Tano nodded. She turned her phone off to conserve its charge and tossed it into her purse. She grabbed a few pieces of red licorice.

"Are you hungry? I was thinking we should stop in Amarillo to eat something. What do you think?"

"Sure. I think I am. That would be great." Holly dug deep into her fabric bag and pulled out some cash. "Here you go. Gas money. I didn't expect a free ride from anybody."

"Put it away. I had to go through here anyway. The only difference now is that I have someone to accompany me. And I'm happy that you're here. Just chill. I don't care about the money." Tano's eyes were on the road ahead. Holly sat cross-legged on the seat and watched the Texas panorama whiz past them. Tano occasionally rested his hand on her leg.

Tano found some music on his phone. Not Badge. A playlist mix that he made for himself. On the road songs. "Turn the Page," Bob Seger. "Running on Empty," Jackson Browne. "Pink Cadillac," Bruce Springsteen. The silence began to feel awkward and artificial as if there was something to be said that neither wanted to say. Holly broke the silence. "So, after Garden City? Where to next?"

"Well, our next stop is actually in Denver. We are opening for Maroon 5. It's the first time we'll open for a band of that caliber. It'll be great exposure. Two nights. I'll get the chance to spend some time in Boulder, check in on the Tumbleweed and see if it's still standing, and say hi to the family. I invited them to the concert, but my dad can't handle the noise and the crowds of people. One of my brothers will be there. Then we are off to Albuquerque, Phoenix, and a couple of venues in California."

"You play some Maroon 5 in your concerts. You know, 'Moves Like Jagger' and 'Harder to Breathe.' Will you perform those when you're with them?"

Tano laughed. "No way. That would be bold. Nah, we'll stick with original stuff and a couple covers. We get about forty-five minutes to open. What about you when you get home?"

Holly looked ahead through the windshield as she gathered her thoughts. "I don't know. I thought I would figure it out this summer, but it flew by and here I am with no real direction. I was just so relieved to be finished with college. I need to find a job and then I might want to move unless I can commute from Sage. I guess it will all fall into place when the time is right. I'm through milking goats." She turned and smiled at Tano.

The sun had never fully emerged from the storm. They drove into Amarillo when it appeared to be dusk, but sunset wouldn't occur for two hours. "Well, what are you up for? Burgers? Tex-Mex? Barbecue? Pizza? Sushi? I know a couple of places."

"Tex-Mex sounds good. And a margarita, too."

"You got it." Tano drove through Amarillo directly to a Tex-Mex restaurant/bar that he knew downtown called Cactus Road. Poles with a flag of Mexico and a Texas flag were posted on either side of the door. Tano grabbed Holly's hand as they walked through the parking lot. To Holly it felt like they were royalty.

Tano directed them through a wide white arch to a booth in the bar. Rusty colored adobe tiles covered the floors. The walls were a marigold color with arched openings between the bar and the sprawling dining room. The seats were covered with brown leather and the tabletops were brown, gold and black granite. Arched recesses spanned the walls of the dining room which held hand-painted murals of villages and brightly dressed villagers. The bar opened into a spacious tiled patio that was surrounded by lush greenery that sprouted red, orange, and purple flowers. Tano had made the right choice to bring them into the bar. Holly knew that she wasn't dressed for a fancy place like that wearing holey jeans and sandals with mud speckled feet. Tano would look good anywhere and she noticed a few of the patrons turn to look at him.

"Good evening, señor and señorita. My name is Federico and I'll be your server tonight. Can I bring you some cervesa, a margarita, sangria?"

"I would like, I guess, just the house margarita," Holly ordered without hesitation.

Tano interrupted. "Bring her a Patron margarita. I'll have a Tecate."

"This place is so big and fancy for Tex-Mex."

"It's the best that Texas has to offer, and we were lucky that it was on our route to Oklahoma." Holly looked down at her hands resting in her lap when Tano mentioned her home state. Each mile that they traveled brought them closer to the end of their experience together. She began to play with the dangly silver and garnet earring on her right ear and looked out toward the patio.

"What's up?" Tano noticed a little change in her mood.

"Nothing. Just looking around. Taking it all in so I remember it." Holly sighed and looked directly at him and smiled and then began to turn the bracelets on her left arm and rearrange herself in the booth.

The waiter brought the drinks, chips and guacamole, and took their order. Holly ordered barbacoa street tacos. Tano ordered carne asada.

"This is the best guacamole and these chips are made fresh. I can tell. And this margarita is the best I've tasted." Holly steered the conversation away from where it was leading. She didn't want to talk about going home. She didn't want to talk about saying goodbye. She didn't want it to end. But it would.

"It's the Patron and the fresh lime juice. But you're too young to have had too many of these," Tano teased. Holly smiled and shook her head. "Holly, you know, it will be dark when we get into Oklahoma. I don't feel good about leaving you there, somewhere, wherever that will be, in the middle of the night. How do you feel about us getting a hotel room—or rooms—for the night and I can deliver you to the Panhandle tomorrow morning? I'm leaving it up to you. I'm not due in Garden City until Thursday. But if you need to be home tonight, we can make it."

Holly felt a little leap of excitement. She wanted to blurt out "yes, yes," but kept her cool enough to casually say, "I don't have to be home tonight. Tomorrow is okay." She had to admit to herself that she was so attracted to Tano and was positively infatuated with him since the thunderous lovemaking in the van. But logic admonished her that it would never be more than what it was. It would end in a matter of hours.

"Okay, it's a deal." Tano wasn't ready to say goodbye either. He was secretly glad that he easily convinced her to stay with him. He guessed he would ask her later if she wanted her own room. She wouldn't.

Federico brought the meals. While they ate, a strolling trio of colorful mariachis serenaded them with *"Te Amaré Toda la Vida."*

"What does that mean?" Holly asked them when they finished the emotional Mexican ballad.

"Te Amare Toda la Vida? I'll love you my whole life. I sing it for you both. *Bella pareja.*" Holly looked inquisitively at the singer in the wide Mexican sombrero. He leaned toward her and said, "That means beautiful couple."

"Gracias, señor," Tano knew very few Spanish words except for those he had just spoken. Holly's eyes widened as she looked at Tano who laughed when he saw her face.

"Let him think I know Spanish. It's all good." And Tano left it at that.

CHAPTER 6

"Another margarita, señorita?" Tano asked with a mock Spanish accent.

Holly rolled her eyes and smiled. "Are you having another beer?"

"Sure, why not. We've got tonight." Tano replied. He motioned for the server and ordered drinks.

Out of the corner of Tano's eye, he saw a trio of giggling, pretty young women, about Holly's age, clumsily approach the table, carrying a black Sharpie. "You look like Tano from Badge. Are you? Can we have your autograph?" one of them asked. The giggling continued. All three of them wore cowboy hats. One of them, a tall, pretty brunette, wore short cutoff jeans that exposed her lower butt cheeks.

"Yeah, I'm Tano. I guess I could." He looked at Holly. He didn't want to be rude. She smiled at him and nodded her head.

"Oh, Tano. I'm your biggest fan. Would you sign the back pocket of my jeans?" asked the brunette in the very short shorts.

"Jeez, I guess so." Tano obliged, calculating where to put his hands while he signed his name.

"Tano, could you sign the back of my T-shirt?" asked the short blonde with long braids and a freckled nose.

"Me, too, please?" asked the last one, a chesty, curvy Latina with curly hair that popped out from under her black cowboy hat and framed her face.

"We just saw you in San Angelo at the concert. Badge is awesome!" She looked at Holly and then looked away.

"Thanks there, ladies." Patrons in the bar witnessed the scene and began to wonder who the celebrity was sitting among them. Tano saw them point and smile at him. The three giggling girls asked Tano if they could take a selfie with him. He obliged. Their faces surrounded his as he forced a smile.

"Thanks, Tano," one of them gushed. "We'll be seeing you next time you're in Texas." They shuffled back to their table. The selfie with them gave Tano an idea. When the waiter brought their drinks, he asked him to take a photo of Holly with him.

"Scoot on over here on my side." Tano motioned for Holly to join him on his side of the booth. "Why are you sitting way over there anyway?" He put his arm around her, they both smiled, as the waiter took a couple of shots.

"One more, please? For me." Holly turned her phone on and handed it to the server, who politely obliged. "Thanks so much. No one will believe that I caught a ride with you." After she looked at the photo, she turned her phone off and tossed it in her purse

Tano pulled her closer to him. "No one will believe that I found a pretty redhead like you on a drive through Texas." While they drank their drinks, Tano googled, found a nearby hotel, and called to see if a room was available. As luck would have it, a room was available at the Embassy Suites which he reserved. "We'll be there in about an hour."

The mariachi band took a break and the server approached their table. "Care for another?"

Holly shook her head no. Tano asked him to bring the check. "Let's go, lovely lady." As they got up to leave, they were faced with the turning heads and curious glances of the others in the bar. Even if he hadn't been, Tano had the looks of a rock star—long wavy dark hair, great moustache, tan, awesome build, faded jeans and cowboy boots, wearing a silver St. Christopher's medal around his neck, a belt with a turquoise and silver buckle. He put his arm around Holly and looped his finger in the belt loop of her jeans as they walked to let everyone know that she was with him.

On the way to the hotel, Tano stopped at a liquor store and bought a six pack of Shock Top beer and a bottle of pinot noir, not knowing where the night would take them. They checked into the hotel with a room on the third floor. The room was dark when they entered, and its picture window revealed the glitter of the city lights as the night sky darkened.

"I really want to take a hot shower." Holly grabbed her bag and began to walk toward the bathroom.

"Go on ahead." Tano grabbed a beer out of the six pack, popped the top, and leaned back on the bed while he waited for her. He turned the TV on, but he didn't really watch it. They were about seventy miles from the Oklahoma panhandle. Holly would be leaving him the next day. Tano liked to live in the moment, but for a few minutes, he thought about the future and not seeing her again. He listened to the shower water run and then turn off.

In a few minutes, Holly emerged, fresh faced, wet hair descending in ringlets down her back and across her shoulders, wearing a large black Badge T-shirt that she must have bought after the concert, and a pair of cutoff jeans.

"I'm glad that I had something clean to wear. I didn't think I would catch a ride with a member of Badge when I bought this shirt." She smiled and looked down at the gold badge imprinted on the front of the shirt. She grabbed a beer from the six pack, popped the top, slid the bottle cap into her pocket, and plopped down on the bed next to Tano. She sat cross-legged next to him.

"Well, it's still early. Want to go clubbing, take in the streets of Amarillo, or just stay here, watch a movie? We don't have to do anything."

"Can we just chill here for a while?" Holly didn't want to share the time she had left with him. She leaned back and stretched out her long tan legs.

"Sure. Whatever you want." They lay there, tipped their beers, looked at the TV, but their thoughts wandered. Holly thought about what her friends would say when she told them she had been with Ben Montano. But Tano thought about lyrics to an old song he remembered that reminded him of her, "Chevy Van."

"I have some weed in the van. Want me to get it?"

"No. Weed just doesn't do it for me. Have some if you want."

"Don't really care to tonight."

Holly rested her left hand on the bed. Tano reached over and laid his hand on top of hers. "Tano, there's still time before you drop me off. I want to know more about you. Tell me what it's like to tour. Tell me what's your favorite Badge song. Tell me who you've met on tour. I want to know more..." Holly's voice faded as she began to wonder if she had pried too much.

"The touring's all right because it's part of my job. Like any job, you just adapt to it. Sleeping in different places every night is kind of a drag. Being around the guys all the time gets old too sometimes. But we've met some awesome people. Like members of The Fray were in the audience one night. Alan Jackson another time. He came backstage to meet us. Hell of a nice guy. One time, we met Eric Clapton. You know 'Badge,' our signature cover song is his. He gave us a thumbs up for our rendition of it. I would have to say it's one of my favorite songs and it is tied to our band's identity. I'm kind of tired of some of the songs in our sets, but the fans love them and that's what they expect from us. I have a couple of favorites." He squeezed her hand.

"So, do you picture yourself, like the Stones, doing this for fifty years?"

Tano laughed. "Naw, nobody will remember us in fifty years. Maybe ten years if we're lucky. Maybe if one of our original songs hits the charts."

"Did you write any of the original Badge songs?"

"Yeah, I wrote a couple of them. 'Somewhere Along the Way,' 'A Trip to Nowhere,' and uh, let's see here—yeah, 'Waiting for the Chance.'"

"Those are yours? Those are great songs."

"Yeah, somebody in the rock business once told me that to make it big, a band had to write its own stuff. The covers are great, but they originally belong to somebody else." Tano slid off the bed, set his beer down. "Just a second. I'll be back." Holly finished the beer and set the bottle on the nightstand. She closed her eyes and began to fall asleep and was startled when Tano entered the room again, carrying a guitar. After all, she had been up all night the night before.

"Oh, man, did I scare you? Asleep already?"

"I musta dozed off—the drinks, the shower, staying up all night. You brought your guitar in? Worried about it getting stolen or something?"

"No, I thought I would play a couple of songs while we hang out here."

"Awesome." Holly sat up and opened another beer.

Tano began to strum and play his original song, "Somewhere Along the Way." It was a ballad with simple melody and lyrics that said so much.

> *"I met someone that I'll never forget*
> *On a road on a rainy day*
> *She was beautiful, kind and full of spirit*
> *Somewhere along the way.*
>
> *Her face gave away her every thought*
> *Although she masked them with words she'd say*
> *I saw in her eyes what she denied.*
> *Somewhere along the way.*
>
> *The days were short, the nights were, too*
> *She had given her heart away*
> *To me, I know, I've held it since then*
> *Somewhere along the way.*
>
> *But the time we had was soon gone.*
> *I left her and didn't stay.*
> *I feel her love encircle me still*
> *Somewhere along the way."*

Holly watched him play. He looked at her face as he moved his left hand from chord to chord on the neck of the guitar. She began to feel a little longing in her heart. The lyrics were taunting her.

"So was that song written for a certain person?" Holly was curious. The poetry seemed to point to someone special.

"No, not one," Tano paused. "Maybe several."

"Did you love 'em and leave 'em?"

Tano scratched his cheek and rubbed his chin. "Yeah, I guess I did."

Holly didn't really want to know about his past with women and let it go at that. She clapped and smiled. "More, more! Encore!" Tano launched into an unplugged acoustic version of "Badge," which didn't rival the electric stage version, but Holly was impressed anyway. She set her beer down on the nightstand and curled up next to him and laid her head against his upper thigh. She could feel the vibration of the guitar strings against her face and heard the echo of his voice in his torso. Tano put the guitar down, stretched out, and laid down next to her, face to face.

"Okay, mystery girl. I know you play the violin, and dance, and studied econ. I know you milk goats and are a Badge fan. What else makes you tick?"

Holly rolled her eyes and blushed. He was so close, and she suddenly felt awkward and embarrassed by her inexperience. "I guess I would have to think about that. I don't know. I've had a quiet life so far. I know that I haven't tapped into my full potential and I'm not even sure what that is either. What can I say?"

"Well, just answer this. What fills your days with happiness? I just want to know you better."

"Music. Writing in my journal. I run. Hang with my friends. I dance. Not much, compared to you."

"Oh, you will find your way. But for now, this moment, you are with me." Tano decided not to press her further. She was clearly uncomfortable with the questions and began to squirm and look away from him. He turned her face toward him and kissed her. And then he kissed her again, deeper, and slipped his hand under the Badge shirt and unhooked her bra. She began to breathe harder.

She unbuttoned his shirt, threw it open and pulled her shirt off over her head, and laid down on his bare chest. Their kisses became more insistent and passionate. He rolled her onto her back and unbuttoned her shorts and slipped his hand inside. She wiggled out of them and laid completely naked on top of the white comforter on the bed. Tano was more than ready for what was to come and threw his clothes off and onto the floor.

The love making was explosive and burned hotter than it had in the back seat of the van earlier in the day. All sprawled out on the bed, they fully experienced each other's bodies in every way, and then over again. They fell away from one another, rolled on their backs drenched in sweat, faces rosy and flushed, glowing with satisfaction. Neither spoke a word for a few moments while they caught their breath and let their bodies cool down. Tano laid his hand on Holly's stomach. She turned on to her right side and snuggled close to him. Beyond the tingle of the love making, Holly began to feel butterflies in her stomach. Adrenalin that comes with the exhilaration of falling in love began to shoot through her body. It was completely unexpected, illogical, impractical, and ridiculous, but she wasn't going to fight it. Let it come.

"That was fantastic." Tano eventually spoke. Holly pulled herself closer to him and nuzzled her nose into his neck. When he turned his face toward her, his moustache tickled her cheek.

"Yes. Unbelievable." Holly smiled and crinkled her nose. She was at a loss for a meaningful word to describe what had just happened. She entwined the fingers of her left hand with his right hand as they continued to embrace. Neither wanted those intimate moments to end, though they knew their encounter would end soon.

After several minutes, Tano sat up and pulled his shorts on. Holly reached down to the end of the bed and found her panties. Tano walked over to the table near the window in the room and opened the bottle of pinot noir. "Want some wine? I feel like a little celebrating after all of that." Tano smiled from ear to ear. Holly grinned back at him.

She got up from the bed, still topless, took a glass of wine and joined him on a tan upholstered loveseat across the room. They tapped their glasses together. "To us tonight," Tano toasted. He looked at Holly and saw a little sadness creep into her crystal blue eyes.

"What's up, baby?"

Holly looked down. "Just that this has to end. I have to go home. You have to go to Kansas." Just then there was a knock on the door that interrupted the melancholy.

"Who is it?" Tano hollered.

"Hello, in there. I've got your receipt for the room," blurted the hotel manager in a shrill voice—a frumpy, but jovial elderly woman.

"Just shove it under the door," Tano hollered. "Jesus, what's the deal with her?" he looked at Holly with wonderment. She continued to sit with him topless, with her long hair flowing down covering her breasts. Tano gestured toward the bed. "Look at the bed. It's a mess."

Holly laughed. "Well, it saw of a lot of action tonight." They resumed drinking wine and talking. Tano turned the television on and selected a movie to watch. Holly felt cold and pulled the Badge shirt on over her head.

"Are you cold? Let's get in under the covers." They jumped in bed, propped their heads up on a stack of lifeless pillows to watch the movie—a superhero movie with a pointless weak plot. Soon Holly fell asleep. Her head rested on Tano's shoulder. He continued to watch the movie with her close to him, but not paying much attention to it. He had been here before—in a hotel room, for one night, with a beautiful girl. Many nights. Many girls. Most of them forgettable. But this one, he knew he would remember. Her gentle and vulnerable demeanor. Her soft voice. She was unpretentious and genuine. Not trying to impress him because of who he was. And her perfect body and face that she was seemingly unaware of. Maybe there was an unwritten song in this.

Tano laid Holly's head down on the pillows. He turned off the TV and fell asleep. Morning would not be welcome to either of them.

CHAPTER 7

Daylight poured in through the panoramic window of the hotel room. As Tano and Holly began to stir, they turned and faced each other.

"Good morning, pretty girl," Tano whispered. Holly smiled and stretched her long legs. "How did you sleep?"

"I think good. But I don't want to leave this bed." Holly stretched her arms over her head and Tano laid his warm hand on her stomach and pulled her closer to him.

"Well, then let's stay." Holly was quiet. When she was fully awake, her thoughts began to race. From the concert, to the long night in the café, to meeting Tano, to the intimate time spent in the van, to the night that had just passed. *What were the chances that any of it could occur as it did? What will happen now? Will he stay in touch?* She wanted answers, but she decided it wouldn't be cool to press him. The same questions circulated in Tano's mind, too.

Tano picked up his phone to look at the time. It was eight forty. "Hungry? Should we order room service?" He picked up a laminated menu from the nightstand next to the bed and held it up so they could both look at it. "Let's see. I think I'll have the Texas breakfast. See? It's a Tex-Mex omelet, home fries, and tortillas. What looks good to you?"

"Hmmm. A large orange juice. I'm so thirsty. And a vegetarian omelet. That seems light enough." Tano used the house phone and placed the order. Holly laid on her back with her arm laying across her forehead. She sat up momentarily, gathered her clothes and went to take a quick shower before the breakfast arrived. Tano remained in bed, silent, staring at the ceiling, thinking.

Soon, there was a knock at the door. Tano pulled his jeans on and opened the door to room service. At about the same time, Holly emerged from the bathroom.

"Just in time, beautiful," Tano smiled. The silence was deafening. Each was lost in their own thoughts. When it began to feel uncomfortable to Tano, he turned the TV on for noise.

"This Texas breakfast is so good. How is yours?" asked Holly softly.

"Great. This should hold me until I get to Garden City."

Holly didn't respond but looked down at her plate, moved the eggs and vegetables around from one side of the plate to the other and put her fork down.

"Not hungry?"

"I guess I wasn't. My dad always told me that my eyes were bigger than my stomach." She looked up, brushed her hair from her face, and smiled at Tano. She picked up her fork and took a few more bites. Tano ate slowly and watched her serious face.

Holly began to gather her things and put them in her fabric shoulder bag. When Tano finished his breakfast, he said, "Well, are you ready to hit the road?"

"Yes." Holly's voice was barely audible. Tano tossed the room key on the nightstand. They both took a quick look at the room and emerged into the reality of daylight.

They would enter Oklahoma in a couple of hours. They drove in silence, each lost in their own thoughts. Music played but it was only background sound for introspection. Holly developed strong feelings for Tano in just two short days. She questioned herself— was it real love or was she just infatuated with him? Holly would never risk her pride by telling him how she felt. What if he brushed her off, laughed at her, rejected and humiliated her? She was never one of those silly, needy girls who clung to any guy who looked her way. She decided to keep her feelings to herself and spare herself the risk of making a fool of herself.

Tano replayed the last two days in his mind. He was puzzled about why he cared about Holly so much. How could that happen?

It never had before. She was unique. Definitely one of a kind. He wanted to stay in contact with her. He thought he wanted her to be a part of his life. But his pride wouldn't let him say what his heart was feeling. He could feel her sadness and so he rested his right hand on her leg and unconsciously rubbed it gently, as if to comfort her. She touched his hand and then held onto his muscular arm with her left hand.

When they got to Texhoma, across the Oklahoma state line, Holly said, "Okay, you can let me out here. I'll just catch a bus or call a friend to pick me up. It's only about thirty-five miles to Sage from here." She looked down at her hands, her long black lashes resting on her cheeks, then grabbed her fabric bag from the floor.

"No, Holly. It's not out of the way for me to take you to Sage. We've come this far together. I'm not going to leave you here—unless that's what you want."

"Well, you've already done so much for me. I can't expect much more."

"I'm good with it. Which way now?" Tano said firmly. Holly gave him directions. Sage was east of Texhoma. The ride continued in awkward silence that became unbearable.

"Tano, let's listen to some Badge music once more. Then every time I hear it, I'll think of this ride with you—and everything else." Her voice drifted off to a whisper.

"Okay, here you go." The playlist began with their signature "Badge" song, then to "Midnight Rider," an Allman Brothers song. It was Tano's voice singing the lead. She began to sway slightly to the rhythm of the song. Her throat was tight. He would think she was an idiot if she burst into tears, but she wanted to.

"Here is Sage. My car is parked at The Farm Store parking lot." Tano was surprised that there was actually a town there when she told him to turn off the main highway. The main street was dirt. On the edge of town was a two-pump gas station next door to a tiny post office that looked like a Swiss doll house with its steep roof. A few yards up the street was a farm supply store with a tiny café attached. Pickup trucks encased in mud loaded with hay or with horse trailers attached were parked randomly in the tiny parking lot.

"My jeep is parked in the back there. See?"

Tano weaved his way through the trucks and stopped next to her car. They both wanted to tell each other that they wanted to stay in touch, that the last two unforgettable days were magic, and that they didn't want it to end. But neither said a word. Holly once again dug into her purse and pulled out a wad of cash.

"Will you let me give you some cash for helping me get home?"

"No. No. It was a pleasure to help out a little lady in distress. Please put that away." Holly lingered in her seat, looking at Tano's handsome, dimpled face, as if to burn it into her memory. She leaned over and kissed his lips. He pulled her closer and kissed her long and passionately, long enough for Holly to feel the electricity between them.

"I guess this is it, Tano." It was going to hurt her to walk away from him. She felt the pain begin at the top of her head and travel all the way through her body.

Tano decided that he wanted her to have something to remember him by. He thought for a moment and then unscrewed the custom T-handle gear shift knob from his Chevy van and handed it to her. It was inscribed with the word "Badge."

"Here you go, Holly. Remember."

Holly leaned over and kissed Tano one more time. The last time. On his lips, Tano felt the tears that were quietly streaming down her face, behind her sunglasses. She opened the van door and said simply, "Thank you, Tano." There was so much more to be said. But the words would not come. She walked in front of the van toward her jeep, her head down, long hair glowing and blowing in the breeze.

Tano rolled down his window. "Holly?"

Just as Holly turned to look at him, he snapped a photo of her. Tears still streaming, she managed a smile and waved to him. He watched her get in her car and followed her out of the parking lot. He watched her drive up the dirt road main street until she was no longer in sight. Tano felt the weight of her absence immediately with the realization that he would probably never see her again. He was hurting, too but he would never admit it to himself.

He began the last leg of his journey to Garden City, Kansas, when he noticed a slight rattling sound on the passenger front door. He turned to look and saw that Holly had hung one of her silver and turquoise bracelets on the door handle. A souvenir for him. He pulled over to the side of the road and reached across the passenger seat to grab it. He hung it over his rearview mirror. He wanted her with him again. Maybe he should go back. Maybe he should find her. Maybe she would travel with him for a while. He pondered the thought. His hands were on the steering wheel ready to turn around. "No, she needs to find her direction. And it's probably not with me. I don't even know her last name." Tano turned the steering wheel toward the highway, toward Garden City, and with each mile, away from Holly.

CHAPTER 8

Five years had passed since Tano had waved goodbye to Holly in that tiny town in Oklahoma. The band had become well known, especially in Colorado. Badge could be more discriminating in its choice of venues. They had played at Red Rocks, the premiere outdoor venue in Colorado, in June. They were no longer an opening band. Their sound had evolved into a country rock sound with an edge. Kind of like Lynyrd Skynyrd meets Keith Urban. Badge had been nominated for AMA and Grammy awards for a song that Tano wrote, "Girl from Yesterday." No one knew who the girl in the song was. It was Holly.

Tumbleweed thrived. Tano was fortunate to have a managing partner he could trust and who made the bar into a destination in Boulder. He spent most of his time there whenever he was home in Boulder. Rochelle, Tano's part-time girlfriend, became tired and bored waiting for Tano to return home following each tour. During one particularly long tour schedule, she impulsively married a local Realtor. It mattered little to Tano. She was too self-absorbed and could not carry on a conversation unless it was about her.

Then came, Delaney, for a year. A statuesque, pretty, narcissistic, brunette with a bad temper and a foul mouth and a proclivity toward tantrums. Nothing serious since. A dinner here, a lay there. He realized that he began to subconsciously compare the women he met to Holly. Even though he barely knew her, in the short time he was with her, he was taken by her warm, gentle spirit and humble lack of vanity. She would pop into his mind randomly. While he drove. When it was quiet. When the rain fell.

And always when Badge played "Free" or "Somewhere Along the Way" or "Purple Rain" or the song that he wrote about her. He realized that he needed to see her once again to either find out for himself if she ever had feelings for him and if not, to free himself from her ghost.

The drive to Sage, Oklahoma from Springfield, Colorado, only took a couple of hours. The time behind the wheel seemed to zip by as he relived the past with Holly. Because she never mentioned her last name, Tano reached a dead end when he tried to find her on Facebook or to Google her. A search of "Holly, Sage, Oklahoma" returned no results. He was intent on finding her. Maybe she wouldn't be there. But the town was small. The people in Sage would know where she was. At least know who she was.

He felt a little jolt of excitement for a minute as he pulled off the main highway into Sage. The main street was still dirt. The buildings were the same, except Tano could see that there was a new light blue commercial metal building at the end of the main street. The first stop would be the two-pump gas station. He decided to fill his gas tank ahead of going into the station to inquire about Holly. He was afraid that he might be viewed with suspicion in such a tiny town when he asked about her. At least he was a legitimate customer.

A disheveled, unattractive, and plain, young woman wearing smudged purple-framed glasses and a red smock greeted him as he walked in the door. "Hello, sir. What can I do fer ya? Gas pump workin' okay out there?"

"Yeah, sure, it was good. I'm looking for a friend of mine who lives here in Sage. And I was wondering if you could tell me where I might find her. I know her parents live near here."

The clerk cocked her head slightly and studied Tano's face. She no longer smiled. As Tano expected, Sage citizens might be protective of their own. Tano held up his phone with the picture of Holly that he took as she walked away from him that day five years before. "Her name is Holly. Do you know her?"

The clerk looked at the photo and narrowed her eyes when she looked up at Tano's face. "I can't be sure if I know her." Yes, she was suspicious. "No, I don't know anyone that looks like that."

Tano swiped to a second photo. "Maybe you can recognize her from this photo?" It was the photo of them sitting together at the Mexican restaurant in Amarillo.

"Nope. Doesn't ring a bell. Sorry." The clerk's tone was snippy. She looked away.

"Okay, thanks." Then on a whim, he approached the candy rack and picked up some red licorice. "I'll take one of these, too."

"One dollar." The clerk looked down and wouldn't look up at Tano's face.

"Okay, thanks." He walked back to the van. He saw the clerk standing at the door and watching him as he drove away. He knew that the Colorado license plates raised her suspicion of him. The main street was so short that he moved up the street a couple hundred feet and thought he would give the post office a shot.

The elderly postmistress stood at a window straight ahead of the door. "Hi, my name is Ben Montano and I'm looking for a friend of mine that I haven't seen for several years. Her name is Holly. Here's a photo of her." Tano held up his phone with the photo of them both.

The post office was tiny with assorted bronze ornate flat vintage mailboxes lining the walls on either side of the window. "Can't say as I do. Can't give out information about mail customers anyway."

Just as she spoke, a tall, husky young man wearing mud stained brown Carhartt coveralls, a baseball hat, and no shirt, walked in the door and angled his way behind Tano to get to his mailbox. While pulling his mail out of the slot, he stretched over to look at the photo on Tano's phone. "Hey, that's Holly. Holly Harris. She a friend of yours?"

"Yes, she is. I haven't seen her for a while. Do you know where I might find her?"

"Not really. Her folks live up the road about a quarter mile or so. On the left-hand side. Look for a white picket fence around a two-story white house. There's a hippie kind of sign with flowers on it. Something about goat cheese. You can see a herd of white goats back behind the house."

"Okay, thanks a lot." He was getting close to finding her. He could feel it. Maybe she wasn't there. But he had a way to find her now. If her parents would talk. The postmistress scowled at the young man, but he seemed unphased by it. Tano got back in his van and began to roll slowly up the two remaining blocks of the main street, looking at both sides of the street even though the chances were slim that she would be walking down the street.

Tano discovered that there was a little park at the end of Main Street. One square block with a small playground with swings, slide, and tetherball pole, a basketball court, some picnic tables. Decades old hackberry and elm trees provided shade to nearly the entire area. On the far side of the park, a lone girl sat at a picnic table near a pine tree and caught Tano's eye. Her vivid coppery hair stood in stark contrast to the deep green of the pine tree backdrop behind her. She appeared to be reading or writing. She was too far away for Tano to see her face. But he felt a little kick of adrenalin. Could it be her? No way. He parked along the street and sat in his van for a few minutes and looked toward her, squinting his eyes, trying to get a clearer view. He had to approach the girl. Could it be Holly? What if it wasn't? That would be embarrassing and alarming to whoever it was. He had to take a chance.

Tano began to stroll along a hard-beaten dirt path which cut through the lawn in the park, as if he was merely taking a long walk. He didn't want to approach too quickly. He took a few steps closer to her.

"Holly? Is that you?" The young red-haired girl looked up from her book. He knew instantly that it wasn't her. How ridiculous of him to think he would find her that quickly, even in a tiny town.

The young girl was speechless for a few seconds as she took in his good looks. "Uh, no. That's my sister. How do you know my sister? Like...who are you?"

Tano was disappointed that it wasn't Holly, but he was a step closer to finding her. The encounter began to feel awkward.

"I met her about five years ago. I'm on my way to Texas, and I thought I would swing by her town and say hi. My name is Tano." He reached his hand out to shake hers. She resembled Holly except she had a stripe of freckles across her nose and a round face. Maybe a few years younger.

The young girl's mouth fell open. "You're Tano? Tano from Badge? You really know my sister?"

"Yeah, I do. Do you know where I could find her?"

"How do you know her?"

"After a concert once. We met. Is she in Sage?" Tano just wanted to know where Holly was, but he soon realized there would be some questions before he could get some answers.

"I'm Haley. She never mentioned you to us. That's weird. Yes, she's here in Sage. At the house. Do you know where that is? It's about a quarter mile from here."

"I think I can find it. Nice to meet you, Haley. And thanks." Haley, still stunned by her encounter with Tano, closed her book and began to walk home briskly.

Tano turned and walked quickly back to the van with anticipation. She was in Sage! He might see her in the next few minutes! As he got into his van, the rearview mirror caught his eye. He drove a different van these days, but Holly's bracelet still hung there. The music of Blake Shelton played in the background, "Sangria."

In less than two minutes, he saw the house that had been described to him. The two-story white house with a white picket fence and a black sign bordered with hand painted, brightly colored wildflowers and white lettering: "Wildflower Goat Milk and Cheese. Homemade Jam and Jelly."

Tano pulled into the dirt driveway alongside the house. Straight ahead there was a herd of varied colored goats nibbling grass in an adjoining field and a couple of clapboard sheds painted barn red. He wasn't sure where he should go. The front door? The back door? One of the outbuildings?

He looked toward the house and when he turned his head and looked through his windshield, he saw her. Holly. She emerged from one of the sheds, turned and latched the door. She was as stunning as ever, just wearing faded jeans, a pink tank top. Her long red-dish blonde hair spiraled down her back. His heart was in his throat which surprised him. He opened the door and stepped out of the van and said, "Holly? It's me. Tano. Remember?"

Holly's crystal blue eyes were wide with disbelief when she turned toward his voice. She clasped her hand over her mouth and blushed. Tears filled her eyes at the sight of him standing there. He was smiling—that beautiful smile, fringed by his moustache, punc-tuated by his deep dimples.

"Tano. How? Why are you in Sage? How could it be that you're standing here? It's been so long." She approached him slowly and stood smiling in front of him with her hands at her sides, not know-ing what to do. Tano stepped closer to her and put both of his arms around her, hoping that she would welcome his embrace. She did. Her emotional reaction told him what he had wanted to know for five years. She did have feelings for him. Like he had for her.

While they hugged, Tano spoke softly in her ear. "I came to Sage to find you. I just wanted to see you again. I can't believe that you're still here. Really here."

Holly clung to him tightly and then looked up at his face and simply said, "I'm still here." She buried her face in his chest, still trying to hold back the tears of joy. Fate had put them together in Sage, Oklahoma. They had come full circle after five years. There was so much to talk about, but neither could speak as the emotions they had suppressed for five years rose to the surface.

CHAPTER 9

Tano and Holly simultaneously pulled apart but continued to hold hands while they each looked at the other's face. Both were aware that their mutual emotional reactions might have been too revealing and that they should dial it back. But Tano could feel that Holly's hand was shaking.

"Tano, Badge is doing so well! The Grammys and AMA award nominations for one of your songs! I check your tour schedule sometimes and download your music. Your new original stuff is so good—great guitar and vocals. And the lyrics, too." Holly gushed and continued. "I saw that Badge will be in Amarillo soon."

"I'm on my way to Amarillo. Yeah, we've had a good run. The sound has come together—we are all on the same page, I guess for now. However long this will last. Holly, what's been going on in your life since I saw you last?"

Holly was silent while she organized her thoughts. In many ways, things were the same, but much had happened in five years. "Well, remember when we talked back then? I told you that I had not found my direction. It took a few months but then, I did. I was hired by a commodities company as an energy resources analyst in Liberal, Kansas. I teach a couple of ballet classes at a local community college. And I have a little house there. It's about sixty miles from here. My job has taken me to Denver a couple of times, and I made a special trip to Boulder once to visit Tumbleweed and have a look for myself. I drank a Tequila Sunrise. You weren't there but I wondered what I would say if I saw you."

"You were in Boulder? Why didn't you look me up? Why didn't I ever see you?" Tano was stunned and surprised. Maybe she had been looking for him.

"I didn't think you would remember me. I was just a passenger in your van for a couple of days. A girl that got left in San Angelo. I wasn't going to force myself into your life. I hate those stalker girls. I would never do that." Holly began to play with her hair.

"Jeez, Holly. Why would you think that I would forget you? You were more than just a girl."

"I don't know. When you left, I had no reason to think that you would ever pass this way again. But now you're standing here. I'm so happy to see you."

"I came here to find you and see you again." Their eyes locked as if each was searching the other for answers to unspoken questions until Tano said, "So, what are you doing here?" He was still holding Holly's hand.

"I took a couple of days off. I try to return home—I guess it's home—to Sage every couple of months or so. It centers me to be here in this place. With the goats and the garden and the rabbits, the homemade jam, fresh baked bread. I guess I'm just an Oklahoma girl at heart." Both realized that it had taken a simultaneous and co-incidental trip to Sage for each of them to reconnect. It was surreal.

"So, Holly...what would you have said to me if I would have been there? At Tumbleweed?"

Holly continued to look down for a minute and then looked up into Tano's golden eyes while she spoke. "I would have said, do you remember me? The girl in San Angelo who caught a ride and played the violin with you in your van during a thunderstorm? And if you said no, I would have died of embarrassment. If you said yes, I would have said I've thought about you many times since then and wished I could see you again."

"We shared more than a ride." Tano pulled her close to him again, crinkling his eyes into a smile.

"Yes, we did. I never forgot it."

"Me neither."

Just then the screen door at the back porch creaked open and a woman stepped out and walked toward them. She was an older version of Holly, with long gray hair in ringlets cascading all around her, thin and tan, dressed in a long, vibrantly colored peasant skirt and a faded denim shirt tied at her waist. Tano thought that she resembled Jane Fonda.

"Who's your friend, honey?"

"Mom, this is Tano. And this is my mom, Liza. Tano is with the band Badge. You know, Mom, you've heard me play their music."

"Nice to meet you." Tano reached out to shake her tan hand.

Liza's eyes were wide with wonder. "Well, yes, I know the music, but I didn't know you were familiar with guys in the band."

"Not guys. Just this one."

"But how...?"

"I met him after the concert a few years ago in San Angelo."

"But you never told me that." Holly's sister, Haley, said the same thing when Tano met her at the park. He privately wondered why Holly didn't mention him to them. Maybe she was embarrassed. Maybe she was hurt or upset. Maybe she wanted to forget him. Maybe she didn't care. Holly didn't respond. "Good to meet you, Tano. I really like your music, even though I'm an old Dead Head— you know, the Grateful Dead."

Tano smiled at her comment. "Yes, I'm from Boulder, Colorado, and the Dead are alive and well there."

Liza smiled and nodded. "Can I get you something to eat or drink? Lemonade? Iced tea? Cookies?"

"Thanks, no."

"Okay, if you change your mind..." Liza's words drifted as she sauntered over to the garden and began to pick tomatoes.

A wooden picnic bench with peeling red paint, surrounded by pink hollyhocks, rested against the picket fence near the driveway. Holly, who was still holding Tano's hand, led him to the bench and they sat down. "So Tano. What would you have said to me if I had walked into Tumbleweed and you were there?"

"I would have said, there's my Oklahoma girl. I wrote a song

about her. You might have heard it, Holly. 'The Girl from Yesterday.'
I guess that's what I would have said."

Holly tilted her head and looked at his face as the tender lyrics
of the song filtered through her mind. "That song was about me?
The song nominated for a Grammy?"

"Yes, it was. I didn't forget you or the short time we had together." Except for a few ballads, Badge music had evolved into raucous
rock and roll. But Holly loved the ballads—songs about love and
loss and about forever and goodbye. "The Girl from Yesterday" was
about all those things. And about her.

"Tano, I don't know what to say. It's a beautiful song. About
me? Really?"

"Yes. It's about you. I think I knew when I left you here that I
would have to come back again. And I tried to find you. But if I never
saw you again, our time together was written forever into a song for
everybody to hear. So now on my way to Amarillo, I gave it a shot. Do
you think I would drive to Sage, Oklahoma, without a reason?"

Holly responded softly, "No." Tano leaned in to kiss her, just as
a tall red diesel pickup roared noisily into the driveway and parked
behind Tano's van. A handsome, muscular young man in his twenties with curly blond hair stepped down from the truck and took a
few deliberate steps toward Tano and Holly.

"Hey, Hol. Who's your friend?"

"Hey, Garth. This is Tano, a friend of mine." Tano reached out to
shake his hand.

Garth ignored the gesture. Tano laid his hand on Holly's. "So,
you're a friend of my sister. Hmmm. Wait a minute. Are you that
Tano from the band—uh, what's it called—Badge?"

"Yeah, that's me." Tano could sense that Garth was not going to
be friendly toward him and he kept his words at a minimum.

"Hol, how do you know this guy? When did you guys meet anyway?" Garth refused to acknowledge Tano and spoke to Holly as if
he wasn't there.

"Garth, jeez, what's your problem? I met him after a Badge concert once. A few years ago."

"I don't have a problem. But Jared might. You remember him, don't ya, Hol?" Garth sneered at Holly.

Holly's face turned crimson with anger and embarrassment. She looked away and then looked up at Garth. "This is none of your business, Garth. Don't be such a jerk."

"Where's Dad? He here?" Garth grunted.

"Yeah, he's in the shop." Holly spoke softly.

Tano looked at Holly and waited for an explanation, as she squirmed on the picnic bench, crossed and uncrossed her legs. Garth thankfully walked away.

"Jared is someone I've been seeing in Kansas. He came with me once when I visited the family here. He and Garth hit it off pretty good. Garth doesn't approve of me having a career and living alone. He thinks I should be at home with little kids at my feet. It's none of his goddamn business." Holly wanted to say more—to tell Tano that she had prayed to see him again. That the feelings she developed for him over the course of those two days never left her. That Jared meant nothing. But that he had meant everything. But she kept those words inside.

"Holly, hey. I took a chance that I might find you here and I didn't even know your last name until today. I wanted to see you again, but I don't want to make trouble for you." Tano wanted to tell her to forget about the other guy. He wanted to know everything about her and needed time with her to do that. They barely knew each other but the attraction was so strong. He kept those thoughts to himself.

"There's no trouble. Only a brother with a shitty attitude." Holly changed the subject. She was embarrassed and hated what had just happened. "So, are you on your way to Amarillo now? For the concert?"

"Yeah. I'm due there tomorrow. I was thinking—so would you like to come with me to the concert? Backstage pass and every-thing. But maybe it's not a good idea after all."

"None of that matters. I would love to. When are you leaving?"

"Well, anytime. I'll leave when you can. Today or tomorrow?"

"I have nothing to keep me here right now. Like I said, just chilling here for a few days. Give me a few minutes to grab a few things and let's go." Holly jumped up. "Come on in with me." Tano stood and followed Holly in through the back screen door of the white farmhouse.

CHAPTER 10

The scent of cinnamon bread wafted through the house carried by a light breeze through the open windows. Two loaves were resting on a wooden cutting board on the stainless-steel kitchen counter. Sheer white curtains billowed softly from the open window over the sink. The windowsill held various tiny pots containing little herb plants. There was a long white pine kitchen table which held six blue calico placemats, and which was surrounded by six heavy matching chairs. A well-used cookbook laid open on the table. In a separate corner of the kitchen stood a stainless-steel prep table cluttered with several metal pails. The little kitchen was immaculate, but clearly well used. The pine floor was worn in places where Liza stood to work—in front of the sink, in front of the commercial stove, and surrounding the metal table in the corner.

Haley was sitting on an overstuffed burgundy chair in the tiny living room looking at her phone. She looked up at them for a second as they walked into the room. "Hey, you found her. You can't get lost in this boring little town."

Holly tilted her head and looked at Tano. "You met up with my sister? How did that happen?"

"I was rolling through town and I saw a girl who looked like you in the park. It turned out to be Haley. And I'm glad that I ran into her. I asked a couple of people in town about you and they weren't willing to say much."

"Hey, Hol, why didn't you say you were friends with Badge? "

"I only met Tano. Not Badge. It was a long time ago."

"Hmmm. I would have told everybody if I knew a rock star." Haley was nineteen.

"I'm going to run upstairs and grab some stuff. Want to come with me? "

"No, I'll hang down here with your sister."

Haley tried to be cool, but after she was alone with him again, her coolness evaporated into self-consciousness and she began to squirm in her chair. "So how long are you going to be here?" Haley couldn't look at Tano while he spoke, fearing that her face would turn red, and continued looking at her phone.

"I'm leaving in a few minutes. Badge has a gig in Amarillo tomorrow night."

"So, what's Holly doing? Is she going too?" Haley still wouldn't look at him.

"Yes, she is." To Haley's relief, Tano turned his head at the sound of Holly's boots on the wooden stairs as she hustled down them. "That didn't take long."

Holly carried a burnished brown tooled leather backpack. She had changed into some clean faded jeans, a white tank top, a belt with a vintage silver and turquoise buckle, and brown cowboy boots. She slid her phone in her back pocket. "I'm ready if you are."

"Okay, let's hit it." Tano put his hand on Holly's back as they walked toward the door. "See ya, Haley. Hey, thanks for helping me find your sister."

"Okay, yeah." Haley still wouldn't look at him.

As they stepped off the back porch, Holly hollered to her mom. "Hey, Mom, I'm going to be gone a few days—to Amarillo. I'll be back before I leave for Liberal." Holly's mom waved to her.

Just then, Garth emerged from a metal building next to the goat pasture. He walked quickly toward Holly and Tano, taking purposeful long strides, yelling in their direction. "Hey, Hol. You going somewhere? With that guy?" Garth's irritation with Tano's presence was apparent in his voice.

"Hey, Garth, not that it's any of your business, but yeah, for a couple of days, to a concert."

Soon Garth stood in front of them, as if to block their path to the van. Holly grabbed Tano's hand as they pushed past Garth and

Cynthia L. Clark

opened the white picket gate. "Hey, Garth, will you move your truck? Now!" Garth walked away and toward the house and opened the screen door. But before he slammed it shut, he hollered to Holly, "Hol, is he the one? Was it him? Does he know?" Holly pretended not to hear his words.

"Come on, Tano. There's another way out of here. Just pull up toward the rabbit shed and my dad's shop and there's a loop around the back of it. "

Tano started the van, but before he put it in gear he turned to Holly. "Are you sure you want to come with me? Looks like there's trouble here." Tano wanted to ask Holly what Garth meant when he asked if he was "the guy." But he didn't.

"Yes. Let's go." Tano pulled forward and followed the path as Holly directed him. When they were in front of Holly's dad's machine shop, Holly rolled the window down and greeted a Golden Retriever laying in the shade on the cool concrete by the door. "Bye, Butkus. See you in a few days." Butkus lifted his head when she spoke and then flopped over on his side, panting in the Oklahoma heat. When they reached the edge of town, Holly rolled her window up as the van began to cool from the air conditioning. Holly noticed the red licorice that Tano had bought at the gas station.

"Hey, red licorice. Can I have a piece?"

"Of course. I never travel without it." Tano smiled at Holly. But Garth's last words reverberated in his head and made him realize that he hardly knew her. *What did his words mean? What guy? What happened? What was she hiding? I guess she will tell me if she wants me to know.* Clearly Holly attempted to move past whatever it was by speaking to the dog and asking for licorice. Both were silent for several miles. Tano turned on some country music. Jason Aldean's "Girl Like You."

Holly sat motionless with her hands in her lap and looked out the passenger window. Tano could see that she was jostling with something heavy in her mind. He laid his hand on her leg. She rested her hand on his. She looked toward him and opened her mouth and took a breath as if she was going to say something. But she turned away just as Keith Urban began to sing "Blue Ain't Your Color." Tano changed the playlist. Something more raucous was needed. Lynyrd Skynyrd. "Simple Man." One of Badge's cover songs. Tano sang along. By the time they reached Texhoma, Holly's usual sunny mood returned. Hearing Tano sing made Holly realize that being there with him, in the present, was fleeting and she couldn't waste a minute in her head and away from him. She tapped her boot on the floor of the van as "Saturday Night Special" pulsated through the sound system.

Tano and Holly. They hardly knew each other and yet they had connected in some cosmic way. Here they were again. On the same road to Amarillo that they took in the opposite direction five years before. Something had happened but would it matter now anyway?

CHAPTER 11

As a little girl in a small town, Holly had to play with her siblings and the few children scattered in the nearby farmhouses or find her own entertainment—picking berries and flowers, climbing a tree, riding her bike, dancing, playing the violin, or reading books that the mobile library brought to town. She spent little time on the internet because the signal was weak and sporadic. She was introspective and spent many hours sitting under a shade tree sorting it all out and recording it in a journal, sometimes words written as poetry, about life as she had known it thus far.

She and her brothers and sister were bussed to Texhoma for school. When Holly was in high school, over the course of a summer, she evolved from a gangly kid into a striking beauty, with her long red hair and round blue eyes edged by long black lashes and her slim figure. Her skin glowed. The few boys in her class became interested. But none of them were of interest to her, other than as friends. She tossed a football with them. She met them for burgers. She paired up with none of them for the homecoming dance but danced with them all. She drank beer with them under the school bleachers. And listened to them when they wanted to talk. But she decided she would never just settle for the first guy who came along and fell in love with her.

She carried the same discriminating perspective with her when she entered the University of Colorado in Colorado Springs. There was a horde of good-looking young men from which to choose. Her college roommate hooked up right away. Holly played the field for a long time, but when she met Davis Montgomery in her junior year, she let her guard down. Tall, dark and handsome basketball player, with hazel eyes and deep dimples, she was instantly attracted to him and he was her first love in every sense of the word. But after a few semesters, his conceited arrogance pushed her aside, as his need for attention exceeded his need for her. She broke it off. Holly was relieved that she never told him that she loved him, even though she probably did. And maybe that would have made a difference. In Holly's way of thinking, using the word "love" made her vulnerable and left her at the mercy of someone who could either stay or go. She believed that once that word was used, it couldn't be taken back. She would not risk heartbreak and humiliation.

Tano's upbringing was much different than Holly's. He spent no time reflecting on life. He was too busy living it. In a cosmopolitan, university town like Boulder, Colorado, there was so much to do. His father was an aerospace engineer and his mother spent her time shepherding Tano and his brothers and sister to and from a variety of activities. For Tano, it was about sports—all of them—and it began in elementary school. Every season was a sports season and he excelled in them all, but he eventually focused on football in the fall, basketball in the winter, golf in the summer and lettered in all of them. He was the homecoming king each year in high school. Girls made every attempt to get his attention and he dated a few of them, leaving broken hearts in the wake. Love 'em and leave 'em. With each passing year, he became better looking. His dark wavy hair and strong, athletic build accompanied by the intense color of his eyes drew attention wherever he happened to be.

Tano's attitude was unchanged when he was in college. And girls behaved the same way around him. Sports were still number one in his life. Academics came easily for him. He smoked some pot and drank some beer. He skied every weekend and spent his summers on his dad's boat. In his junior year, he picked up a guitar at a friend's house and began to pluck the strings and played around with the feel of it. Before he knew it, a couple of hours had passed. He knew sports wouldn't carry him forever and into the future and a new passion developed. He taught himself to play the guitar and he played it well, mimicking the sounds of Joe Walsh, a favorite of his, and Keith Richards, of the Stones. Soon he and a couple of friends formed a garage band. They called themselves Band on the Run and played at a few venues around Boulder. Word of mouth and some demo CDs brought them gigs outside of Boulder. Slowly their fan base grew. They changed the band's name to Badge.

Tano knew that he had to make a living and that playing in a local band would not do it for him. He and a friend bought a bar on the downtown Pearl Street mall, where the action is in Boulder, renamed it "Tumbleweed" and made it into a destination, with its reputation for great music and fine tequilas. Always successful in everything he did. He had never experienced loss or failure. He still wouldn't commit to anyone but had plenty of women who gave themselves willingly to him, hoping that eventually they would be the one.

On their way to Amarillo, the music Tano chose continued to brighten Holly's mood. "Listen to this one. It's an oldie that I found. 'Chevy Van.' It's about a guy who gave a girl a ride in his van." The lyrics could have been written about their first encounter. Holly smiled at Tano as she listened to it. Her eyes caught sight of the rearview mirror in the van where the turquoise and silver bracelet that she left him five years before still hung. She reached up and touched it with her fingers for a minute. Tano smiled at her and lightly rubbed the top of her leg.

"You still have it!" Tano could hear amazement in her voice. "I almost forgot that I left it. I hoped you would find it."

"Glad that you did. It reminded me of you every time I looked at it." She was stunned to hear that he thought of her at all. Even more stunning, he came to look for her. Holly felt warm inside and cautioned herself. The reunion between them happened so quickly and without warning. The adrenalin rush she felt was like a high that she couldn't ignore. She wanted to pounce on him again, like she impulsively had done five years before.

"I still have the Badge shifter knob that you gave me. I keep it in a safe place." She hooked her left hand around his muscular arm while she spoke. "So Tano, what is happening when we get to Amarillo?"

"Well, Badge and the roadies are staying at the Embassy Suites for the next couple of nights. We'll just hang out tonight. Have dinner. Tomorrow there will be a little bit of rehearsing and a sound check when the roadies get the equipment set up. And then we'll decide on the set list. It's usually pretty much the same setlist for the lighting techs. But, hey, I'll let you pick a couple of songs that you want."

"I would love to." They were about twenty miles from Amarillo. Holly began to think about being alone with him again, making love. It's what she wanted. Would it be the same? She put the thought out of her mind. If it was to happen, it should just unfold naturally.

Tano's thoughts were the same. It hadn't been his plan to ask her to come with him to Amarillo, but when he saw her again, he knew he needed more time with her. And there was no room for him in Sage, especially with her hostile brother. Garth's last words still trickled into Tano's head. *What did they mean? What happened to Holly? What could it be?*

When they arrived at the hotel, they grabbed their bags and let the valet park the van. They checked into the room. Tano texted the guys in the band and let them know he was there, and they made plans to meet for dinner in an hour. Tano kicked off his boots and sprawled out on the king-size bed.

"Come here, sweetness. Let me get a hold of you." Tano reached his hand out. Holly grabbed his hand and Tano pulled her on top of him and spoke softly in her ear. "I'm glad you were able to come with me today. "

"I know. I didn't expect that my day would end up like this." Tano smelled so good. Just like she remembered. He held her tightly around her waist. His hands moved to her soft rear end and he kissed her deeply and passionately. Holly felt the electricity from the kiss throughout her body as she returned the intense passion to Tano. But without warning, she rolled off him and laid next to him with her leg resting over his looking up at the ceiling. Tano felt confused by her mixed signals.

"Holly...what's up?"

Holly didn't answer at first. She was trying to find the careful words that she needed to say. Tano waited and then she responded in a hushed voice. "Tano...I should tell you something." Tano pulled her closer to him to let her know that she could. "You know back there at home—in Sage—when Garth yelled that stuff at me when we were leaving?'

"Yeah? What was that all about? Listen, you don't have to tell me if you don't want to."

"Yes, I do. I should. Well, it's like this... When I got home after the ride from San Angelo with you, a few weeks later, I discovered I was pregnant...." Before Holly could say another word, Tano sat up halfway, leaned on his elbow, and looked at her face while she spoke. "I wasn't with anyone other than you, so I knew how it happened. I took a pregnancy test twice to be sure. I kept it to myself not knowing how to tell anyone about it. But above all, I knew that I'd have the baby and I'd keep it and raise it. Never a thought not to. When I told you that I hadn't found my direction yet, I knew then that I had. But I didn't plan to contact you about it or cause trouble for you. But for me, I saw it as a blessing." Tano was silent while he absorbed what she said. Then Holly blinked hard and began to regret that she decided to tell him, but she had to finish.

"So I continued to keep it to myself. I still wasn't showing at about two months. One day, my mom was gone somewhere to a cheese festival or something like that when I began to cramp badly, and hemorrhage. Only Garth was home and I had to ask him to take me to Texhoma to the hospital. He had no idea what was going on. I wasn't sure myself. I had to tell him that I was pregnant, and something was wrong. He beat the steering wheel with his fist yelling, 'I'll kill the bastard that put you through this. Who is it? Who is the son of a bitch?' I would never tell him or anyone. It's been almost five years. I lost the little baby that night." Tears welled in her eyes, but she held them back, refusing to cry.

Tano laid his head back down on the pillow next to Holly. He pulled her closer to him and kissed her on top of her head. Holly was finished talking about it and was afraid that she ruined everything. Tano was stunned by what she said and let her words wind through his head while they laid there. Finally, after what seemed like an hour, he spoke. "Holly, are you okay? I'm sorry you had to go through that all alone. And I'm sorry the baby is gone. But I have to ask—why didn't you tell me?"

"How could I? I didn't have a phone number for you. It was too important to message you on the Badge Facebook page or write a letter. I wasn't part of your plans. You barely knew me. Maybe you wouldn't have believed me. Maybe someday I would've told you. Let you meet him or her and decide. It was a tiny miracle for a while. And yes, I'm okay." Tano was silent.

Holly wanted to ask him what he might have done if she told him but Tano began to speak anyway. "I'm not sure what I would have done if I knew. It was five years ago. But I think that I would've helped you and the baby as much as I could. I would've wanted to be involved as much as I could, I guess. I've never given kids much thought before. Was it painful?"

"Yes, the cramping was painful, but it was over in a few hours once I made it to the hospital. But the pain of disappointment lasted longer. Partly hormones, partly pure sadness."

"Holly, I'm just blown away by what you told me. I'm here now. I don't know how to even try make it up to you."

"I wanted to be honest with you, especially after Garth's outburst. And I'm sorry if I bummed you out."

"No, I needed to know. Right now, I have a mix of thoughts. It'll take me a while to sort it out. But tonight, let's go out and celebrate our reunion."

Those words were needed to move them away from the solemn mood generated by that conversation. He hugged her softly as they laid next to each other. Her honesty had somehow made his affection for her even stronger and deeper than before.

CHAPTER 12

"Let's head to the restaurant and meet the band and grab something to eat. I'm starving."

Holly was relieved that the conversation about the miscarriage didn't appear to change anything in a negative way. She guessed that they might talk about it again. But not tonight. He was right. It was time to celebrate their reconnection.

Surprisingly there were several Thai restaurants in Amarillo. The band picked one within walking distance of the hotel. Holly loved Thai food mainly because it wasn't as common as the down-home southern cooking that she was used to in Oklahoma. Tano held her hand as they maneuvered the street. Tano caught the eye of many people on the street as they walked toward them. They could see he was somebody special, but they weren't entirely sure who he was. He just had that look about him. Tano noticed the attention but humbly thought it was about them as a good-looking, well-matched couple, and not just about him.

Holly felt a little nervous as they approached the large table of people that had been reserved for Badge. She was an outsider, a stranger to all of them. They had a history and a string of experiences that she wasn't a part of. She trusted that Tano wouldn't let her feel uncomfortable.

Tano was still holding her hand as they approached the table. "Hey, Tano," someone at the table said. There were two empty seats together at the end of the table. Before they sat down, Tano introduced Holly. "This is Holly Harris. And Holly, that is Rocky and his girlfriend, Janet, Randy and...you are?" Randy was with a petite freckled brunette with purple tips in her hair that he didn't know.

"This is Shiloh," Randy said.

"Okay, good to meet you, Shiloh. And that is Jack." Tano pointed to the Badge drummer.

Holly smiled at all of them and gestured with a little wave of her hand. "I recognize all of you from Badge. Nice to really meet you." Holly couldn't help but notice that Janet's eyes narrowed to a glare when she first saw her. Tano saw it too. Janet was big boned and tall, slightly overweight, with long straight blonde hair, and big facial features. They took their seats at the end of the table. The server brought menus and took drink orders. "Jeez, Tano, what kind of drink goes with Thai food? "

"Wine or beer, sweetheart. I don't believe they have tequila here." Tano winked at her and rested his arm on the back of her chair. Janet looked at them and rolled her eyes when Holly asked the question about drinks.

"Whatever is on draft for me. And Holly? A pinot noir?"

"Yes, that works."

The restaurant was spacious and full of noisy patrons. The tables, chairs, bar stools, and the bar had clean lines. Black wooden spindle chairs, rectangular gunmetal-colored tables, with rust-colored concrete painted floor, which echoed the noisy talk. The walls were covered with sage green grass cloth. The band began to discuss the concert venue and a schedule for the next day. None had seen the event center before and would need extra time for set up and sound check. Holly whispered quietly to Tano that she was going to the restroom. Janet and Shiloh were engrossed in conversation as she walked away and were unaware that she left the table.

While Holly was in the bathroom stall, she heard Janet's loud voice as she and Shiloh entered. "Yeah, and Rocky told me that he just picked her up on the road or something. Like a hitchhiker. Or homeless or something. Tano deserves better than that. After all, he was with me for a while."

"I think she's pretty and nice. You only went out a couple of times. And you're with Rocky now. Why does it bother you so much?"

"Maybe, but she's not pretty enough or good enough for Tano. Yeah, I'm with Rocky but if I ever get my hands on Tano again, I'll—" Janet's remarks ended quickly when she looked in the mirror and saw Holly standing behind her waiting to wash her hands.

"Oh, I didn't know you were in here." Janet's eyes bulged with surprise, but she was unapologetic. She loomed over Holly. Holly looked up at her and smiled slightly although her heart was racing from anger.

"Well, apparently, but I'm right here. And it's none of your business but I met Tano after a concert and he gave me a ride home a few years ago. I'm not a hitchhiker and I'm not homeless. Tano is free to decide who he wants to be with and tonight, it's me." Holly squeezed past Janet and began to wash her hands in the sink in front of them.

"Oh, whatever." Janet shrugged it off. Shiloh was mortified and red-faced by the awkward encounter. When Holly left the restroom, Shiloh said, "Jesus. Janet. That was embarrassing."

"I don't care. She won't be with him for long. She will never be part of his life and we'll never see her again."

Janet and Shiloh quietly returned to the table. The band members were still engrossed in conversation. Janet saw that Tano put his arm around Holly. When the drinks arrived, he raised his glass to toast only her. "To us, tonight." The server brought their meals. Tano and Holly both had ordered Thai barbecue beef.

"Oh, Tano. Remember the time you and I ate Thai food at that cozy little café in Vail? Remember? It was tucked away near our hotel," Janet smirked and looked at Holly as she spoke to clue her in on their history. Rocky took no notice or didn't care and continued to sample his spicy beef and broccoli.

"Not really." Tano looked at his plate when he mumbled the answer.

"You know, a couple of years ago. I know you remember." Janet's voice became a little shrill as she realized her attempt to insert herself between Holly and Tano was failing. Everyone at the table was silent waiting for Tano's answer.

Tano looked directly at Janet. "Nope, I don't." Janet's attempt to recreate a memory had humiliated her. Her face burned with embarrassment and anger. She ate her meal in silence.

"Tano, I can't eat all of this. Do you want some?" asked Holly as she took another sip of the pinot noir.

"No, baby, I have enough here. I might not be able to finish mine either." Tano leaned in close to Holly and whispered in her ear, "But what do you say—let's head back to the hotel soon?" Tano wanted nothing more than to be alone with Holly. He was finished with the band for the night. He would be with them the next day for set up. Holly and her sweet little body were on his mind.

"So, we're headed to the hotel," Tano announced to the table. "Check in with you guys tomorrow at four at the Arena? Roadies and light techs done by then?" Janet scowled at them.

Rocky answered. "Yeah, they should be or close. They're down there now checking out the stage. We'll go over the set list then and do the usual sound checks."

"Well, goodnight, everybody. This little lady and I are calling it a night."

"It was nice to meet all of you." Holly scanned the table and smiled, even at Janet.

As they walked to the hotel, Tano held Holly's hand. She was curious about the history of Janet and Tano, but not enough to mention it and ruin the romance that was building for them. When they entered the hotel elevator, Tano leaned against the wall and Holly put her arms around his neck and pressed her body against his. Tano pressed back. Holly could feel that her body wanted time alone with Tano as much as he did with her. The elevator doors opened, and they walked quickly down the long hallway to the room. Tano unlocked the door to the room and before it latched shut, he pulled Holly's tank top over her head and began to unbuckle the turquoise and silver belt buckle while Holly unbuttoned his shirt and pulled it off him. The lacy white bra came off next and Tano held a perfect little breast in each hand. He bent down to kiss each one and then picked Holly up and laid her on the oversized king-size bed. Holly kicked her boots off. In a matter of seconds, both had slipped out of their jeans.

"Lay on top of me. I want to feel the weight of your body." Holly whispered.

Tano laid on top of her. He heard her sigh and felt the curves of her body under his. They kissed, with a passion so deep that their bodies felt a charge of electricity flow through each of them. A passion that was born five years before on a two-day trip through Texas was fully ignited again at that moment.

Tano looked into Holly's bicolored blue eyes and whispered, "I can't believe I'm here with you again. I can't believe it's been five years."

"Yes, it has been. And here we are," Holly whispered breathlessly as the excitement between them grew. Tano put his hands under Holly's little rear and she pulled him into her. They lost track of time as they gave themselves intimately to each other, exploring every body part from every angle and every position until the intensity of the love making erupted in a breathtaking finish. Their bodies were slick from sweat. Tano slid off and laid next to her to cool off. Holly felt the sweat evaporate from her body, but she could still feel Tano. It had been ecstasy that each would never forget, and both wanted it to happen again.

Tano and Holly continued to lay naked, bodies touching, face to face. Tano brushed Holly's damp hair out of her face and kissed her forehead. Holly snuggled in close to Tano. "Holly, you know, you're the kind of girl that guys fall in love with." Holly smiled and nuzzled her face into his neck. *I hope it happens to you.*

CHAPTER 13

Thoughts about the lost pregnancy floated in and out of Tano's head. As he laid close to Holly, he pondered his conflicted feelings about the unexpected news. On one hand, it was over and in the past and now that he knew about it, they should move on. And there was nothing to say. On the other, his feelings for Holly, although undefined, softened his perspective of what might have been.

"Tell me—what did you truly think when you found out you were pregnant?" Tano winced as he asked the question feeling awkward bringing the subject up again. But the truth is he wanted to know the answer.

Holly was surprised that he mentioned the miscarriage again so soon. After she told Tano about it, it seemed that it had been enough for him to know. He said he would sort it out, but she believed that meant he would forget about it.

"I was surprised but I shouldn't have been. We had unprotected sex twice. So for a few minutes, I was upset and stunned, but I suddenly started looking at it in a different way. A warm feeling came over me and the thought that the baby was a tiny miracle that came about from a chance encounter with you and I chose to believe that maybe it was supposed to happen. I don't know—that sounds kind of mystical. Maybe silly or unrealistic. It's hard to put into words. But I was happy and at peace with it. I kept it a secret until that awful day when I lost it."

"What did your mom and dad say when they found out?"

"My dad is a man of few words. He didn't scold, or lecture. There were no questions. He looked at me with his usual expressionless, stoic face, but in his eyes, I saw a little sorrow. He hugged me." She paused for a minute while she recalled the day. "My mom asked me why I didn't tell her. She said that having a baby is a blessing and that each one is a tiny wonder. I told her that her knowing wouldn't have changed what eventually happened. She agreed but she was so sweet to me. Neither of them has ever mentioned it again."

Tano didn't know what to say or why he felt he had to talk about it. He was wordless and continued to hold Holly close. Then he spoke. "Having a baby would have changed everything—if I knew about it. For one thing, we wouldn't have spent five years apart. And looking at you now, and knowing what I know about you already, that baby would have had an exceptional mom."

It was Holly's turn to be wordless after she heard what he said. The sadness that had been buried for years, began to surface, but she pushed it away. It was all hypothetical now and in the past tense. "Maybe. Thank you. It would have been a beautiful baby." She hoped that he wouldn't say anything else about it or she would burst into tears. He hugged her tightly and rubbed her arm lightly with his hand. Then he sat up.

"How about some beer or wine? Should I order some drinks up from room service? We are celebrating, remember?" Tano reached down on the floor and found his jeans and pulled them on.

To Holly's relief, he dropped the conversation about the baby. "Yes, I do. How about a bottle of wine?" Holly found her panties and threw her tank top on and sat up, too.

Tano ordered a bottle of wine and a platter of assorted gourmet cheese and crackers that were on the late-night room service menu. He turned the TV on and began to flip through the channels.

"What about *A Star is Born* or *Bohemian Rhapsody*? Both movies with music. Seen 'em?"

"Yes, loved them both. Let's do *Bohemian Rhapsody* again." Holly thought that *A Star is Born* might bear some similarities to them and she didn't want to see the sad ending with him.

There was a knock at the door. "Room service." Tano answered the door and brought in the food and set it on the end of the bed.

"Okay, my lady. We have drinks and snacks and are set for the night."

Both remained in bed with a plate of cheese and crackers and glasses of wine. Tano sang along with the Queen music and brightened what had become a pensive mood. Holly knew that listening to him sing those songs was a singular moment that she would never forget. She closed her eyes to commit the flash in time to her memory. When Freddie Mercury began to sing "Under Pressure," Tano and Holly simultaneously jumped out of bed and began to dance, holding glasses of wine, bodies gyrating to the repetitive rhythm of the bass guitar and strong beat. When the song was over, Tano took Holly's wine glass and set both glasses down on the nightstand next to the bed. He wrapped both arms around Holly and picked her up and laid her down on the bed and laid on top of her. Holly felt a buzz from the wine. She wrapped her legs around Tano as his kisses became deeper and deeper. She never wanted anyone more than she wanted him at that moment and her body let him know it. And once again, their passion for each other ignited and set in motion an intimate series of give and take, each wanting to please the other until their bodies could no longer wait for the orgasmic finish. Breathless and sweating, they separated and laid apart to cool down. Tano held Holly's right hand in his left and after a few moments, pulled her over on top of him, just to be close to her again and whispered in her ear, "I know now why I missed you so much."

Holly whispered, almost inaudibly, "Did you? Why is that?"

"Because you give so much of yourself. And with a nice body, too." Then he patted her bottom and held her tight. His feelings for her were strong. Was it love? Or just a lot of fun? Or both? She was a girl unlike any other he knew, and she had gotten to him. "I think that the movie is over now. Do you want to call it a night?"

"I guess. At least turn out the lights." Holly didn't know if Tano had it in him for a third round of love making. As much as she knew they needed rest, she could not get enough of him. It had been a long drive from Sage, and an even longer drive from Colorado for Tano. And five years apart.

When he fell asleep, she laid awake, wanting the day to never end, wanting him again, wanting to capture each moment in her memory since she knew their time together would end soon. She listened to the soft rhythm of him breathing as he laid on his back. She turned on her side, toward him, and surrendered herself to sleep.

CHAPTER 14

The peaceful solitude of the night was interrupted by a light *tap, tap, tap* on the door of their hotel room. Holly and Tano stirred unaware at first that the knocking was on their door. Another light *tap, tap, tap* then a woman's muffled, slurred voice, "Tano. Tano, you in there?"

"Jesus, it's Janet and she's drunk. Be still. Maybe she will go away," Tano whispered to Holly. They both laid still and held their breaths, as if she could hear them.

"Tano, Tano, let me in! Rocky and I had a fight." She continued tapping on the door. "I don't know where to go. Let me in." Then the knocking stopped. Tano pulled Holly closer to him. They both laid curled up together, eyes closed, and listened.

Soon there was loud pounding on the door. Janet slurred and shouted, "Come on, Tano! Let me in! Let me in! I don't care if she's in there with you. Let me in! Now!"

"I've had enough." Tano sat up, reached for his phone. "I'm calling Rocky." Tano dialed Rocky's phone. No answer. He spoke quietly as he left a voice message so Janet wouldn't hear him speaking. "Jesus, Rocky, your girlfriend is up here pounding on the door and yelling. Would you come get her the hell away from my door? I'm in 333."

The loud knocking and slurred shouting continued. Tano picked up the hotel telephone, and called hotel security. "This is Room 333. Someone is at my door, drunk, knocking and yelling. I'm sure that everyone on this floor can hear her. Could you come up here and get her to leave?" The pounding and shouting continued. "Can you hear that? Okay, hurry up."

"Tano!" Then there was a loud thump against the door. Janet had collapsed and fell into the door.

In a few minutes, Tano and Holly heard, "Come on now. Let's get you up. What is your room number? You're disrupting hotel guests."

"Don't know. Was with a guy and we had a fight. Don't know..."

"What's your name? What's the guy's name? We'll get you back there."

"It's Rocky. Rocky is his name. But I want to stay here in this room." Hotel security called the main desk to find out who she was staying with.

Tano was tempted to open the door and clear up the confusion. But he continued to wait silently. When security could get no answers, they finally picked Janet up by both of her arms and held her up as she stumbled to the elevator. Janet vomited in the hall on the way. When security reached the lobby, they dropped her onto a cushioned chair and approached the desk.

"Do you believe that dumbass Janet?" Tano whispered when the noise stopped. "Maybe I should text Rocky and tell him what's going on."

"I know it's none of my business but jeez, Tano, what is with her? I had a little confrontation with her in the bathroom at the restaurant."

"I took her out a couple of times. Don't know why I did. She seemed okay at first. Nothing special though. She turned into a possessive psycho stalker right away. She finally quit harassing me when I blocked her messages but then she got her claws into Rocky and here we go again. Rocky could do better than that. She's not even hot or pretty. I don't think Rocky really cares anyway. She said something to you at the restaurant?"

"Yeah, I overheard her talking about me to Shiloh in the bathroom and I set her straight. I see the picture now. Looks like she still has a thing for you."

"Maybe, baby. Let's go back to sleep."

"I'll try. I'm just so wide awake now." Holly laid on her back and studied the ceiling. In a matter of minutes, she could hear Tano's soft, steady, rhythmic breathing as he fell asleep. She looked at her phone. It was three thirty a.m. She tossed and turned and rearranged her pillow. Suddenly in the stillness of the predawn night, there were gunshots outside the hotel. Pop, pop, pop!! And the loud long piercing scream of a woman. Then silence.

"Christ, what is going on out there?" Tano sat up suddenly and stepped toward the window to get a look. Holly followed behind him. Light from the hotel illuminated the sidewalk below where a woman laid. Someone rushed to the scene from the hotel lobby. They crouched down near the woman and took out their phone and made a call. More hotel employees rushed out to the sidewalk. Tano saw the woman move her legs slightly. "I want to see what's going on down there, but if I show up, the press will link me and Badge to it somehow."

The night silence was pierced by sirens rushing to the scene. The rotating red lights created a strobe light effect in the room as they reflected from the windows. Undecipherable radio chatter from the emergency equipment echoed below. Tano closed the curtains tightly, they returned to bed, where they spooned, with her back side pressed against his front. But adrenalin from sudden disrupted sleep had made them restless for the rest of the night.

Dawn appeared too soon. Tano and Holly laid still with their eyes closed hoping to drift off a while longer. Holly rolled onto her back and stretched her arms over head. Tano reached over and put his arms around her waist and pulled her closer to him and held her tight. Within minutes, Tano heard the text tone on his phone.

I know it's early man, but can I come up and talk to you?

"It's Randy. He wants to come up here and talk." Tano texted *yes* back. In a couple of minutes, there was a knock at the door and Randy hurried into the room. Holly had pulled her jeans on and was sitting on the brown tapestry couch. Tano sat next to her on the edge of the cushion, leaning forward waiting to hear what Randy had to say.

"Well, we have a situation, man, but I'm not sure what to do about it. Maybe nothing. But early this morning, Janet was wandering around outside of the hotel. Drunk. Totally wasted. And was shot somehow. She's alive and in surgery now. Rocky is pretty upset. He's at the hospital. I guess they had a fight and she left. From what he told me, hotel security said she was disturbing hotel guests, knocking on doors, yelling. So they put her in her own room because she wouldn't go back in with Rocky. She left the new room again, went out on the street, and got shot somehow."

"Jesus, like, where was she hit? What was she doing anyway? Do they think she was mugged or what?"

"She was shot twice—in the shoulder and in her right side. She lost a lot of blood. No one knows what happened. She didn't have her purse with her. It's still in the room. So, she had no ID either, but the hotel security knew that she was a hotel guest. They are looking at the security footage now. So anyway, there's the concert tonight, man. I don't want to cancel it. Rocky might want to. What do you think?"

"I think we should talk to Rocky. But I'm thinking that if she pulls through surgery, we should go ahead with the concert. But if she doesn't make it, I don't know." Tano looked at the floor and thought. "But if we publicly react to this incident, then it will appear to the press and the fans that we are linked to it somehow and not that it was just a random thing, like it is. Is Rocky really into her or what?"

"I can't tell. You know he doesn't talk about his women. He ignores them mostly. I think he feels bad, maybe a little responsible, because he let her leave his room. I wanted to let you know about all this, man, before you got slammed with it."

Tano unconsciously began to rub the top of Holly's thigh while he absorbed all that had happened. Randy noticed the gesture and said, "Oh, hi, Holly. I didn't mean to be rude. It was just urgent that I talk to Tano."

"I'm good. I didn't think anything of it. How is Shiloh doing with this?"

"She doesn't really know Janet well. I met Shiloh in Boulder when we were home a couple of months ago. She's only been around Janet for a couple of times. She's upset though."

Tano walked over to the window and opened the heavy dark drapes. Yellow tape encircled the crime scene. There was a brown puddle of what appeared to be dried blood on the concrete sidewalk. A small group of reporters stood near the scene talking among themselves and taking photos of the hotel and the scene. "Ya know, I wanted to go down to the restaurant and get breakfast, but I think we should order room service. What do you say, Randy?"

"I better head back to the room and stay with Shiloh. She's pretty freaked out

"Okay, so, the plan was to meet at the Arena at four. See you there. I guess if everything goes as planned." Randy mumbled and nodded and hurried out the door.

"Okay, little lady. Take a look at this menu." Holly came from a farm family where breakfast was the biggest meal of the day. Tano was surprised when she ordered green chile quiche, hash browns, and jalapeno bacon. "Can you finish all of that?"

"Yes, I think so. It feels like we've been up for hours." Tano ordered huevos rancheros with hash browns and turkey sausage.

Tano turned the TV on while they waited for room service. He walked over to the window and looked out at the shooting scene again. Holly began to wonder if his intense interest in the shooting meant that he had some feelings for Janet. She wouldn't ask him. She would just watch.

The TV was set to a local station which broke into the broadcast with news about the shooting.

"An unidentified woman was shot in the early morning hours in front of the Amarillo hotel where the Boulder, Colorado–based country rock band, Badge, is staying. Badge is scheduled to give a concert tonight at the Arena. Spokespersons indicated that it is unknown if the shooting is in any way connected to the band. An investigation is underway and nearby surveillance footage is being examined by police. The condition of the woman is currently unknown."

A few seconds later, Rocky texted Tano:

> *Janet is out of surgery. In fair condition. Concert is on. See you at four at the Arena.*

Tano had questions for Rocky, but he didn't want to text them to him. They would talk later. He read the text out loud to Holly. Room service arrived with breakfast. Holly and Tano ate quietly. "My quiche is so good. I'm glad I ordered it, but you know all of this looks like too much again." Holly wanted to break the silence.

"Eat as much as you can. It's all good."

"Tano, what's on your mind? I can see the wheels turning. Are you worried about the concert?"

Tano didn't respond and took a bite of the hash browns and then said, "Nothing, really."

"Okay." If he wanted to talk, he would. She wouldn't press him for conversation. After a few long silent minutes, Holly's phone alerted her that she received a text message. She walked across the room, picked up her phone. Tano heard her sigh loudly and mutter under her breath, "Oh, jeez." When she looked up, she said, "Garth is flipping out. He heard about the shooting. He just texted me."

"What did he say?"

"Oh, just that he wants to know what's going on. I'm just going to tell him that we are fine. And that I'll be home tomorrow."

The text actually read *What the fuck is going on there? Tell that Badge son of a bitch that you're coming home now!* Garth was Holly's problem. Her feelings for Tano had grown intensely in just one day. There was no way that she would impose on him in any way that would cause him to doubt a relationship with her, if it was meant to be. And she silently prayed. *Please let it be.*

CHAPTER 15

Holly and Tano showered and took their time getting dressed. "Let's get out of here for a while. Let's see what there's to do in Amarillo." Tano thumbed through the visitor brochure that he found on a table in the room. "How about the zoo? Are you up for that? And there's a place called the Cadillac Ranch on Route 66 that looks kind of funky. What do you think?"

"Sure, let's start at the zoo. It looks like it's not far from here," Holly said as she looked over his shoulder at the brochure. They made their way to the elevator. "I wonder if there's any news," Holly said as they walked, referring to the shooting.

Tano shook his head. "We'll know soon enough." The elevator dropped one floor and a woman stepped in.

"Hello, Tano." The woman was thirty-ish, short, chunky, with a prominent underbite and red hair in a flat, short, nondescript style wearing a brown hoodie, baggy white T-shirt, brown jeans and white Converse tennis shoes. She had an almost troll-like appearance.

"Donna?" Tano was clearly surprised by the appearance of the woman who he obviously knew. "This is unexpected. What are you doing here?"

"Oh, there are reasons. I saw that Badge was in town and decided to stay for the concert tonight." Donna moved closer to Tano and reached for him as if she expected a hug, but none was forthcoming. He took a step back.

"Okay, well, enjoy. We are getting out of here for a while. Reporters appear to be everywhere. You know a woman was shot in front of the hotel last night."

Donna nodded her head and then turned and looked directly at Holly. "And is this your girlfriend?"

"This is Holly. I guess I should have introduced her." He turned to Holly. "Donna was a bartender at Tumbleweed a couple of years ago."

"Nice to meet you," Donna said, continuing to stare intensely at Holly's face with brown eyes so dark that the pupils were barely visible.

"Well, see you around." Tano grabbed Holly's hand, exited the elevator, walked quickly to the van and hopped inside. They had made their way to the hotel parking garage without fanfare. "Wow, that was weird. That Donna is kind of psycho. When she worked for me, she told people that she was my girlfriend. She screened my calls at work, left notes on my van and in my office, sent me Valentine kinds of stickers in Messenger, called me at all hours of the night for random made-up reasons. I had to let her go from Tumbleweed a few years back and I didn't expect to see her again. Ever. And she shows up here? It's weird."

"How did you let her go? Did she react badly? Did you date?"

"No way! I never went out with her. Not my type. One day, I had enough of her possessiveness and lies and told her to leave. That was the last time I saw her until today." Reporters seemed to be camped out by the scene of the shooting and unaware that one of the band might leave the premises from a different exit. Tano started the van and drove from the parking lot. Donna disappeared among the parked vehicles.

The zoo was just a few miles away. Tano was silent as they drove. But it wasn't his silence that bothered Holly. It was the vibe she felt from him. Something was different and she couldn't resist mentioning it.

"Tano, I can see that something's on your mind. It's probably none of my business, but you've been different since you found out that Janet was shot. Are you worried about her? Or is it that Donna?"

Tano scratched his head, adjusted his sunglasses, and ran his fingers through his hair before he answered. "No, I'm not worried about Janet. It crossed my mind that maybe I should have let her in and maybe she wouldn't have been shot. She'll be fine. She's Janet." Then he rested his right hand on Holly's left thigh. "It was when I looked down from the hotel window at her body laying there on the ground and the blood that reminded me of something that happened a really long time ago that I kind of blocked from my mind for a long time."

"Okay." Holly laid her hand on his and gave it a little squeeze. He was clearly bothered by something and she would have to let him decide whether to talk about it or not.

About ten minutes later, Tano pulled into the parking lot of the Amarillo Zoo and began to speak about it again. "When I was about nine or ten, my brothers, my sister and I spent a week with our cousins in Bailey. They lived on a farm and had this big old barn with a hay loft in it. So one day all of us were playing around up there. My cousins, Dan and Greg, got down from the loft and went into the house and came out with a pistol. They were messing around with it and Greg accidentally shot Dan in the stomach. Dan didn't make it. I remember hearing that gunshot and looking over the edge of the hayloft and there was my cousin, Dan, sprawled out on the ground and blood spilling out all around him and Greg screaming his name and shouting 'no, no, no.' Looking down at Janet laying there in the blood just reminded me of that awful day that I didn't want to remember. But I'm good, Holly. Let's go look at some animals and forget about the shooting. And Donna, too."

Holly leaned over and rubbed her hand on Tano's right upper arm and kissed him lightly on the cheek. *He could use some tenderness*, she thought.

Tano was moved by the gesture. *She has a such a generous heart.*

The Amarillo Zoo housed a mixture of exotic and western domestic animals. The warmth of the morning sunshine brought the animals out of their shelters to sun themselves before the heat of midday. Mixed among enclosures for lions, tigers, monkeys and kangaroos were pens which housed bison, goats, several multicolored mustangs, and a silver fox, which was Holly's favorite. They meandered through the reptile and amphibian exhibits before Tano decided they should get ice cream cones.

Tano had been oblivious of the attention he attracted from some of the zoo visitors. When they reached the concession stand, a couple of people approached him and said, "Oh, Tano! We are coming to your concert tonight. Can we get a selfie with you?" Tano humbly obliged and then turned his full attention to Holly.

"What will it be?"

"A scoop of vanilla and a scoop of chocolate. And some chocolate sprinkles, too?"

"A double dip, huh? Same for me." They found a metal park bench under the shade of a pecan tree. The bench was divided in half by a center armrest but they both sat together closely on one side. A light breeze lifted Holly's hair away from her face and Tano could smell the light floral scent of Holly's shampoo. *I'm so happy that I found her*, he thought. As he looked at her, Holly turned and smiled at him.

"Okay, country girl. Let's go see what this Cadillac Ranch is all about."

The Cadillac Ranch was west of Amarillo and about ten miles from the zoo on Route 66. Neither of the them knew what to expect when they arrived. They parked on the side of the road behind a line of other parked cars. And there it was. Ten vintage Cadillacs in a single row were buried hood deep, vertically, covered with bright multicolored paint and graffiti.

"Do you think it's a work of art or just a roadside attraction?" Holly asked Tano.

"I don't know. I guess it's how each person looks at it. I think that some cars are an art form. Holly, stand over there in front of that one. Let me take some photos of you." Tano pointed to the first Cadillac and took a photo of Holly with the full line of vertical Cadillacs positioned behind her. A little whirlwind of dust spontaneously appeared in the stark background just as Tano took the photo. "Look at this. It looks like a tornado above your head."

"Okay, now you." Holly snapped photos of Tano. A sign near the site said that the "sculptures" had been placed there by an Amarillo millionaire who chose the 1948–1963 Cadillacs to depict the "Golden Age of the Automobile." The sign said that Bruce Springsteen had written a song about it called "Cadillac Ranch" that was a selection on *The River* album.

"Let's listen to that song when we leave, Tano."

"Great idea. I'm not quite sure what to think of this place. I've never seen anything quite like it," Tano said, as he attempted to decipher the graffiti on one of the cars. "Are you hungry? Do you want lunch?"

"I'm not hungry but if you are…"

"Rob usually has a big spread when the band gets to the venue. I can wait until then. Let's head back to the hotel."

"Good idea. I want to change into some different clothes." As Holly suggested, they listened to "Cadillac Ranch" on the drive back to the hotel. Pure classic Springsteen rock and roll.

When they returned to the hotel, Holly changed into a rhinestone laden black short sleeved cropped T-shirt that exposed her little midriff. She slid on the bracelets that she often wore. Before she slipped her jeans on, she walked over to her bag to grab the skinny tooled black belt with the silver rose buckle that she was going to wear. Tano couldn't resist grabbing her from behind and he carried her to the bed. "Hey, you know we don't have to be at the Arena for another hour. Want to play?" Tano laughed.

"Well, apparently you do. So, I say yes." Holly winked at him. Tano laid down beside her, kissed her tenderly, slipped his hand under her shirt, unbuttoned his pants and let the passionate give and take begin.

Afterward, Tano rolled onto his back and laid his arm across his forehead and turned to her and said, "Well, sweet thing, after that, playing the guitar tonight will be boring."

Holly laughed. "It will be great. I'm excited to see Badge tonight. And yes, what we just did…was electric. Let's try and get ready to go again." Although Tano wanted to shower with Holly, he knew that they would never make it to the Arena on time for the sound check if he did. So they quickly showered and got ready. Holly thought Tano looked especially handsome in his black T-shirt, faded blue jeans, brown and white cowboy boots, with his long tousled wavy black hair. *I'm so lucky.*

"Let's go, Holly baby, and make some memories."

CHAPTER 16

Tano drove around to the loading entrance and parked at the Arena to avoid the horde of reporters waiting at the main entrance. Unfortunately, they had positioned themselves at every entrance and exit to snag someone from Badge with a statement about the shooting.

"All of us should have taken a limo together and then we wouldn't have to encounter these vultures one at a time. Walk fast and don't even acknowledge them." Tano and Holly emerged from the van. Tano put his arm around her and held her close to him as they hustled to the building. TV cameras captured the swift walk.

Reporters began to hurl questions. "Hey, Tano, over here—what do you know about the shooting this morning?"

"Was the woman who was shot part of your entourage?"

"Do you think the shooting is related to Badge?"

"Did you add extra security?"

"Are you going ahead with the concert tonight?"

Questions were tossed at them from all directions. Tano looked straight ahead and did not respond to the frustration of the news corps.

When they got inside, Tano said, "Maybe we do need extra security. Never thought of it. I guess I'll talk to Arena security and see what they have planned for us."

The roadies had already begun to set up guitar stands, drums, and risers, and to test the mikes, amps, and the lighting techs were programming the lighting effects. Rob, the band's manager, greeted Tano when he walked in. Rob had just recently been hired by Badge to manage the band's tour schedules and bookings. He was tall and slim, with long wavy brown hair, and dark, deep lashed eyes, and a deep dimple on his chin. He looked as if he belonged in a rock band.

"Hey, Tano," he said as he shook his hand. "What the hell happened at the hotel? Those reporters were already camped out when we came in this morning."

"I don't know anything except that Rocky's girlfriend, Janet, was shot by somebody outside the hotel. The news people probably know more about this than we do. But hey, do you know what the security situation is for this place? Security for us didn't even occur to me until one of those jokers out there asked me about it."

"Hell, maybe we need to check it out, Tano. I'll go talk to them."

"Okay. Rob, this is Holly. She's going to be with me today and backstage during the concert. See to it that she gets anything she wants." Tano still had his arm around her and slipped his hand into the back pocket of her jeans and pulled her closer to him.

"Nice to meet you, Holly. You been to a Badge concert before?" When Rob reached out to shake her hand, Holly noticed a tattoo on the back of his right hand of a small cactus with a barbed wire coiled around it.

"Yes. A few years back in San Angelo. I loved it. Nice to meet you, too." She looked at Tano and smiled.

"Well, I see Randy and Jack are here. Rocky on his way?"

"Yeah, he should be here soon. He's probably at the hospital checking on Janet this morning. Or smokin' some weed."

"Okay, well, I'm going to go look for the security guy and I'll catch up with you later." Tano and Holly walked into the seating area and pulled two cushioned seats down. Tano wanted to look at the stage setup from the audience's perspective. He rested his right hand on Holly's thigh.

"Well, Holly, remember I told you that you could pick out a few songs for us to play tonight. Have you given it any thought?"

"Yeah. I have. How about 'Free'—remember we played it together in the van? Do you guys still play that? And those originals of yours: 'Somewhere Along the Way' and 'The Girl from Yesterday' that you said was about me. Too many quiet songs? And of course, you always perform 'Badge.'"

"No, that's not too many. We slow it down three or four times at each concert. All of those songs are on the setlist. You can count on it." Tano leaned over and kissed her on the cheek and patted her thigh as he stood. Rocky emerged on the stage and picked up his guitar. The band members surrounded him to get the latest news on the shooting. Holly saw Rocky shrug his shoulders as he spoke. Evidently the incident was still a mystery.

Holly watched and listened as the band began to play song after song and then stop in the middle to fine tune them and then begin again. Even though they knew all of the music by heart, their trained ears could detect where minor musical adjustments should be made. Occasionally, Tano looked in her direction and smiled or nodded. Holly was so wrapped up in the rehearsal, she didn't even notice that Shiloh had quietly sat down near her.

When Holly turned and saw her, she said, "Oh, Shiloh! How long have you been there? I'm sorry. I was watching the rehearsal, and I guess I wasn't paying attention."

"Oh, that's okay. I didn't feel like coming to the Arena for a while, so Randy let me stay in the room and I caught an Uber."

"That was really something—Janet being shot. We don't know anything, do you?'

"No, they—well, the police and hotel security are looking at camera footage to see what happened. Our room—Randy's and mine—is next to Rocky's and we heard them arguing in the middle of the night. Later we heard the door slam. That must be when she left. I don't know Janet very well, and I hope that she will be okay, but she makes things so difficult. Insisting on her way all the time. Like she is entitled or something. Oh, I shouldn't talk about her like that." Shiloh's freckled face flushed as if she was embarrassed.

"It's okay. I don't think she likes me because of Tano and their history. I guess that's why." Holly wanted to change the subject. "They sound good, don't they? I've been a big Badge fan since college. I'm just so happy that Tano brought me with him."

After an hour or so, Badge seemed satisfied and ready for the show. Rob ordered catering for the band, a case of Corona, and bottles of Jack Daniels and Coke which were set up in a nearby dressing room. Tano motioned to Holly and Shiloh to come with him. There was a full table of Texas barbecue with potato salad, macaroni and cheese, pinto beans, and all of the condiments. Tano poured himself a shot of Jack. "Want one?' Tano asked. Rocky, who reeked from pot, poured himself a shot, slammed it down, and then poured another.

"Sure, why not?" *It must be one of their preshow rituals*, Holly thought. She and Tano found an oversized stuffed chair in the corner of the room and squeezed into it together while they ate.

After a few minutes, Holly received a text from Garth.

> *I just saw your face plastered all over the news with that Tano bastard. You better come home.*

She read the message and put her phone in her pocket. About five minutes later, her phone rang. It was Garth. She didn't answer.

"Everything good?" Tano asked Holly when he saw her face grow serious as she looked at her phone.

"Well, it's Garth. He heard about the shooting and I guess there was footage of you and me going into the Arena this morning on the news. Nothing ever happens in Oklahoma and so they depend on Texas for news stories."

"Maybe you should talk to him."

"No, I might text him. Yeah, I will." Holly pulled her phone out.

> *I'm fine. Someone was shot outside our hotel. It doesn't involve Badge. I am safe with Tano.*

As they sat huddled together in the big comfy chair, Tano and Holly heard Rocky talking to Jack, the drummer. "Yeah, she was just waking up from surgery. She was lucky. No organs were involved. One bullet lodged between the ribs. The bullet in the shoulder just grazed the collar bone. It will take a while to heal. It must have been a small caliber gun or she might have been killed."

"What happened? Is she talking yet?" Tano asked.

"Don't know. Either a robbery or just a nut job. Footage showed a person with a dark hooded sweatshirt and white tennis shoes emerge from somewhere near the entrance to the hotel. She was probably too wasted to know. I'm going to the hospital now to see her. Man, I shouldn't have let her leave the room last night. "

"Hey, steer clear of those vultures." Rocky nodded and left.

"I think we should stay here until the concert. Are you good with that? Hey, come out on stage with me and let's you and I jam a little. The doors don't open for another hour."

"Is that okay?"

"Of course. I say so." Tano and Holly walked out onto the stage. Holly picked up Rocky's violin from the stand and Tano grabbed his guitar. Holly ran the bow over the strings a couple of times, while Tano was getting set up, and then began to play a little of the hoe-down yet intricate, fast-paced fiddle solo from "The Devil Went Down to Georgia."

"Seriously, Holly? Classical and country? You're so talented."

"Oh, I was just playing around. I told you that when there was nothing to do, I listened to rock and roll and country music and then played my violin along with it. An Oklahoma girl has to play some-thing other than Chopin."

"Well, now you're a Kansas girl, too. Do you know this song?" Tano played soft chords on the acoustic Fender guitar and began to sing "Dust in the Wind" by the band Kansas. Holly knew the vio-lin accompaniment to that song very well and began to play when she figured out the key. They sounded so perfect together that the band members, roadies, light techs, and Arena staff gradually gath-ered around the stage to listen. When they finished the song, the stunned watchers applauded. Tano clapped, too, and Holly bowed.

"Jeez, Holly. Want to join the band?"

"That was fun. Sure." Holly knew he was joking. "How about an-other?" Holly picked up the bow and began to play a violin solo so beautiful that the onlookers paused and stood motionless, trans-fixed on the copper-headed girl who had appeared onstage with Tano. Not a sound was heard except for Holly's haunting version of "Hallelujah." When she finished playing, the astonished makeshift audience that had gathered was silent for a few moments, waiting for more, and then they erupted into applause. Tano, who had been standing near Holly during the spontaneous solo performance, was stunned and beamed with pride. Holly blushed, grinned, pretended to curtsy and bow.

"Man, sweetness, you rock! I don't know what to say. That was amazing." He pulled her close and kissed her on the forehead.

"Okay, that's it for the preshow," Tano waved to them and laughed. He and Holly put the instruments back on the stands, just as Rocky returned from the hospital.

"Hey, Rock, what did you find out?"

"Not a lot. Janet's in pain, but the doctors think she will make a full recovery. She doesn't know what happened for sure. The only things that she thinks she remembers is that the person who shot her was a woman—at least she remembers a woman's voice—and that she said something about Badge and you. She has no idea why she was shot."

Tano looked at Holly. Holly looked at Tano. A woman? The same thought popped into of their heads. Could it have been Donna?

CHAPTER 17

Donna Lynn Brown was born thirty years ago to the family of Bob and Linda Brown in Fort Collins, Colorado, and became the baby sister to a brother, Bob Jr., and a sister, Cathy. From birth, she took on the appearance of a rubber baby doll, a troll doll to be precise, with a turned-up pug nose, chubby cheeks, tousled dark red hair and short chunky legs. Linda dressed her in the finest little smocked dresses and baby doll shoes. Passersby would comment about how cute she was and that she didn't look real. Baby Donna loved the attention and would coo and smile.

As Donna grew into a toddler, she continued to draw attention for her unusual looks. Her eyes were walnut brown, almost black, which enveloped her pupils giving her a lifeless, cartoon like gaze. She had developed a slight underbite and her troll-like features continued to make her stand out among the other children at school and made her the center of attention. As the elementary school years unfolded, she became conceited. Some of the kids called her a brat. She didn't care.

Her childhood was unremarkable and as uninspiring as her name. There was no drama. And fortunately, no trauma. Her dad went to work each day as a manager of a Fort Collins hardware store. Her mother worked part-time at a local preschool. Donna and her siblings rode their bikes, played soccer, went to summer camp, and caught crawdads and dragon flies in the summer. Donna took baton twirling lessons.

When the middle school years arrived, her female classmates suddenly began to develop long legs and curvy figures and their facial features began to mature. They began to wear makeup and to gain the attention of the pubescent boys. Donna remained short, and chunky and paunchy with her moppet facial features and short flat trendless red hair. The slight underbite became more prominent. Suddenly and without warning the years of positive attention faded away and Donna fell into the background. The few friends she had lost interest in her self-absorbed personality and drifted away. The high school boys gave her no notice and her social life was nonexistent. She convinced herself that they were just jealous and that she just needed a new environment.

She enrolled in Front Range Community College after graduation since she had no real idea what she wanted to do with the rest of her life. She got a job as a banquet server at a local hotel and eventually was trained as the bartender in the hotel bar. There she met Melvin Smith who would become her husband. He was serious, plain spoken, average height and about thirty pounds overweight. Also as unremarkable as his name. He worked in the oil fields. He was completely infatuated with Donna. They were married at the Larimer County Courthouse on a sunny May day.

Even with a devoted husband, after a couple of years, Donna was bored. Melvin was boring. Their life was boring and she was tired of it. One summer day, she and her sister, Cathy, decided to take a trip to the Pearl Street Mall in Boulder to check it out. They were tired of the Fort Collins shops. As they strolled past Tumbleweed, there was a small sign in the window that read, "Bartender Wanted."

"Hey, I'm going inside to see what this job is all about." Donna impulsively opened the door. "Come on, Cathy. Come in, too," she said as she waved her hand. Cathy, who was never comfortable with impulse, grudgingly followed her.

Donna approached the shiny gray granite bar and sat down on a round red bar stool. Anthony, the interim bartender and Tano's business partner, was standing behind the mirrored bar looking at the inventory of tequila bottles and jotting notes on a clipboard. He was dark and handsome with light blue eyes, and a deep voice like Sam Elliott. He wore a gold wedding band. "What can I get for you ladies today?"

"We don't know yet. But I wanted to ask if you still need a bartender. I saw the sign in the window."

"Yeah, we sure do. I'm just filling in here until we find a permanent bartender. There's going to be a big festival here on the mall this weekend and Barb, the bartender, just quit suddenly to travel to Spain with her boyfriend. Why? Do you know somebody?"

"Yes, I do. Me. I'm TIPS alcohol certified and have been bartending in Fort Collins for three years."

Cathy audibly gasped when she heard what Donna said. "Donna, what will Melvin say about this? Are you going to commute or what?" she whispered to her.

"Okay. Come around here," Anthony motioned to her, "and make a basic margarita for me. Let's see what you got." Donna hopped off the barstool, went behind the bar and quickly and methodically made a Patrón margarita. Anthony tasted it and said, "Not bad." He had been looking for a pretty young bartender to draw in customers and Donna did not fit that profile at all. But he was so desperate to fill the position, he decided to make Donna an offer anyway.

"So, when could you start? This position is between twenty-five to thirty hours a week. Some day shifts, some nights. What do you think?"

"I think yes. I could start in a couple of days. I need to clear my schedule in Fort Collins." Anthony shook her hand and handed her an application to complete.

Cathy was aghast by what had just happened and squirmed on the bar stool, wanting to leave. "What are you doing? Are you insane? Let's go."

"No, I'm bored and I need something new. Some new people. Some new friends. What's wrong with that?

"The commute is long and Melvin isn't going to like it."

"Tough. He'll just have to get used to it. Anthony, I'll take a peach margarita to celebrate. What about you, Cathy?"

"I'll just have a Coke." Donna rolled her eyes at Cathy. Cathy's eyes were still bulging from shock and she was still squirming on the bar stool.

While they sat there sipping their drinks, a man walked behind the bar and greeted Anthony. A man so handsome that Donna's mouth fell open. Black wavy hair that rested on his shirt collar, light brown eyes, dimpled cheeks, dark moustache, great body, dressed in torn denim jeans, and denim shirt with sleeves rolled up to his elbows, and wearing brown cowboy boots. He smelled heavenly.

"Hey, Tano, I didn't expect you until this weekend. I just hired us a bartender. Donna, right?"

"Yes, I'm Donna and this is my sister, Cathy."

Tano reached across the bar and shook her hand and smiled at her. "Glad to meet you and glad you can help us out."

Donna didn't want to let go of his hand and continued to stare at his face. Cathy poked her in her side and whispered, "Donna, I think that's Tano from that group Badge?"

"What? I don't think so. Whoever he is, he is unlike anybody I've ever seen before." Donna continued to watch him while he talked with Anthony.

Again, Cathy whispered to her, "Yes, I think it is him. Badge is based out of Boulder. Ask him."

"No way. What if he isn't? That would be embarrassing."

"Okay, then I will. Tano?" Tano turned and looked at her. "You wouldn't happen to be Tano from Badge, are you?" Cathy shyly asked him. Her face was red with embarrassment.

"Yep, that would be me."

Cathy and Donna turned and looked at each other, jabbed their elbows together, with mouths open in disbelief. "See. I told you."

"Wow, this is a better set up than I thought," Donna muttered under her breath.

Donna began to work at Tumbleweed in time for the festival on Pearl Street and was a top-notch bartender. Anthony let her know that she could work additional hours if she chose. As Cathy predicted, Melvin was not happy with Donna's new career. But Donna didn't care. She had seen someone who had swept her off her feet. Just the sight of Tano sent shivers of excitement through her body.

To her great disappointment, he spent most of his time away from Boulder. But each day that she arrived to work at the bar, it was her hope that he would be there that day. And when he was, she tried desperately to get his attention of which Tano was totally unaware.

One afternoon when Tano was standing behind the bar checking on the inventory, Donna abruptly and impulsively walked up behind him, put her arms around his waist and laid her head against his back. Although Tano was taken by surprise, he thought she was just trying to squeeze past him, but she continued to hold on.

"Uh, Donna. Do you need to get past me? Or what?"

"Oh. No. I...uh..." Donna's troll-like face flushed so red she resembled a Christmas elf. "I...uh..." She scurried away.

Tano thought nothing more of it until he began to receive calls from vendors who told him that when they called or stopped by to see him, Donna told them that she was his girlfriend and that they could talk to her when he wasn't there. To test what he had heard about her, he asked a female friend of his to call Tumbleweed and ask for him to see what she would say.

"Hi, is Ben Montano there?"

"No, he's not. I'm his girlfriend. Could I take a message?"

"Oh, really, well, then tell him to call Becky. He has my number." Tano heard all of it on Becky's phone.

Tano immediately drove to the bar, threw the door open, and fired Donna.

"Tano? Why? What happened?" Donna's mouth fell open.

"You know damn well what's been going on. Anthony, could you get a final paycheck for Donna? Today is her last day. In fact, she's leaving now."

Donna's bulldog face crumpled into a wrinkled grimace and she began to sob heavily and rushed out the door. Tano never saw her again. But she saw him. She continued to hang out on the mall hoping to catch a glimpse of him. She figured out where he lived and drove up the canyon and parked near his house and imagined herself inside. Her marriage to Melvin fizzled out with no regrets. As weeks turned into months, her fixation grew, and she convinced herself that Tano didn't really mean it when he fired her, that he really wanted her and if she could just be with him once, he would know it, too.

In recent weeks, with each passing day, the quiet internal desperation that churned within her had reached a new plateau with no boundaries. Donna looked at the Badge schedule online, bought a couple of guns, impulsively rented a car and drove to Amarillo, Texas. *There can be no competition for Tano. Nothing or no one will stop me from having him. I know he wants me. Maybe I can move in with him. Maybe I can tour with him.* Those twisted thoughts replayed over and over in her mind. Donna's overwhelming obsession was about to lead her on a relentless course of destruction with Tano, she believed, as the final reward.

CHAPTER 18

Holly whispered to Tano. "Do you think it could be Donna? Would Donna do something like shoot someone?"

"It's hard to know what she is capable of."

Rocky tapped Tano on the shoulder. "Hey, the police and hotel security want to talk to you and Holly sometime before we leave tomorrow to get your take on what you know."

"Yeah, sure."

The band members and entourage returned to the backstage waiting room. The venue doors were open, and noisy and excited fans began to filter in. As was the Badge custom, Tano and the band each drank three shots of Jack Daniels while they waited to go onstage. As was his custom, Rocky smoked a joint.

"Here, Holly, want a shot?"

"Maybe one."

Tano faced Holly and put his hand on her shoulder. "Okay, now, I want you to be where I can see you during the concert. You stand over here with Rob. You're my special guest. My special girl." He pointed to the side of the stage. Holly smiled and drank the shot of whiskey. It warmed her lips and throat as she downed it. Tano pulled her close and kissed her hard and she tasted the whiskey on his lips. She felt a surge of electricity shoot through her body. *Was it the whiskey or the kiss?*

At a few minutes past seven, Badge stepped out onstage to a packed arena of cheering fans and began the set with their signature "Badge." Colored lights shot up behind them like fountains and white spotlights scanned the audience. The fans expected "Badge" would be the first song and they stood and sang along. Then Badge launched into a series of raucous, hard driving rock and roll, all of them Badge originals, written by Tano or Randy. "Leather and Chrome," "A Trip to Nowhere," "Waiting for a Chance," and "Dusty Highway."

Toward the end of the set, Tano emerged solo under a single white spotlight with his Fender acoustic guitar. The audience hushed to listen as Tano spoke.

"Let's take it down a notch for a minute. I wrote this song about a special lady that I met around five years ago and I'm happy to say that she is here with me tonight. Holly, this one's for you. 'The Girl from Yesterday.'" Tano looked toward Holly, who was beaming with happiness, and nodded. He began to gently strum the guitar and to sing the poignant words he wrote about her.

> I saw her once, then I looked twice.
> She seemed like she might be lost.
> I asked and then I gave her a ride
> But it wasn't without a cost.
>
> I kept myself free for all this time.
> No one could hold on to me.
> But after a few minutes and a couple of miles
> She captivated me.
>
> What she couldn't know or see
> Or even understand,
> For the little while we were together.
> She held my heart in her hands.
> The girl from yesterday.
>
> I dropped her off in a tiny town.
> I didn't want to let her go.
> I knew that I would never see her again.
> I wouldn't let my sadness show.

I'm still free and want it that way.
That's how it must be, I know.
But if I ever meet her again,
I'll never let her go.

What she couldn't know or see
Or even understand,
For the little while we were together,
She held my heart in her hands.
The girl from yesterday.

The Arena was alive with applause following Tano's solo. Some of the girls in the audience were so moved by the solo performance that they wiped tears from their eyes.

"Who is she anyway?"

"Where is this 'Holly'?" some were heard to say.

The stage lighting became brilliant again and pulsated with the beat of the drum as Badge sang the cover of Lynyrd Skynyrd's "What's Your Name?" and the iconic classic audience favorite Deep Purple "Smoke on the Water." The audience was still standing, dancing and clapping along. When the songs in the set were over, Badge set their guitars down waved to the audience and left the stage for a twenty-minute break.

Tano immediately headed in Holly's direction, grabbed her, pulled her close, and hugged her tightly. "Well, girl from yesterday, what did you think?"

"I loved it. What a great set! The band was rockin'. And my song—you sang my song." They stood face to face, just inches apart. His deep dimples glistened with sweat. His eyes revealed a softness she had not seen before.

"Of course. You asked me to. And we always do that one anyway. It's a special one and the fans seem to like it, too. It's hot out there. I need a drink."

Tano took Holly's hand, and when they reached the waiting room, Tano grabbed a bottle of Coca-Cola and gulped about half of it. Rob had replaced the Texas barbecue with light snacks—chips and salsa, guacamole, hummus, veggies, fruit, and protein bars. Holly took a bottle of water and grabbed a small plate of hummus and veggies. Jack, the silent drummer, stood in the corner talking on his phone with his wife, drinking a bottle of Coors. Randy and Rocky were each smoking a joint and talking to one of the road-ies. Tano poured some Jack Daniels whiskey in the bottle of Coke he was drinking and took some veggies and hummus from Holly's plate. "Fuel for the second set."

When there was a light knock on the door, Tano looked away from Holly toward the door and saw, to his amazement and shock, frumpy, overweight Donna standing in the doorway wearing a bag-gie white top covered with large sunflowers, white leggings, leop-ard print flats, holding a large leopard print purse across her chest.

"Donna? Damn! How did you get back here? Hey, Rob, did you let her come back here?" Tano shouted.

"No!" Rob hurried over to the door. "Hey, how did you get back here?"

"Oh, it's okay. I'm an old friend of Tano's. We go way back. I just told the security guy. He waved me on back." Donna cheerily spoke and waved her hand. Rob rushed out the door to get the security guard.

"Well, it's break time and you don't belong here right now. Go on out of here!" Tano's face and voice showed he was clearly annoyed.

"I just wanted to tell you that the concert is great. You know I'm your biggest fan." She walked toward him. Tano backed up, and then Donna stopped and turned toward Holly, narrowing her eyes as she spoke. "So, you're the girl from yesterday. I always thought it was me." She winked at Tano and shuffled out the door when a security guard grabbed her arm.

"Man, that chick gives off a bad vibe," said Tano. "Do you think she could be psycho enough to shoot Janet? Or hurt somebody? One of us?"

"I don't know "said Holly. "But she clearly has a thing for you and doesn't care much for me."

"Rob, see to it that she gets nowhere near us again. There's something wrong with her. I don't like it," Tano said.

"Sorry, Tano. I really don't know how that happened."

The break was over and one by one the band members took their places onstage and the audience came alive again. Tano brought his spiked Coke out, took a swig of it, and slipped his bass guitar over his shoulder. The fountain lights began to shower the stage with blue as Badge began to sing the old Rolling Stones ballad, "Heart of Stone," and launched into a timeless British rock set, performing The Animals' "We Gotta Get Out of This Place" with its driving bass guitar; Emerson, Lake & Palmer's "Lucky Man" with its deep harmonies; followed by a condensed version of Led Zeppelin's "Kashmir," accompanied by strobe lights alternating among green, purple and red, changing with Jack's heavy drum beat and the repetitive guitar sounds.

As Tano had promised Holly, Badge performed "Free" and then their originals "Tumbleweed Blues," "Somewhere Along the Way," "Tequila at Midnight" and "Kiss Off." It was the end of the concert. But the crowd shouted "More! More! More! Badge! Badge! Badge!" Badge emerged for one more song, but it had to be about Texas. They chose to sing Waylon Jennings' "Lukenbach, Texas" to close out the night.

"Thank you, Amarillo, Texas! Love y'all. We'll be back!" Tano shouted to the screaming audience. The concert couldn't have gone better. Everything and everyone were in sync. Rob recorded the concert. He planned to talk to them about a concert album. Tano was hot and sweaty when he left the stage. He kissed Holly when he saw her and his moustache was wet. The band members met with the roadies and the techs quickly and congratulated them on a job well done, but their focus had already shifted to the next venue.

"Great job tonight!" Jack surprisingly spoke to the band members. They each took a shot of Jack Daniels, as was their custom at the end of each concert, too.

"Rob, we're heading out. Meet up in the morning?" Tano put

his arm around Holly. She could feel the heat from his warm body through his shirt. His hair was wavier than usual from his body heat and it curled over his shirt collar.

"Yeah. I'll text all of you."

"It's good." There was a general agreement among the rest of them. "But we have to talk to Amarillo police and the hotel guys about the shooting before we leave. I don't know when that will be."

"Okay. Check with you tomorrow."

Holly and Tano made their way to the van in the loading area where they had parked earlier. The area was lit by only a couple of streetlights and spotlights on the building. As they backed out, Holly saw the movement of a streak of yellow out of the corner of her eye. When she turned her head, she only saw parked cars. For a second, she thought it was Donna but dismissed the thought and didn't mention it to Tano. But she believed he was right to be wary of her.

As the van drove farther away from the Arena, a short heavy figure wearing a white shirt covered in large yellow sunflowers holding a leopard print bag emerged from among the parked cars. *So that's my competition. But I could tell by the look on his face he's still into me. He's going to forget all about her when he's with me. And "The Girl from Yesterday" will be my song, not hers.* Donna reached into her bag and clutched the pistol inside it in her hand. *And it's gonna be soon.*

CHAPTER 19

"Hey, it always takes me a couple of hours to unwind when it's over. My ears are still ringing, and lyrics are spinning in my head. How about getting a drink at the hotel bar when we get there?"

"Sounds good. Let's do. I'm not ready to go to bed—well, to sleep anyway."

Tano turned to Holly and smiled. She could see that he was still physically feeling the energy of the concert and he turned the radio off in the van.

"I usually hang with the guys for a while, but I didn't want to tonight. I'm taking you home tomorrow and I want to be with you," he said as he rested his hand on her leg. When they arrived at the hotel, Tano left the van with the valet to park. Once again, Holly felt like they were royalty as they walked together. She thought that he made her look good. Tano was so good-looking from every angle. It was obvious with each step he took that he was somebody exceptional. Tano's thoughts about Holly were the same. He loved standing next to that exquisite redhead.

They slid into a corner booth in the bar. The bar was dark with its walls encased by dark cherry wood paneling. The black slate tables were dimly lit by a candle in the middle. There was a young curvy woman with spikey black hair singing bluesy ballads backed by a piano, a guitar and a drum. Her voice was husky and full of passion. When she began to sing "Trust Me," the old Janis Joplin ballad, Holly could see that Tano was beginning to relax as he took in the emotion of the song.

"Slide on over here. What are you doing over there again?"

Tano pulled Holly close to him and kissed her on her cheek when she slid into his side of the booth and continued to hold her close. He took a long copper strand of her hair in his fingers, twisting and playing with it.

"What can I get you two?" a dark-haired waitress with a long braid wrapped with a purple ribbon asked.

"Jeez, after all the Jack... Let's see—how about whatever you have on draft?"

"Well, I have Fat Tire, Sam Adams, Coors, Budweiser, and..."

"Sam Adams. Holly?"

"I guess just a sparkling water. I don't want to mix alcohol."

"Thanks, y'all." The singer spoke with a husky voice to the bar patrons with a distinct Texas drawl when she finished the song. "You like Janis Joplin? How about another? I'm in a Joplin mood to-night. You know that Janis was a Texas girl—born and raised in Port Arthur down by the Gulf." The guitarist began to play a few notes, and she launched into "A Woman Left Lonely" with a passion that made it believable that the lyrics belonged to her. Holly got chills as she listened to her.

The waitress brought the drinks, but Holly and Tano were so mesmerized by the woman singing that they didn't notice. Another Joplin ballad, "Maybe," followed with the same deep emotion. When she finished singing, she laughed and said, "Whew, I don't know about you folks, but I'm emotionally drained. Let's lighten it up some. How about a little lady country?"

"Well, that cleared the music that was in my head." He pulled Holly closer. "I'm ready to head up to the room now. How about it?"

"Yes, that sounds good." As they left the bar, the singer chose Miranda Lambert's raucous "Gunpowder & Lead" to liven up the crowd.

"Oh, shit," Tano said. "I left my phone in the van. Damn. You go on up to the room and I'll ask the valet to get it for me." He handed her the key card for the room.

"Oh, no. Okay. Hurry on up." Tano leaned over and kissed her lightly on the lips and walked toward the hotel entrance. Holly went in the opposite direction.

What neither of them knew was that someone in a dark brown hooded sweatshirt, which covered a yellow sunflower covered top, had been watching them from the bar and saw them go in opposite directions. Donna. *Where's he going? Maybe he's looking for me. But now is my chance to get that one alone and do some damage.*

Holly walked over to the elevator and pressed "4" for the fourth floor when the doors opened. Before the doors could close, Donna shoved her way through the opening in the elevator doors. Holly was alarmed by the sudden entrance. "Which floor?" she asked before she realized who was standing there.

"Same as you." Donna coldly stared at Holly without blinking. She was wearing the hood of the brown sweatshirt on her head. It was zipped up to her neck with the bottom of the yellow flowered top hanging below it. She surveyed the elevator for cameras and saw one perched in the corner of the ceiling above Holly. She positioned herself with her back to the doors facing Holly. The elevator began to move.

Holly was alarmed, fully conscious of their suspicion that Donna may have shot Janet. She watched Donna and noticed that she was clutching her big leopard print purse tightly with one hand inside as if she was holding something.

"Donna...?" Holly quietly spoke to her, trying to appear calm although her heart was in her throat. She knew she was trapped there with her. "Are you staying here, too?"

To Holly's relief, within a few seconds the elevator stopped on the second floor and an elderly man and woman stepped on and pressed "3" for the third floor. Donna continued her dark gaze at Holly with a fake, almost corpse-like smile plastered on her face, big teeth showing, and didn't respond to her question.

"We were just visiting our daughter and grandsons on this floor," the elderly woman said in a creaky voice. The elevator stopped on the third floor and when the doors opened, Holly immediately left with the elderly couple, just as four young people poured in. Donna moved to the corner.

"Hey, that's not your floor!" Donna shouted to Holly. Holly

continued to walk next to the elderly couple hoping that they would provide cover for her. She didn't know what Donna was planning but the whole scenario felt foreboding and sinister.

"Crap, what do I do now? Damn old people!" Donna did not know what to do—whether to get off and follow or to let it go. *There is no time to think. It would do no good to get caught. Tano wouldn't want that. Then he couldn't be with me like he wants to.*

When the old couple found their hotel room, Holly ran ahead to the stairwell exit at the end of the hall and shot down the three flights of stairs to the main floor lobby. Her heart was racing with fear that Donna was close behind her. Holly shot out of the stairs exit into the lobby just as Tano was coming through the main doors holding his phone. Holly rushed toward him and put her arms around his waist and held on tightly.

"Holly! What's wrong?" Holly was flushed, shaking, and breathing hard.

"Donna! Donna!" she gasped as she tried to catch her breath.

"What about her?"

"She followed me onto the elevator wearing that brown hooded sweatshirt, hood pulled up on her head, holding something in that big purse! She was..." Holly took another deep breath. "She was...oh, Tano, believe me, something was going to happen! I know it. I felt it. Then some people got on the elevator and I got off with them and ran down the stairs! But she saw that I was headed to the fourth floor. She knows that we are staying up there! I don't think I'm just being paranoid. "

Tano held her tightly and spoke calmly to her but he was churning inside with fury. "You should have come with me." He paused for a minute to think, still holding Holly. "Okay, here's what we are going to do. We are going to move to another room on another floor right now. I'll ask hotel security to go with us to the room to get our stuff. I believe you. Something is wrong with that chick. Man, she was acting weird at the concert, but I didn't think it would go beyond that. I wish I never met her."

"Okay," she said as she continued to hug his waist. She was

beginning to calm and catch her breath. "I don't know what she was up to, but she didn't even try to disguise herself with that ridiculous flower top hanging below her jacket."

"I won't let anything happen to you. To us. I'm going to call Rob and have him give a heads up to the other guys about Donna. They might still be at the Arena hanging out." With his arm around Holly, he walked over to the concierge desk and requested a different room and explained that there was an uncomfortable encounter with an unstable fan.

"Of course, Mr. Montano. Henry, please accompany Mr. Montano and his guest to their rooms and help them move out. Let's see—what floor would you like, sir? We have a few available rooms, but you know your concert brought so many people into Amarillo that we are quite full."

"Move us where you think we would be most comfortable, but I would like some security on that floor near our room at all times. We are only staying until tomorrow. If you can't arrange it, my manager will. Can you tell me if someone named Donna Smith is registered here at the hotel?"

"Henry, will you help them move to the sixth floor, room 633?" Then he turned to Tano. "I'll contact hotel security immediately. We cannot disclose who our hotel guests are. It's a privacy thing, but I can tell you who is not a guest here and I can tell you that no one by that name is registered here."

"Okay, thanks for your help. How does that sound, sweet thing? I took care of it."

"Yes, you did. I know that I wasn't just being paranoid. She was acting very strange and looked that way, too. Something was about to happen."

Tano and Holly sat stiffly on cushiony tan and teal chairs in the lobby to wait for hotel security to arrive to accompany them to their room and for Henry to return with a luggage cart. Tano kept his eyes trained on the elevator expecting that Donna would emerge. He called Rob and let him know what was going on.

Holly listened to Tano as he spoke to Rob on the phone. "Yep that was her. We think that she might have had something to do with Janet getting shot. So just be on the lookout. We're leaving Amarillo tomorrow."

"Sir, are you ready? This is Vance Miller, with hotel security." Henry approached with the luggage cart.

"Yep, let's get it done," he said, as they walked to the elevator and began their ascent to the fourth floor.

"Mr. Montano, I had a chance to look at video footage of the security camera in the main elevator. I saw the woman that you identified as an unstable fan. She appeared to be acting a little strange but didn't do anything criminal. But I have to say that she bears a possible resemblance to the perpetrator in the hotel shooting early this morning, so you're wise to be cautious about her. I'll be in touch with Amarillo police about her."

"Thanks for your quick assistance."

It was nearly midnight when Holly and Tano entered their hotel room and began to pack their luggage while Hotel Detective Miller stood in the corridor outside their door. Out of the corner of his eye, he thought he saw the stairwell exit door at the end of the long hall open slightly and then close quickly, but he couldn't leave his post to investigate.

Detective Miller had seen something. Donna had been hiding in the stairwell. She knew that Tano and Holly would return to their room and she wanted to catch a glimpse of him but had not expected security to be there. But if Holly was alone again, her .22-caliber pistol would be put to work. *That dumb bitch. I'll get her next time she's alone. She's standing between Tano and me.*

While they were clearing out their room, Donna took off her sweatshirt, jammed it into her bag, trudged down the stairs, and made a clean exit out the front door of the hotel completely undetected. She returned to the nearby parking garage where she had been sleeping in her car. *Okay, time to hatch a new plan. Oh, Tano, wait for me.*

CHAPTER 20

At about twelve thirty a.m., Tano and Holly settled into the new hotel room. They both flopped down on the king-size bed with deep simultaneous sighs. Tano rested his right forearm across his forehead and let thoughts of the past couple of days run through his mind. With great happiness, he had just found Holly the day before, but then she told him of the miscarriage and he hadn't had much time to process that piece of news. Then there was the shooting, the visits to the zoo and the Cadillac Ranch, the Badge concert and two close encounters with psycho Donna. All within a little over twenty-four hours. His head was spinning.

Holly snuggled up next to Tano, rested her left hand on his chest and kicked her left leg over his legs. Her thoughts were hopping from one happening to another, but she primarily thought about the sudden appearance of Tano the day before, how he had looked for her, the resurface of her deep feelings for him, the warm feeling of his body next to hers at that moment. As she had done five years earlier, she began to feel a little sadness knowing that their time together would be coming to an end the next day. But this time, maybe there would still be a thread to hold on to, to stay connected, and to commit to that connection. There was no doubt that she was in love with him. And she questioned how difficult it might be for her to go on without him as they resumed their lives. Time would tell.

"I'm beat. How about let's just hit the sack?" said Tano.

"Yeah, it's been like a runaway train."

Tano and Holly kicked off their boots. Tano stripped down to his black boxers and Holly slipped on the Badge T-shirt she wore to bed the night before. With the lights out, they still struggled to sleep until fatigue finally won the battle.

A few hours later, Tano reached for Holly and pulled her close to him. He knew that he would regret not making love to her one more time before they separated. Holly stretched her arms over her head and then rested them around his back as she felt the weight of his body and the penetrating kisses. The passion almost allowed her to tell him she loved him. But she couldn't. She had been in love with his ghost for five years, reliving many times every moment they had together on that fateful ride from San Angelo. Not able to forget, not able to move on emotionally. But on this night, still not able to expose herself to possible rejection that way.

Both began to stir about eight a.m. "Good morning, pretty girl."

"Hello there this morning. I wonder what will happen today." Holly smiled. Feeling somewhat refreshed, they showered and ordered breakfast from room service. A full Texas breakfast for Tano and a pecan waffle and fruit for Holly and a big pot of coffee for them both. They were to meet with hotel security and the Amarillo police at nine thirty to provide a statement about what they knew about Janet's shooting, if anything, and then check out at noon.

Tano texted Rocky before the meeting:

Hey, Rock, so how is Janet and does anyone know anything more about what happened?

Rocky replied:

She's doing better. Talking more. Still in pain but on meds. Still not saying much about the shooter. Too drunk. Probably leave the hospital tomorrow or the next day.

Hotel security was still on guard outside the room. "Hey, thanks for the security. We'll be back in about a half hour. Have to meet with police. Are you planning to keep watch?"

"Yes, sir. Nothing to report so far."

"That's good news." When they entered the elevator, Tano felt Holly stiffen a little as she held his hand. She knew there was nothing to be afraid of—she was with Tano—but the memory of the encounter with Donna was so fresh.

Amarillo Police Detective Braden Messina met them at the elevator and took them to a conference room on the main level where Hotel Security Officer Paul Podesta waited.

"Have a seat, Mr. Montano and Ms. Harris. So, as you know, a woman, Janet Longwell, was shot outside the hotel in the early morning hours yesterday. Can you fill us in on what you witnessed or know about the incident, if anything?"

Tano spoke. "Well, I think around one or two a.m., Janet began knocking on the door to our room and asking to be let in. She was clearly drunk. We ignored her and she kept it up. Each time louder and more urgent. I tried to call her boyfriend, Rocky, who is in the band with me, to come and get her but there was no answer. So I called hotel security to come and take her away because she was disturbing us and probably others. From the sound of things, they did. That's all I know. But then at about three, an hour or so later, we heard gun shots outside of the hotel. We both got up and looked out the window. It looked like a woman lying on the ground on her back, but we couldn't say who it was."

"So why didn't you let her in when she was knocking on the door? Exactly how do you know her?"

"She was here with Rocky from the band. She was staying in his room, I thought. I dated her a couple of times. A long time ago. I was in bed with my lady and I didn't want to be interrupted." Tano looked at Holly and smiled.

"And you, Ms. Harris?"

"I saw and heard the same things that Tano said he saw. I don't know her at all. I met her for the first time at dinner the night before she was shot."

"I'm going to show you footage from the exterior security camera taken at the time of the shooting. But before I do, Janet told me that a woman approached her and said something to the effect like,

'Do you know Tano?' And she said 'Yeah, he's my boyfriend.' And the woman pulled out a gun, Janet reached out to push her away and she shot her. She remembers nothing else. Can you think of a reason why she would have said that?"

"No," Tano said. "There is nothing between us. At all!"

"Did either of you see or notice anyone or anything suspicious when you entered the hotel or room?"

"No. I noticed no one acting suspiciously."

"Me neither," Holly said.

"Okay, here's what the security camera picked up." Detective Messina opened his laptop. From the camera angle above the front door, they saw Janet stagger out the door to the sidewalk and stand looking toward the street. In less than a minute, she was approached by a boxy figure, shorter than her, wearing a dark sweatshirt with the hood pulled up, and distinct white Converse tennis shoes. They could see that Janet was talking, then reached her arm out in front of her, and was shot. She doubled over and then collapsed in a heap, landing on her back. The shooter put the pistol in her pocket and turned and walked casually away from the scene and out of sight. Tano looked at Holly. Both had wide eyes.

The detective spoke. "So what can you add to this picture?"

"I'm not sure. But the shooter looks like it could be a woman I know. Just her body shape and that sweatshirt and the shoes."

"Why do you say that?"

"Because Holly and I've had encounters with her twice in the last couple of days. She's someone who used to work for me a few years back and I had to fire her, but she seems to have some kind of obsession with me. She's kind of unstable."

"Her name?"

"Well, it was Donna Smith."

"Can you tell me anything else about her? Where's she from?"

"At one time she lived in Fort Collins, Colorado, and then Boulder. I think she got divorced. That's all I know."

"Smith, huh. Why do you say she is unstable?"

"She somehow slipped past security and barged into the waiting area of the Arena during the Badge concert and made comments like she was my girlfriend. She must have been at the concert. And then Holly here had an encounter with her in the elevator last night. She was acting strangely holding something in her purse. And she was wearing a dark brown hooded sweatshirt, right, Holly?" Holly nodded. "Come to think of it, we ran into her as we got off the elevator near the parking garage yesterday, too."

"Can you describe her?"

"Well she's about five foot two or three. She has a squarish fat body. Her hair is a dark red, about to her jaw line and flat. She has these teeth—they are big and she has an underbite. Distinct mouth. She's probably in her thirties."

"Dark brown eyes," Holly added.

"Well, she is someone to look into. Thank you for your time today, Mr. Montano and Ms. Harris. We'll be in touch if we have any more questions. Please write your contact information on this sheet of paper for me."

When they left the police interview, they headed up to their room and began packing. The valet brought a cart and they began to load it with the few pieces of luggage they brought. The valet took the cart downstairs. Tano and Holly walked by Jack's room just as he opened the door.

"We're heading out soon. I'm driving Holly back to Oklahoma. Then I'm driving back to Boulder for a few days. Meet up with you in Denver next Thursday for the Fiddler's Green concert? We'll talk before then. Is Rocky staying until Janet is released?"

"Yeah, he is. Sounds good. Heather and I are taking the kids to Grand Lake to fish this weekend."

"That sound great. Hey, great job last night—especially on Kashmir. We couldn't do it without you."

"Thanks, Tano." Jack slapped him lightly on the back.

Tano and Holly entered the lobby and he handed the valet the receipt to retrieve the van. When the concierge saw Tano, he beckoned to him to come to the front desk. When Tano and Holly walked over to him, he looked at Tano and then looked down and then looked at Holly, and immediately looked down again. He continued to look at the desk when he said, "Mr. Montano. Your wife left this message for you," and he handed him a note.

"What? I'm not married. Who gave you this?"

"I can't say for sure. A short woman. I didn't really look at her. A lot of bottom teeth though."

"Thanks. I guess." Tano opened the note card.

> *"Hello, Tano. Great concert last night. Looking forward to seeing you at home soon. With love, D. Montano. Don't you just love the sound of it —Donna Montano"*

"Goddamn it! Read this fucking thing!" Tano handed the note to Holly.

"Oh, no. She is really a psycho. Tano, what are you going to do?"

"Well, get the hell out of here as soon as I let the police know that she might be going by the name of Donna Montano." Tano made a phone call, grabbed their bags and they piled into the van. Someone else was planning to hit the road, too and she was waiting in a tan Buick sedan on the street as Tano pulled away from the circle drive in front of the hotel.

"Going home with me, baby," Donna whispered to herself.

CHAPTER 21

They were only about 120 miles from Amarillo, Texas, to Sage, Oklahoma. It was almost noon and if they drove straight through, they would arrive in Sage in two hours. Tano was not ready to let Holly go so soon. He looked at his GPS map and saw that there was a less direct route to Sage. One that would take longer. There was a lake—Lake Meredith—on the way. They could stop there for a picnic or a hike, even while wearing cowboy boots. Holly didn't ask questions when Tano exited Amarillo onto a different road. She was trying not to dwell on the end of their time together, but it was imminent, and it made her throat ache like she could cry.

"I'm so glad you came with me. It wouldn't have been the same there without you."

"Well, it was memorable anyway," Holly said referring to the shooting and Donna. "I seriously believe that Donna shot Janet and that I was her next target. You need to be careful. You could be her next target. Remember—some obsessed crazy killed John Lennon and there have been others like that."

"Naw, she wouldn't shoot me. She wants this bod." Tano managed a little laugh and tried to lighten the conversation.

"Yep, she does. But so do I." Holly leaned her head on his hard, well-defined shoulder. He was wearing a white T-shirt. She had never seen anyone look so good in a plain white tee. She buried her face in his shirt sleeve and could smell the scent of his skin. An assortment of country and rock music played as they drove. She didn't know if it was a playlist or SiriusXM. No matter.

About a half hour into their trip, they arrived in Fritch, Texas, a small town that was nestled next to Lake Meredith and the Canadian River.

"In case you haven't guessed, I'm not ready to take you back to Sage. Wanna hike or have a picnic? Or just sit by the lake and do nothing? Say yes."

"I'm not ready to go back either. Just like last time." She smiled and looked at her hands in her lap for a second. "I say 'yes.' Let's do."

"We should grab some water and some snacks for lunch." He followed the signs that took them to the lake and on the way there was a fruit stand. They pulled in and began to browse the fruits and vegetables.

"Nectarines! Should we get some?" Holly held two nectarines in her hand and brought one up to her nose to smell it.

"Of course. I think I'll grab a couple of these peaches and an apple."

Near the makeshift check stand, there were small boxes of whole grain crackers and individual containers of spreadable Swiss cheese. Holly picked up one of each. Tano grabbed small bottles of water and cherry cider.

"Here you go, sir. Enjoy the taste of Texas," said the middle-aged lady, wearing a brown cowboy hat and a blue denim apron, as she handed him a bag.

"Thanks. Do you happen to have a plastic knife or two?"

"Sure thing. Have a nice day." The lake was about a half mile away. As they drove away, a tan Buick pulled into the fruit stand parking lot. Tano hadn't noticed that they had been followed from Amarillo. Chunky, square, Donna got out and pretended to peruse the fruit stand, keeping her eye in the direction that Holly and Tano had driven.

"May I help you find something? Anything in particular?"

"Well, I guess whatever those two that just left here got."

The clerk frowned, puzzled by her answer but said, "They got nectarines, peaches, apples and crackers."

"I'll take the same."

"Help yourself." The clerk gestured with her hand toward the bins of fruit. Donna picked out some fruit and some crackers, paid for them, and got in her car. She took a big bite of the apple and ripped into the crackers. *Now is not the time for me make a move. But I got to see what's going on.* She drove to the parking lot at Lake Meredith. Yep, Tano's van was there. But where were they?

Tano and Holly found an unoccupied dark green pine picnic table chained to a tree in the sun. "It's pretty hot out here." Texas in August. It was 94 degrees. "Let's move this table around to the other side of the tree and into the shade." They slid the heavy wooden table out of the entangled brush and shoved it to the north side of the tree. They slid next to each other, ducking under the overhanging low branches.

"That's better." Holly took a nectarine from the bag, poured a little water over it and then dried it on her tight, light green T-shirt, rubbed it on the thigh of her jeans and took a bite.

"Nectarines are my favorite fruit. And this one is perfect." She took another juicy bite.

"Well then I'm glad we stopped." Tano opened the crackers and spread some cheese on a few of them. "So, Holly Bear, what's next for you?"

Holly smiled. *Holly Bear—so cute. I love it.* "Do you mean like soon or long term?"

"Both."

"Well, I'll return to Kansas tomorrow morning. Resume the things I always do—work, my garden, my music, my friends, and I'm taking a ballet class to keep in shape."

"It's working." Tano rested his hand on Holly's lower back.

"And long term. I don't know. I'm not exactly thrilled about being in Kansas but I felt like I needed to set a foundation financially and career-wise to support myself, and that was where the best opportunity was at the time." Holly looked toward the lake. "Someday when I settle down some, I would like to have a baby." She took in a breath and sighed.

"Well, that sounds like a plan." Tano pulled her close.

Holly didn't want to go any further with those thoughts. "What about you?"

"After I drop you off, I'm heading back to Boulder and will be working at the Tumbleweed until the Denver concert on Thursday. Anthony's taking his wife to Yellowstone for a few days. I'm actually looking forward to being there. It grounds me."

"And for long term?"

"Who knows. I guess it depends on Badge and how long we can keep an audience. I plan to keep the Tumbleweed and live in Boulder—well, keep my house there. I haven't given too much thought to kids or a family yet. I'm in no hurry. It has to be right and I hope that I recognize it when it is." Tano pulled Holly close again. Holly continued to look toward the lake. *Is it me?*

The conversation had created a serious mood. Holly was uncomfortable with the silence. "Hey, I'm going to go wade in the lake. Want to?"

"Sure, why not?" They slid off their cowboy boots, rolled up their jeans to mid-calf, held hands and cautiously made their way barefoot over the rocky beach to the lake shore.

Holly dipped her toe in first, still holding Tano's hand. "It's cool. Feels good." And she stepped in with both feet. "Come on," she said, and pulled him in.

"Hey!" Tano kicked a little water in Holly's direction. Holly laughed and kicked water a little harder, splashing Tano's jeans. Tano reached in with both hands and threw water at Holly, splattering her face and clothes.

"Okay, this means war!" Holly laughing reached into the lake water and threw water at Tano, drenching his face and the front of his shirt and jeans. Tano chuckled and grabbed Holly's arm and pulled her close, chest to chest, face to face, with lake water dripping from his moustache and kissed her. "Battle's over. Truce," he whispered.

Donna got tired of waiting for Tano and Holly to return to the van. It was hot in the car and she had already devoured an apple and the entire box of crackers. She decided to get out of the car and try to catch a glimpse of them. She weaved her way between parked cars until the lake was in view. And there they were. Tano and Holly standing face to face in an embrace kissing. Donna felt the blood rush to her head with fury. Her face was red, and she began to shake. *Tano—you're mine! Get rid of her! Or I will!* Then she saw them walk toward a picnic table, slip on their boots. If they were leaving, she needed to be ready, and ran back to her car.

"It's too hot to hike. Are you ready to go? I don't want you to be late."

"No, not yet. Let's just sit here a while. I want to get some photos of the lake. And here—how about some selfies?" Tano complied. "And you take one of me and I'll take some of you."

They looked at the photos, held hands, gazed at each other, took in the wilderness around them and then without speaking about it at all, they both stood, grabbed the fruit and drinks, and walked to the van. The drive to Sage would take a little over an hour. They were silent for most of the trip. Tano pointed out sites along the way. Holly pointed at antelope. Badge music quietly played in the background. It was like they were reliving the trip to Sage five years earlier with the same sadness building for them both. But it would not be over like last time. Their connection was strong now and they would stay connected. Like in the song, "Girl from Yesterday," Tano had found her and would never let her go.

Still unnoticed by Tano, following a few cars behind them was Donna talking loudly to herself. "Where is he taking that bitch? Better not be to Boulder! That's my turf!" She grabbed another apple and took a bite. She looked at her face in the rearview mirror. "I'm so pretty. I can't wait 'til he sees me again!" When she little, her mother found two old rock-and-roll "Donna songs" and played them for her whenever she asked. "Donna the Prima Donna" by Dion and "Donna" by Ritchie Valens. Her mom convinced her that the songs were about her. As she followed Tano on the road to Oklahoma, she listened to the two Donna songs over and over on her playlist, reinforcing her deluded belief that she was special—special to Tano.

Once the van turned east out of Texhoma, Holly knew it would be a half hour or less when they reached Sage. As she sometimes did subconsciously when she was anxious, she began to rub both hands on the tops of her thighs as if they hurt. They didn't hurt. Her heart did. Tano noticed the gesture and took her hand in his and squeezed it a little and she stopped. Still silent, they drove past the gas station, the post office, the park, the farm store/café until the Wildflower Goat Cheese sign was in sight. Tano slowed down and pulled into the driveway of the Harris house. The tan Buick that had been following him from Amarillo, without his notice, zoomed past him as he turned and continued straight on the county road. Tano and Holly turned in their seats toward each other, holding hands, looking at each other.

"Can you stay a while? Come see the rabbits and goats. Meet my dad?" *Please say yes. Stay with me a little longer,* she thought.

"Yes, I can. I planned to make Springfield today and then a short trip home tomorrow."

They hopped out of the van. The screen door slammed and Holly's mom came outside to greet them. "Hello, you two. How was the concert?"

"It was great, Mom. I had the best time. I'm an even bigger fan now."

"I made oatmeal chocolate chip cookies a while ago. Go on in and help yourself."

"Okay, first I wanted to give Tano a little tour of the place."

"Thanks, Mrs. Harris."

"Just call me Liza." Tano nodded.

"Come on." Holly took Tano's hand and they walked toward the goat pasture. The curious goats came running over to see them. Holly reached over the fence to pet one and several of them ran over and began to nudge her hand to be petted. "Go ahead. Pet one. They love the attention."

Tano reached over the fence, petted one little white one with a few black speckles. The hair was stiff but fine. When he took his hand away, the little goat began to bleat loudly. "Okay! Okay!" he said, and petted it again.

After a few minutes of bleating and petting, Holly took Tano's hand and led him to the rabbit shed. Inside the shed were about a dozen rabbits in cages on shelves lined with straw. They were of all colors and sizes. Long eared, short eared, brown, white, black, long hair, short hair. Some resting, some eating or drinking water. They took notice of Holly and Tano and began to sniff the air as they watched them. The shed was lined with a single row of little awning windows on the north side opened for ventilation.

"What do you do with all of these rabbits?"

"Well, some are used for breeding and some for meat. The meat tastes like chicken. Here on a farm in Oklahoma, we don't think twice about eating rabbit. It was hard for me when I was younger if I got attached to certain ones. I used to name them all but now I try not to because I feel an attachment when I do. However, I call this one Snuggles. He is a breeding rabbit." Holly pointed to a little quiet gray rabbit. "But I have to admit that I haven't eaten rabbit in years. I just can't. Come meet my dad."

Tano surveyed the property to see if Garth's tall red diesel pickup was there. It was not in sight. They walked to the red shop where Holly's dad was working on the carburetor of a big green John Deere 4030 tractor. He was wearing greasy blue coveralls and his hands were black with grease. He was tall and thin, wearing wire glasses and a grease-stained yellow John Deere hat on his head. He looked up when he saw Holly, pulled a rag out of his back pocket and wiped his hands on it. They were still black. He walked toward them.

"Hi, honey." He looked at Tano. "I'm John Harris." He reached out to shake Tano's hand.

"I'm Ben Montano, but I go by Tano."

"So, you're that rock star that Haley has been going on and on about."

Tano smiled. "I don't know about that but yeah I'm in a rock band. I met Holly a few years ago."

"Yes, I heard." He tilted his head back and studied Tano's face, looking out of the bottom of the lens of his glasses. "Where ya from there?"

"Boulder, Colorado. It's my hometown. I have a business there, too."

Just then, they heard the roar of a diesel truck outside as it pulled up and parked near the rabbit shed, and then the sound of a slamming door. Holly muttered almost inaudibly under her breath, "Oh, shit. Garth." Tano heard her. They heard the back-screen door slam when Garth went in the house and then a few seconds later slam again when he came out.

Holly said, "I'll get this over with." Tano and Holly left the shop and walked toward the house. Garth met them near his truck.

"Holly, you bringin' this son of bitch to the house again!" Garth hollered, coldly staring at Tano.

"It's none of your damn business and I can bring whoever I want here anytime. Have some respect, jack ass!"

"Respect for this guy? What about respect for you? After he left you like he did? After what you went through?" Garth shoved Tano hard.

Tano shoved him back. "Yeah, have some respect for your sister! "

Garth shoved him again and yelled. "You left her, son of a bitch! You left her, you prick!"

Tano tried to restrain himself. After all, he was a guest at the Harris house but he had to defend himself. He took a swing and landed a punch on Garth's face. Garth charged him and they both fell to the ground, rolling and punching while Holly screamed, "Garth stop it! He didn't know! He didn't know! Hear me? I didn't tell him!"

When Butkus, the golden retriever, heard the loud scuffle, he came running from the shady spot where he had been laying peacefully asleep. Holly bent down and grabbed him by his collar before he could get involved in the fight. But just as Holly bent over, several bullets whizzed over her head and hit Garth's truck and the side of the rabbit hutch.

Tano reached over and grabbed Holly's hand and pulled her hard to the ground. "Stay down! Everybody stay down!" Garth and

Tano stopped fighting as they listened for more bullets. There were no more.

"God damn son of a bitch! You done nothin' but brought trouble to this house every time my sister sees you," Garth sneered at Tano, still laying on their stomachs on the ground.

"Garth! Knock that shit off!" John Harris came out of the shop, walking toward them. "Get up now! Don't you think you oughta go see who mighta took a shot in this direction? And when you get done, go on home to your wife and kids!" John walked to the house to call the sheriff. Liza had been in the house and came running out to see if everyone was all right. "Go in, Liza. It's all over out here now."

Holly was so upset that she thought she might throw up. Adrenalin was pumping hard and she was shaking. She had nearly been struck by bullets from somewhere. She could have been killed. If Butkus hadn't charged up to the fight, she would have been standing in the range of the bullets. And her brother had just attacked the man she loved. She stood up and held her head which was pounding. Tano stood up, brushed the dirt off of his clothes, and put his arms around her. "I'm so sorry, Holly. I'm so sorry. I just couldn't put up with that shit. I don't even know the guy." She couldn't be mad at Tano. She loved him whether he knew it or not and none of it was his fault. She hugged him tightly and laid her head on his chest. She could feel his heart beating hard in his chest. He appeared to be unscathed by the fight, but Garth had a bloody nose.

Garth wiped his nose on the sleeve of his T-shirt and surveyed the damage to his truck. He couldn't drive it with glass all over the seat. "Dad? Can I borrow your truck? I can't drive mine. I want to head over the hill—over there. I think the shots came from that direction. Now! Damn it! Before the bastard is gone!" Garth turned to Holly and pointed at Tano. "You better send pretty boy home. Jared is on his way here to be with you." He got in his dad's white Ford service truck and left in a hurry, leaving dust behind. John began to survey the damage to Garth's truck and the rabbit shed. Surprisingly none of the rabbits were injured

Holly was in shock. So much had happened to her in the last couple of days. She didn't want to see Jared. Why was he coming? She just wanted to bask in the glow of the magical time she had just spent with Tano. But she couldn't think.

"I should go," Tano said. "I want to make Springfield today. Maybe as far as Trinidad or Walsenburg. Besides, Garth won't be happy if I'm still here."

"Please stay for a while. Please don't go yet. I'm not ready to say goodbye."

"It's not goodbye. Not at all. We will stay in touch. We will see each other again. I promise."

Tears began to flow heavily as she clung to Tano with her head on his chest. He touched her chin and turned her face to his so he could kiss her. The more she tried to stop crying, the worse it became. She held her breath and tried to stop. Tano kissed her anyway. "Walk me to the van?"

"Okay," Holly answered with a shaky voice. Tano had his arm around her and could feel her shaking. They walked toward the van.

"I'll call you tonight or tomorrow. I want to know what you find out about the gunshots, too."

"Tano, I...I..." Holly began to sob again. "I'm so sorry. I just can't stop crying. I'm going to miss you so much. I missed you for five years. Did you know?"

"Yes, I do. Because I felt the same." Holly's sadness was breaking his heart. He got in the van and rolled down the window. "Come here, Holly. I have something for you." He reached into the console of the van and pulled out a little white box and handed it to Holly. When she opened it, inside was a necklace with a silver pendant in the shape of a badge with a heart inscribed inside it. Engraved in tiny letters inside the heart was "Tano." "I had this made for you in case I found you. A little more personal than a gear shifter this time. So you don't forget me."

"How could I? I care so much. Thank you. Put it on me." She turned, lifted her hair, leaned back into the window, and Tano clasped the necklace at her neck.

"It looks great on you. Come here, sweetness. One more kiss to go." Holly leaned into the window of the van and kissed Tano good-bye. "Be good to yourself."

"Tano. Thank you for everything." Tano blew a kiss her way and backed the van out slowly. When he got to the road, he waved goodbye. Holly waved goodbye and said softly to herself, "I love you." She watched the van until it was no longer in sight. Then she walked over to the bench with the peeling paint by the fence and buried her face in her hands and cried. Butkus laid at her feet, panting in the heat, to comfort her.

"Damn! I didn't hit my mark! Damn! I didn't fucking hit her! Not this time."

Donna shouted and hit her steering wheel with the palm of her hand over and over. She had fired a gun like that many times when she and Melvin went target shooting. *How could I miss? I had her in my scope. How could she bend over just as I fired?* She had tossed the .300 Winchester Magnum in the trunk of the car and proceeded to drive away from the elevated area about a half mile east of the Harris house where, with Holly in her scope, she had fired the shots. Donna drove slowly so as not to attract attention. She knew someone would come looking for a shooter. In a matter of minutes, Garth in the service truck came up behind her and waved at her to pull over. It would make no sense to run. But it would make sense to play dumb. She pulled the Buick over.

"So, hey. Did you happen to see or hear anyone in this area shooting a gun in the last ten or fifteen minutes or so?" It didn't occur to Garth that a woman driving a tan Buick sedan could be a shooter.

"No, I was just driving from my grandma's house. I didn't see or hear no shooting, but a pickup passed me going pretty fast a few minutes ago."

"What did it look like?"

"Let me think. White with hay in it. Dirty."

"Okay." *That matches the description of just about everybody around here*, Garth thought. He decided to drive into Sage to see what he could find out. Donna, on the other hand, laughing to herself, drove past the Harris house. Tano's van was gone. *Yay, he's coming back to Boulder to be with me. I'm on my way, baby.*

CHAPTER 22

"Hello, there John. So, what happened? Everybody okay?" Young, dark, and handsome Sheriff Troy Martinez arrived in the sheriff's black Ford SUV and quickly scanned the scene.

"Everybody's okay. Don't really know what happened, Troy."

"Well, tell me what you observed." Troy took off his hat and rubbed his hand over his dark wavy hair and put it on again. He carried a camera and a clipboard with a form ready to jot down information about the incident.

"I didn't really see anything," John said. "I was there in the shop. Just heard the shots and a big ruckus. But Holly was nearly hit by them bullets. You should go talk to her. She's settin' over there on that bench."

Holly was still sitting alone on the peeling red painted bench by the gate with Butkus at her feet resting his head on her boots. She took her face out of her hands and looked up when she heard Troy approach. Her face was red and covered with tears. She took a deep breath.

"Hey, Troy." She spoke in a soft voice. Troy had always been fond of Holly. Years ago, he had even asked her out a couple of times. He kissed her once and never forgot it. Seeing her so distraught made him feel less like a sheriff and more like a good friend. Troy sat down on the bench next to her and spoke gently.

"Hey, Holly. Can you tell me what happened?"

"Well, Garth—you know what a hot head he is—got into a shoving match with a guy that I was with and they ended up on the ground fighting. I was standing over them yelling at Garth when

Butkus came charging up. I bent over and grabbed him by his collar just as bullets whizzed over my head and blasted the windows in Garth's truck and hit the rabbit shed. They must have come from that direction." Holly pointed toward the eastern horizon. "Then Tano—that's the guy that was with me—pulled me down on the ground and the shooting stopped."

Troy made a few notes on the clipboard, then leaned over looking directly at Holly's face. "Holly, you're so upset. Do you need for me to get ahold of someone to help you out?"

"No. It's not just the gunshots. It's more than that. It's some other personal stuff and it all came crashing down on me at the same time. I know I'll be fine." Troy put his arm around her. Holly put her head down. Try as she might stop them, the tears continued to flow.

"So, where is the man who was here with you? The guy Garth was fighting with? I may need to talk to him so I should get his name and contact info, too."

"It's Ben Montano. You know, Tano from Badge." Troy raised his eyebrows when she identified her friend. "He left to return to Colorado. If he stayed, Garth would start up something with him again. But I'm sure he would talk to you if you needed to. None of us really know what happened. I have his phone number." She took her phone from the back pocket of her jeans and showed the phone number to Troy.

Just then Garth roared into the driveway in John's service truck with a trail of dust billowing behind it.

"Jesus, Troy! Took you long enough! I been out looking for the son of a bitch. Where you been?"

The sheriff ignored Garth's comments and said, "So what can you tell me about what happened here?"

"You know, I just drove over yonder there to see if I could spot the dumbass coward who shot at my sister. There wasn't anybody but a dumpy looking gal that I never seen before driving a Buick. I made her pull over and asked her if she saw something and she said somebody passed her going real fast in a white pickup with hay in the back. That don't mean much around here."

"Look, Garth. It could have been a stray bullet from somebody shooting rabbits or antelope from over there. Holly tells me you were fighting with a male friend of hers. What's that all about?"

Garth raised his voice and said, "That doesn't have nothing to do with it. I don't like the prick and I don't want him coming around my sister. That's all there is to it. That son of a bitch already left her."

Holly said under her breath and only Troy heard. "Don't make me choose between you."

The sheriff, realizing that no one really had anything significant to add, said, "Okay, let's take a look at the truck and the shed and see what was left there." Holly stepped over Butkus who was still at her feet. She was beginning to compose herself.

Holly took a quick look at both windows shot out of Garth's truck and the holes in the wall of rabbit shed with Troy, Garth and John. She took some wood fragments from the shattered wall out of a few of the rabbit cages when she went inside.

"Well, that was some big ass gun they were using to shoot at some rabbits or a prairie dog, if that's what was going on. Must not have used a scope or the bullets wouldn't have strayed this far," Troy said when he spotted one of the bullets nestled in some straw on the ground in the rabbit shed. "Winchester .300 Mag," he said.

"Jesus, any of the guys around here could have a gun like that. How would we ever find out what happened?"

"Leave that to me, Garth. How do you know that it was somebody from around here? You don't. I don't want you to go snoopin' around Sage acting like some kind of detective. Let me do my job and you cool that hot head of yours. Look—there was some property damage. Holly was nearly shot and is so upset, so the scene here could have been so much worse than it is."

"Aw, she's not concerned about the bullets. She's all heartbroken over that rock star son of a bitch. I really shoulda let him have it."

"Well, it looks like he got to you pretty good," Troy said, looking at the blood on Garth's T-sleeve and his swollen nose.

"That ain't none of your goddamn concern," Garth sneered.

"Not this time."

Holly had heard enough. They were talking about her as if she wasn't even there. "I'm going in now, you guys."

"You take care now, Holly. I'll be in touch. If you need anything," Troy said. Garth glared at Troy when he smiled, winked at Holly and gestured goodbye with his raised hand. She attempted a smile and walked up to the house. Her mother had been standing on the back steps talking with John. She was wearing faded bib overalls with a flowery red peasant shirt underneath with one hand in her pocket and the other holding a metal pail. It seemed she was always carrying a metal pail. John reached over and patted Holly's back and walked down the steps and toward his shop with Butkus trotting along behind.

"Honey, are you all right? Your eyes are so puffy. Your face is, too." Liza reached up and moved Holly's hair from her face.

"I'm okay." She began to open the back-screen door and turned. "No, I'm not. I don't know if I'll see Tano again. We had the best time together. And Garth picked a fight with him. And now Jared is coming here, too. And the bullets. It's too much. But I'll sort it all out."

"Yes, you will. The good Lord was looking out for you today and He will help you figure it all out. Honey, I made some chicken tortilla soup. It's simmerin' on the stove. Help yourself. And there's some of my whole wheat rolls that I made fresh this morning. And some of my homemade strawberry jam."

It was just like Holly's mother to attempt to fix the situation with food. "I'm not really hungry. Maybe later. I'm going up to my room." Liza hugged her tight.

Holly went upstairs to what used to be her bedroom and plopped down on her back on the pink and lavender quilt her mom made for her bed years ago. Her bedroom remained unchanged after she moved away to Liberal. It felt safe and nurturing. She laid motionless with her right arm over her eyes. Her thoughts raced from Tano, to the shooting in Amarillo, to the Cadillac Ranch, to the impromptu jam session before the concert, to the encounter with

Donna, to the lake, to the gunshots in the past hour. One thought bouncing off the other. It was too much. She opened a drawer to her nightstand hoping there were earbuds inside. She pulled out a pair of pink ones, took her phone out of her back pocket, selected a playlist of ballads, closed her eyes and laid back down to listen.

When Tano left Sage, he wanted to turn around and go back just like he had wanted to do five years before. His feelings for Holly were even stronger now, even though he wasn't sure how to describe them. He knew that he wanted to spend more time with her. Maybe he even loved her. But maybe only for today. Maybe he would forget about her in a day or two. Probably not.

It seemed like he had just left Sage when he arrived in Springfield, Colorado. He decided to get some dinner and stopped at the Four Corners Diner once again. Rosie, the server he had seen on his last trip through Springfield a few days earlier, was working the night shift.

"There you are again! Rock star back in these parts! And so soon!" Rosie gushed and blushed. The customers sitting at the lunch counter turned to look at him as he walked in the door. Rosie handed him a menu. "Where do ya wanna sit?"

"In that booth by the window over there would be good. Yep, done in Texas and Oklahoma for now. Heading back to Boulder. "

"Well, did ya do good in Texas?"

"Yes, Rosie, I did great in Texas. I could live the last three days over again."

"Good concert? Them Texans liked ya good enough?"

"Yes, Texas was good to me."

"I listened to that there CD that you gave me. That band of yours is top notch. Lots of different stuff on there."

"I'm glad you liked it. So, Rosie, let me have a cup of coffee and a Philly cheesesteak sandwich."

"Fries come with that or do you want something else?"

"Naw, give me fries. No, make that onion rings."

Tano looked at his phone while he waited for his dinner. There was a voice message from Rocky. Janet was released from the hospital and they were flying back to Colorado. There was nothing new about the shooting. Janet remembered very little. Badge would meet up Thursday before the concert for a sound and light check. There were a few text messages from friends who heard about the shooting in Amarillo. No word from Holly. They were probably still in a whirlwind over the shooting. Suddenly, he felt a pang of guilt. *I left her so quickly. She was nearly shot and so upset. Why didn't I wait a little longer? It wouldn't have made any difference. Well, except for Garth. I have to apologize. The truth is, I miss her already.*

"Here ya go, Rock Star." Rosie approached, brought the coffee and food and jarred Tano from scolding himself. "Ketchup's right there. Can I get ya anything else?"

"No thanks."

While Tano silently ate his food, unbeknownst to him, someone was sitting in the parking lot watching him through the café window. Donna was eating a giant-sized Hershey Bar and drinking a Diet Mountain Dew while she waited. *I knew he would ditch that scrawny redhead after he saw me. I didn't have to shoot her after all. Now I can have him all to myself.* While Donna was daydreaming, a big chunk of chocolate began to melt in her fingers. She licked her fingers and wiped them on the big yellow top with the sunflowers she had been wearing for two days. *That won't matter. When I get to be with Tano, I won't be wearing no clothes anyway.* She laughed to herself and looked at her face in the rearview mirror. Melted chocolate was smeared across her right cheek. She rubbed her cheek on the sleeve of her shirt. *Shoulda got some pork rinds instead.*

"More coffee, Rock Star?" Every time Rosy called him "Rock Star," a customer or two would look her way to see who it was.

"No, I'm good. Heading to Trinidad but I don't want to be awake all night." Rosie left the check. Tano pulled out a ten-dollar bill and left it on the table as a tip and walked up to the register to pay.

"You come on back here anytime, Rock Star. Thanks."

"Ya know, I plan to," Tano, believing that he would visit Holly again in Oklahoma, agreed.

Donna started the rental car as Tano emerged from the café and got in his van. She waited for a half minute and pulled out onto the highway. She could see him ahead. *He won't drive to Boulder tonight. He will stop somewhere to sleep. With me tonight.* He drove for about twenty minutes when he reached the tiny town of Pritchett. He pulled over. She stayed a few blocks behind. *What could he be doin'? Probably making a hotel reservation.*

Tano couldn't wait until he got to Trinidad to call Holly. He was concerned about her and the way he left her. He dialed her number.

Holly continued to lay back on her bed listening to music. Music had always had a way of soothing her and allowed her thoughts to transcend beyond the present. It was working. Her phone rang and she yanked the earbuds from her ears.

"Holly, baby. What's going on?"

Holly was surprised and so happy to hear his voice so soon. She felt a little surge of adrenalin. "Hi. Well, not much now. The sheriff came and checked things out and found bullets from a .300 Winchester Mag. A big gun. Garth, of course, went looking for the shooter and only encountered a lady driving up the road. So, nothing there."

"How you doin'?" She was so upset when he left. He had to know if she had calmed herself.

"I'm good, I guess. Tano, I...."

"Yeah, baby?"

"Oh, nothing. I forgot what I was going to say." She didn't forget. She lost her nerve. She wanted to tell him that she missed him so much, that she wanted to be with him, that she might be in love with him. That she was in love with him.

Tap. Tap. Tap. There was a light knock on the bedroom door. "Hold on a sec," she said to Tano and held her phone to her chest.

"Honey, someone is here to see you. It's Jared. Can you come down?"

You've got to be fucking kidding me. He is here already? Holly took a deep breath. "No, I just can't right now. Tell him I'll see him tomorrow. I want to be alone for a while. I just can't."

"Okay, I'll tell him. Are you okay?"

"Yes, Mom, just overtired. Please tell him not tonight. Make him understand." Holly put the phone back to her ear and said to Tano, "Oh, no! Jared, the guy from Kansas, just got here. I'm not going to see him tonight. I'm heading to Kansas tomorrow. I don't know why he couldn't wait until I got home. Garth had something to do with this I'm sure. I don't want to talk to him or about him. So where are you now? Where are you staying tonight?" Tano could hear that she was annoyed, so he led the conversation in a different direction. "I just drove through Springfield, ate some dinner, and pulled over to call you. I'm staying in Trinidad tonight. I'll be in Boulder tomorrow. Oh, hey, I talked to Rocky, and Janet was released from the hospital. There's nothing new about her getting shot."

"Two random shootings in a few days. Unreal, don't you think?"

"Yes. Kind of surreal. I'll let you go. We can talk tomorrow. I just wanted to know that you were all right. You were so upset when I left. I'm sorry that I left so abruptly, but it seemed like under the circumstances it was best. I liked it when you're riding with me though." That was the best he could do to let her know that he cared for and missed her. He could only hope that she got it.

"I'm good. I wasn't ready to come back. I had fun with you." That was the best that she could do to let him know that she cared for and missed him. Her throat began to ache as she thought about telling him goodbye just hours before.

"Well, I should be on my way. It's a couple of hours before I get to Trinidad. Thank you for coming with me to Amarillo. Bye, baby."

"Thank you for asking. Bye, Tano." Her eyes welled with tears thinking of her words that were left unsaid. She put the earbuds back in her ears and closed her eyes.

Tano pulled back out onto the highway thinking about Holly. About seeing her once again. He could still smell her scent in the van—lilies of the valley. Without him knowing, Donna was close behind, driving the tan rental car listening to the Donna songs. The sun was beginning to set. Pretty soon she could move right up behind his van without him seeing her and spoiling the surprise that she had planned for him. *Surprise, lover boy! Donna's gonna take care of you. The next song you write will be about me.*

CHAPTER 23

White daylight dissolved into streaks of yellow, pink and orange across the darkening sky as Tano traveled west to Trinidad. Masses of stars gradually appeared and sparkled like dangly crystal earrings over the remote highway. *Holly would have noticed the stars.* Thoughts of her consumed him as he drove alone. Her calm presence and gentle touch, her bright observations, her humble lack of vanity, the peace that she brought him when she was there. He listened to his road trip playlist. "Drive" by The Cars played as he rolled into Trinidad.

He had not made hotel reservations but took a chance that La Quinta would have an available room. He was in luck. He was assigned a room on the second floor above the hotel lobby. He was happy to learn that a swimming pool and fitness center were amenities that he could take advantage of in the morning before checkout at noon. He parked, grabbed his monogrammed leather bag. When he found his room, he set the bag down, looked out the window, sat on the bed for a minute and then fell back onto the mattress. He stared at the ceiling as he pondered the events with Garth and the shooting in Sage. *What are the chances that something like that would happen? WTF?* He kicked off his boots, pulled his phone out of his pocket and texted.

> *I'm in Trinidad for the night. Boulder tomorrow. Goodnight, sweet thing. Talk tomorrow.*

Holly returned a message.

Goodnight, Tano. I'm in Sage for the night. Liberal, Kansas tomorrow.

Tano picked up the remote and began to scan the TV stations for something to watch as he unwound from the past few days. Before he could settle on a movie there was a light tap, tap, tap on the door. Being cautious as well as a little perplexed, Tano went to the door and looked through the peephole. *No way! No fucking way! Donna? Seriously? How?* There she was standing there wearing a baggy sleeveless red top with multiple layers of ruffles on it, wearing a silver concha belt that made her look as wide as a refrigerator, white short shorts, red high heels with that silly bulldog grin on her face. *Oh, my God! She looks like a clown!*

"Who is it?" He didn't open the door.

"It's me. It's Donna."

"Well, where did you come from?" As he spoke, he cringed like he had been pinched.

"I was driving home from Amarillo and saw your van in the parking lot here at this La Quinta off the highway and I thought I would stop and spend the night here too and say hi. Can I come in?"

Tano thought fast. "No, Donna, I'm feeling sick right now. Like a stomach virus or something. Don't want you to get it too."

"Oh, maybe you got food poisoning from that fruit at the lake." Donna said without realizing what she had just disclosed.

She saw us at the lake! She was there at the lake! She was following us! What a dumb ass to tip her hand that way! Tano had to think fast again. He couldn't reveal that he noticed her stupid mistake.

"Maybe. Yes. I don't know."

"Well, they have a free continental breakfast here in the morning. Do you want to meet for breakfast?"

"Are you staying here?"

"Yeah. I got a room downstairs. They serve until nine thirty. Wanna meet at oh, let's say nine?"

"Maybe, if I'm feeling better. Doesn't sound good right now."

"Okay now. Take care. See you in the morning. Meet you there." Through the peephole, he could see her ruffled backside swaying like a heifer as she walked up the hall. He stood by the door and thought for a minute. *Okay. She really has been stalking me. She most likely shot Janet. Maybe she was the shooter of the Winchester in Sage. Whatever she's up to, she is fucking dangerous.*

Tano was tired and his head pounded but he couldn't sleep after the shock of seeing Donna at his door. But he had a solution to avoid her this time. He would check out at five a.m. long before she would figure out that he was gone. Before she could follow him. Before she could hurt him or make trouble. This time anyway. He turned the TV off, set an alarm on his phone for four thirty a.m., turned on a white noise app on his phone, laid it next to his head on a pillow and eventually fell asleep.

At five a.m., Tano set the room key on the nightstand, tiptoed his way to the elevator, headed to the parking lot and made his escape. He still felt sleepy, but he would stop for coffee when he felt that he was safely away from Donna.

Promptly at nine a.m., Donna made her way to the hospitality room for breakfast wearing the same ruffled outfit she had on the night before, guessing that Tano had not seen her in it. She grabbed herself a cup of coffee, found a cozy corner table, and waited for Tano. At 9:10, when he had not arrived yet, she began to fill a plate with waffles, sausage, bacon, eggs, and toast, and poured herself a glass of Diet Mountain Dew. At 9:20 she began to get concerned. She couldn't call or text him because he blocked her years ago. She gobbled up her plate of food and went to his room. When she got there, housekeeping was busy cleaning it.

"Where is Mr. Montano? Where's the man who was staying here?"

"I don't know, ma'am. I didn't see a man. The front desk just told me that the gentleman in this room left early this morning and I could get a head start on clean up." A young girl with a Spanish accent was sliding clean pillowcases onto the bed pillows. Donna walked in and surveyed the room. *He musta forgot. He wouldn't leave if he remembered that we were supposed to meet.* Donna was perplexed and had no clue that he would ditch her there. *Oh, no. I hope he's all right. I have to catch up with him.*

Before she went to her room to pack her things and check out though, she headed back to the hospitality room for another plate of food. The breakfast was over, but it had not been removed yet. More sausage and this time, cinnamon rolls to go with her Diet Mountain Dew.

Although her stomach was satisfied, Donna was not. When Tano fired her from Tumbleweed, she convinced herself that he only let her go because he was so attracted to her. That he didn't want to be tempted by her. That it was inappropriate for a boss and an employee to get involved. As the weeks grew into months and then years, her thoughts became more delusional until she was no longer able to distinguish reality from the fantasy she created in her mind. Her obsession with Tano had already led her to fire guns on two occasions, both times with the intent to kill.

As she rested her hands on the steering wheel of the rental car while travelling north on I-25, she glanced at the cubic zirconia ring that she wore on the ring finger of her left hand. It sparkled in the morning sunlight. She had ordered the ring from Amazon several months before. When it was delivered, it included a gift card with a message that she had written to herself: "For you, Donna. For our life together. Love, Tano." She clutched the card to her chest and pretended that it was really a gift from Tano. In a matter of days, the pretense dissolved into a reality that only existed in the growing insanity in her head. When her family questioned the veracity of her claims of romance with Tano, she cut all ties, particularly with her sister.

She spoke out loud as she rehearsed a conversation that she intended to have with Tano when she returned to Boulder. "Tano, you and I need to have a talk. I know you're just playing hard to get. This has to stop. We are engaged after all. We need to plan a wedding. I'm ready to move in anytime and have some babies." She squealed at the thought of making babies with him and continued.

"I know you're just using those women to make me jealous and damn it, Tano, it's working. That Janet person told me that she was your girlfriend in Amarillo. So, I shot her. Wanted to kill her but I got scared. And that hippie hick chick from Oklahoma? I shoulda blown her head off. I tried. And I ain't done yet and I ain't gonna get caught. Nobody's gonna stop us from being together. Doesn't this ring mean anything?"

She held her left hand up and looked at the ring again, closed her hand into a fist, and banged the steering wheel with it. She began to breathe hard as anger built within her while she thought about the women who were trying to "step into her shoes."

"Tano, look at me! Look at me! I'm the perfect woman for you!" she yelled at the windshield. Then she caught a glimpse of her reflection in the rearview mirror and smiled at herself with her prominent bulldog grin. Gradually her breathing slowed as her anger evolved into anticipation, believing that she would see Tano in Boulder very soon.

CHAPTER 24

When Holly opened her eyes, she closed them again. The morning light permeated the sheer white shade in her room. She dreaded seeing Jared. He was responsible, nice, considerate, from a wealthy ranch family. Salt of the earth. A nice-looking guy. A good guy, but he wasn't Tano. Try as she might, now that she had been with Tano again, there was no way to purge him from her psyche or shake him from her heart. There was no adequate substitute for him. She was never more certain of anything. His strength, his talent, his outlook on life, his sexy handsomeness, the way he made her feel. No one else would ever come close. She knew it. And as minimal as it might have been, they had a history together. She loved him even though she didn't know how he felt about her, if anything. She held the Badge pendant that Tano gave her in her hand. She opened her eyes again to the daylight and to the truth.

She took a shower, got dressed, and skipped down the stairs, like she always did. Liza was making a big breakfast of pumpkin pancakes—Holly's favorite.

"Grab some juice and have a seat."

"Thanks, Mom. I'm not real hungry but you know I can't resist those pancakes. Did you whip cream, too?"

"Of course, it's not every day my oldest daughter is here with me."

Soon Haley came dragging into the kitchen wearing a gray bathrobe. "God, Holly, what happened here yesterday? I heard about it some from Garth but he's always waving his arms around and doesn't always make sense."

"Everything is okay. There were some stray bullets that somehow ended up here and shot out Garth's truck windows and put a hole in the rabbit shed."

"Yeah, I saw all of that. I'm talking about the big fight."

"It wasn't a 'big' fight. Garth picked at Tano until he couldn't take it anymore and they got into a fight. "

"So are you going to see Tano again? Did he kiss you? Did you get his autograph?"

"No autograph, but he gave me this necklace." Both Liza and Haley got up close to Holly to get a look at it.

"That is a very unique piece of jewelry," Liza said. "Symbolic."

"Can I borrow it sometime?" Haley enthusiastically asked. "You know—to show my friends."

"Never!!!" They heard a car drive into the driveway and two car doors slam. Liza had just handed Holly a plate of pancakes with whipped cream and syrup. In walked Garth and Jared.

"Hi, hon," Jared said when he saw her. He smiled and bent over her and kissed her on the forehead.

"Hi, Jared. What brings you here? I was planning to head home this afternoon. I'm sorry about last night. I guess you heard that it was kind of a rough day

"Yes, I heard. Are you okay, honey? I was so worried when I heard what happened from Garth. He called me a couple of days ago and thought that I should pay you a visit anyway. But I needed to see if my sweetheart was really okay. I know you've only been here this week. But I missed you and…" Words rushed from Jared's mouth.

Holly interrupted him before the sentimentality could begin. "Have some of my mom's pancakes." Liza handed a plate to Jared with a stack of four pancakes slathered with whipped cream.

"Garth? Did you eat at home or do you want pancakes? Your dad already patched the rabbit shed and is in the shop now."

"Yeah, give me a couple of them." Garth looked up occasionally at Holly as he ate, giving her a stern, disapproving look. "Where'd ya get that necklace?"

"Tano gave it to me." Jared looked at Garth.

"He probably hands them things out to all the girls. A dime a dozen. You're no different."

"Garth, that was uncalled for. She's never going to visit us again if you keep it up. I've had about enough and so has your dad. So, knock it off and act like an adult." Liza scolded.

Holly had been bracing herself for a comment about Badge or Tano or the trip to Amarillo. Although she wanted to respond, she remained silent. She wanted to talk to Jared later privately. The kitchen was silent as its occupants finished the pancakes. Holly got up, gathered the plates from the table and took them to the sink.

"Come on, Jared. Let's go see the old man." Garth pushed his chair up to the table.

"I will later. I want to spend some time with her." Holly was uncomfortable with the thought but tried not to let it show. "Let's go outside and sit for a while and enjoy the cool part of the day," Jared meekly said. He wanted to know what had been going on with Holly and her trip to Amarillo. But at the same time, he didn't want to know.

"Okay, for sure."

Jared took her hand in his as they walked out to a couple of green metal lawn chairs under a black walnut tree and sat down.

"Holly, I know you just had some kind of a fun adventure with a rock band. But I know you, Holly, and I know that kind of lifestyle isn't for you. And maybe you just needed to blow off a little steam, and I don't think I want to or need to know what happened while you were gone. But it's important to me that you're back here with your family, with plans to head back to Kansas and return to the normal way of life that is truly you."

Holly wanted to say but only thought to herself as he spoke, *Jared, you don't know me at all. And no, you shouldn't know what happened between Tano and me. Those moments belong only to us. And no, things will never be the same here or in Kansas. I'm not the girl that you want me to be.*

She sat silent for a minute and thought before she spoke. "It's too soon to know what I feel about the past week and how it fits with my life. It was significant in many ways."

Jared looked down as he felt the pain of those simple words. But he had a plan and he was going to go through with it. "Holly, you and I have a solid, stable foundation in Liberal. And solid family ties. And with that foundation, we could build a good long life for ourselves and children someday. As a couple. Maybe this isn't the time to do this. Maybe Garth's panic is pushing me. Maybe no time is perfect but, I want to ask you to marry me. We don't have to hurry. But I want to be part of your future plans. I love you. Will you marry me?" Jared got down on one knee and handed Holly a little silver jewelry box. Holly opened it. It was a beautiful yellow gold ring with a marquis-cut diamond and two diamond baguettes on either side. She subconsciously reached for the Badge pendant and held it in her other hand.

"Jared. This is so sudden. I don't know what to say. This is a big permanent decision. I had no idea this was coming. Can you give me some time?" She smiled at him and he got up from the ground, sat next to her and pulled her close to him. He leaned in to kiss her lips, but she turned her head and he kissed her cheek. *Oh, jeez, I already know the answer. I just can't say it right now. He is so vulnerable.*

"You keep the ring for now and wear it when you're ready. If nothing else, I wanted you to know that I want what we have to be permanent. I can't imagine my life without you in it."

Holly's insides hurt for Jared. *Damn Garth pushed him into this. I need to talk to Tano. What would he say? And if I tell him, he will think I'm trying to trap him somehow. I would never do that. But I don't ever want to hide anything from him.*

"I'm so flattered. I do need some time. I'll keep the ring in a safe place for now. Thank you, Jared, for wanting me that way."

Jared looked down at the ground, and then looked up at Holly and smiled. "I want you to be sure. I'll wait."

Holly put the ring box in the breast pocket of her pink polo shirt. She had to do something to end the intense conversation. "Come on. Let's go play with the goats." She grabbed his hand and walked toward the goats, stopping to pet Butkus on the way. "Hey, Butkus. Another hot day, huh, buddy?"

Garth popped his head out of John's shop when he heard Holly talking to Butkus and with a big smile on his face, hollered, "Did she say yes?"

CHAPTER 25

"Not yet." Jared flashed Garth a hopeful smile, trying not to look embarrassed. Garth slammed the door and stepped back inside the shop. Holly looked down at the grass and continued to make her way to the goat pasture.

"Come here, little ones." Holly gently spoke.

The goats scampered over to the fence to be petted. Liza had finished the morning dishes and was in the goat pasture circulating among them. Holly looked at her standing there in the sunlight, with a breeze gently blowing her long gray strands of hair and ruffling the long denim skirt she wore, carrying a metal bucket. Her serene face, with the hint of smile, was a portrait of contentment with the life she chose. But was it really satisfaction or merely acceptance? Holly's mind flashed on a vision of Tano. *How could I make a life with a man who loves me, when I'm in love with someone else?* Her stomach churned and her neck and shoulders tightened as she recalled the earlier awkward moments when Jared proposed. *I wouldn't physically feel like this if Jared was the one. I just know it.*

Liza sauntered over to them.

"Mrs. Harris," Jared said, "I've asked Holly to marry me." Holly cringed. She planned to mention it to her mother later in private.

Liza looked directly at Holly's expressionless face and saw nothing. She looked at Jared who was smiling.

"It was a little bit of a surprise to her. She's thinking about it, aren't you, hon?" Jared put his arm around her waist and pulled her closer to him. "Show her the ring."

Holly reached into her shirt pocket and pulled out the little box and handed it to Liza. "I'm going to keep it for now. I'm just not ready to wear it yet."

Liza looked at the ring and then looked up at Holly's face again. Still nothing. "Yellow gold," she said. "It's quite lovely, Jared." Liza recognized that if Jared really knew Holly, he wouldn't have picked out a yellow gold ring. She only wore silver. Never yellow gold.

"There's no hurry or anything. I'm just happy that I got the chance to ask her," Jared blurted. *Before someone else comes along. Like that rock star. I can't let her get away.* The silent glances between Holly and Liza were making him uncomfortable. Jared resumed petting the goats, and Liza took her bucket and headed toward the back door.

Garth came charging out of John's shop as the insurance agent, Pete Schofield, drove into the driveway. He was anxious to clean up the truck and get the windows replaced but the agent needed to see it first. He walked around the truck, took photos, shook Garth's hand and left. Garth got a broom and a Shop-Vac and began to clean the glass out of his truck, ignoring Holly and Jared.

Jared's phone rang. "Excuse me a sec. It's my brother." Holly walked over to the red paint-peeled bench by the gate and sat down to wait for him. She heard him say, "I'll be there this afternoon. Bye."

"Holly, I'm heading back to Liberal soon. A cattle buyer is coming in this afternoon and my brother wants me there for the meeting and we'll take him to dinner tonight. Still planning to come home today? You could join us for dinner."

Holly drew in a deep breath and exhaled. She was so relieved that he was leaving. "No, I think I'll stay one more day. And head home tomorrow." She needed some time alone to think. To clear her head. To talk to Tano.

Holly followed Jared into the house. When Liza learned he was leaving, she filled a baggy with oatmeal cookies for him to eat on the way home.

"Bye, hon. See you tomorrow?" Jared pulled Holly close and hugged her around her waist. He wanted to kiss her but she deliberately took a step back from him. He was worried. Something was different about her. She stiffened when he touched her. She avoided eye contact with him. Interaction with her was awkward and superficial. Maybe the proposal was too much. Too soon. Or maybe it was too late.

Holly walked him to his car. She smiled and waved to him as he backed out of the driveway in his King Ranch edition black Ford pickup. He blew her a kiss. The morning air was changing from warm to sweltering. She went in the house, put on a loose lime green tank top, black yoga pants and her running shoes when she decided to take a run through Sage. When she ran up the driveway, Butkus followed her along the perimeter of the property a way until he found a shady spot where he laid to wait for her return.

As she wound her way through the tiny town, people who knew her waved to her and one hollered "Hey, Holly. Looking good." The Oklahoma sun was becoming unbearable. She slowed to a walk and returned home. Butkus greeted her with a wagging tail and accompanied her to the house.

She had left her phone at home and when she returned, she saw a text from Tano.

Home in Boulder

Holly texted back.

Can I call you later?

Tano responded.

Sure. I'll be at Tumbleweed. Would love to talk to you.

Tano had rolled into Boulder at nine thirty a.m. It was a four-hour drive from Trinidad to Boulder, but he only made one stop for gas on the way home. He couldn't risk Donna catching up to him. *Donna—what a piece of work! A psycho packaged like a troll.*

Although his suspicions about her were strong, he continued to resist going to the police. She definitely shouldn't have a gun. He suddenly remembered that she mentioned once that she and her husband went target shooting on the weekends. Could she have fired shots at Holly in Sage?

His house was nestled among pine and aspen trees a few miles up the canyon from Boulder. The log exterior was dark with a sloping shiny copper metal roof that always caught the eye of travelers on the highway. The interior was open and sprawling with lightly stained wide plank pine flooring. A few Two Grey Hills rugs in natural hues of greys and reds lay on the floor near the massive burgundy leather couches and dark brown chairs. Glass-top end tables with heavy twisted pine legs flanked the furniture. Lamps with copper and brass bases rested on the tabletops. On the walls were several paintings by a local artist in the hues and style reminiscent of Georgia O'Keeffe. In one corner of the room, two Fender acoustic guitars in brown shades and a black Fender Stratocaster similar to one of Eric Clapton's leaned on their stands. In the opposite corner, his golf clubs rested. The pine-covered vaulted ceiling stretched to a second story loft where the master bedroom was located.

Tano turned the key in the lock, tossed the keys on a dark pine table by the door. He dropped his bag, walked over to the couch, which faced the massive fireplace flanked by river rock, kicked his boots off and rested his feet on the heavy oval blue agate coffee tabletop, leaned his head back and closed his eyes. He dozed for a half hour. When he awoke, he felt that his head was clearer. The little nap had separated him from the events of the previous days. But it didn't lessen his continuous thoughts of Holly. He decided that he couldn't put a label on what they were, because he clearly couldn't define it for himself. Maybe he loved her. Maybe it was just a short-lived adventure. A fun fling. Maybe she was just a sweet memory that he would recall from time to time. Is that what he wanted? The clear answer was no. But he wanted what was best for her. A down-to-earth girl, smart, sensible, beautiful for sure. Did she belong in his world? How would she handle weeks away from him?

He flipped through the mail. Went to the refrigerator and pulled out a grapefruit LaCroix water to drink. He sent the text to Holly letting her know he was home. He would be on his way to downtown Boulder to the Tumbleweed to touch base.

"Hey, Tumbleweed. I'm back," he said as he walked in the door of the bar.

"Hey, Tano. How'd it go? We heard about the shooting near your hotel. I remember Janet. How did she end up there?" Anthony was standing behind the bar looking at some paperwork when Tano walked in.

"She was with Rocky somehow. It's still kind of a mystery how that happened. Let's just say that the last few days were kind of intense in many ways. The concert was great."

"I heard. So, did you find her? The girl from yesterday?"

"I did." Tano nodded, smiled, and looked toward the windows as he pictured Holly standing there.

"And?"

"It was good. I'm glad I did." Anthony didn't prod him with more questions. "So fill me in on the events of the last week and what needs to be done before you get back." They discussed inventory, a new margarita recipe, a change in vendor.

It was around four in the afternoon and the early evening bar patrons had not begun to arrive yet. Storm clouds were building above Boulder and Pearl Street was less crowded. Tano's phone rang and he could see that it was Holly. He walked into his office and closed the door.

"Hi, baby. How's it going?"

"I'm good. How was your drive back?"

"Well, I left Trinidad pretty early. You will never guess why."

"No, why? Did something happen?"

"Yep. When I got to the hotel in Trinidad, guess who knocked on my door?"

"Who? A fan?"

"Yep, a fan all right. Donna! You should have seen her. All decked out like a circus clown in ruffles and short shorts. It was unbelievable."

"Did you let her in? Oh my God."

"No! I could see her through the peephole in the door. She wanted to come in, but I told her I was sick. And then she made some comment about how maybe I got food poisoning from the fruit that I bought at the lake. Jesus, she was at the lake when we were! Stalking us! So I got out of Trinidad before she knew I left."

"Wow. That's scary. You haven't seen her in Boulder yet?"

"No. Oh, I wanted to tell you that Janet and Rocky are flying home today. There's still no word about the shooting there." Tano wanted to know about Jared's visit but he wouldn't ask. "So what did anyone find out about the shots fired at your house?"

"Nothing new. Insurance guy came to look at Garth's truck so he can clean it up. The sheriff may be giving you a call."

"Okay. So has Garth settled down?"

"Well, he's not talking to me so that means he's not yelling at me either."

"So are you heading to Kansas yet today?" *Please tell me about Jared*, Tano thought.

"No, I wanted to stay here one more night."

"So..." Before Tano could finish his sentence, Holly began to speak in a gentle tone.

"Tano, you can't believe this—I sure couldn't believe it myself, but Jared came here with a ring and asked me to marry him. It was so unexpected and random. I think Garth pushed him into it. I was shocked."

Tano recoiled like the breath had been knocked out of him. There was dead silence for what seemed like eternity to Holly.

"Tano? You there?"

After another long lapse of silence, Tano said, "What did you tell him?"

"Nothing. I didn't tell him anything. I put it in my pocket and told him that I had to think."

"What do you need to think about?"

"How to tell him no."

There was another long pause. "Listen, I'm not going to tell you what to do but I'm going to tell you to do what's best for you. I only want the best for you. And if the life he can offer you is what you want and need, you decide. You need to think about it."

Holly was stunned and held her breath. Her throat began to ache, and her eyes burned with tears. She wanted him to tell her that she belonged with him. To tell Jared no. That he wanted her. That maybe they could have a life together. That maybe they could give it a shot anyway. That he loved her. What was he implying? When she spoke, her voice was strained and tight from the pain her throat. "Do you mean what you said?" Lightning flashed and thunder began to roar as a heavy downpour of an Oklahoma deluge suddenly descended on the roof of Holly's bedroom.

Tano was silent for a moment again as he pondered an answer and gently spoke. "Yes. I want you to have everything you ever wanted." He felt the weight of his own words pressing down on his chest.

"Okay." Holly could not say more. Tears streamed down her face, but she tried not to let him hear the pain and sadness in her voice. Then she had to say it. "But Tano...what about us?"

Tano didn't know what to say. Holly had no idea how much he was hurting. At that moment he knew that he truly loved her and in fact, he loved her so much, he would let her go if that was the choice she made. "I don't know." Oddly rain and hail began to pour in Boulder simultaneous to the deluge in Sage.

"Okay." Tears streamed down her cheeks in unison with the rain on her windowpanes. "Tano? Thank you for the past few days."

"You're welcome, baby." Tano couldn't bear the pain he heard in Holly's voice any longer. "I gotta go. Take care."

"Okay, bye." Holly sat cross-legged on her bed looking at the black screen on her phone. *Why did I tell him about Jared's proposal? Why? Why? I didn't want to be dishonest. I can't take those words back. I told him I would say no. Why did he react like that? It's all my fault. It's all my fault.*

Tano sat back in the swivel chair in his office. He never felt worse. He didn't mean to imply it was over between them. But that's how it must have sounded. He wanted to call her back. To straighten it out. To tell her the truth. *I fucked it up. Why did I react like that?* One of the bartenders knocked on his door. There was a customer at the bar who was a friend of his who wanted to say hi.

"I'll be out in a minute. Thanks." He put both hands on the top of his pounding head and leaned back in his chair. *I missed her for five years, I got her back, and did I let her go? Maybe that's how it was supposed to be.* He rubbed his face in his hands, stood up, opened the office door and stepped out into the bar.

CHAPTER 26

"Hi, Tano! Where'd ya go? I thought we were gonna meet for breakfast this morning?" Donna chirped. She was sitting on a bar stool wearing the same ruffled red top, red high heels, and white short shorts smeared with a streak of chocolate. Her hair was flat and stiff. She was wearing that pasted-on smile, drinking a blackberry margarita. Tano's eyes grew wide with disbelief and anger and his face was burning. Unfortunately, Anthony had left the bar for the day. If he had been there, he never would have let her in the bar or at the very least, he wouldn't have let her know he was there. He glared at the bartender who had knocked on his office door.

Tano quietly spoke through gritted teeth as he leaned against the bar. "Donna! What do you want? Are you stalking me or something? Jesus! You're everywhere that I am. This has to stop!" She was oblivious to his obvious anger.

"So, do ya feel better now? Remember you were sick."

"Donna, you have to go. I don't want to talk to you. Please leave!" Tano was clearly frustrated and wouldn't look at her. He was quietly reeling over the botched conversation that he had just had with Holly and then she appeared.

"Oh, Tano. You don't mean it. So, are you done with that red-headed hippie girl from Oklahoma?"

Tano was struck by that comment. Words raced through his mind. *How could she know that Donna was in Oklahoma? The same way she knew that they stopped at the lake in north Texas. She must have followed them from Amarillo.*

"Look! I have no interest in you now or ever. I want you to leave.

Get a life and leave me out of it! I'm goddamn serious! I don't want to see you ever again!"

Donna's eyes grew wide and she gasped. "Well, that was harsh."

Tano couldn't take another minute of interaction with her. He stormed back to his office and slammed the door. He called the bar from his personal phone. When the bartender answered, Tano angrily told him not to serve Donna another drink, to make sure that she left, and to let him know when she was gone.

Donna continued to sip on the margarita and look at her reflection in the mirror behind the bar. *He didn't mean any of it. I could tell he liked my outfit by the way he checked me out. He's just tired from being sick and driving that hippie redhead all over the place. He just needs to rest.* She took out her phone and scrolled through her e-mail for a confirmation. She had just bought tickets to the Badge concert in Denver in a few days. *With that skinny redhead gone, he will sing to me this time.*

Holly laid her head back on the bed pillows. She closed her eyes. She still held her phone in her hand. Tears burned her eyes and ran down the sides of her face and formed little puddles on the pillowcase. She replayed Tano's words in her head over and over. *Did I misunderstand? Did I get it wrong? And Jared? What was he doing? We don't know each other well enough to marry. He just wanted to claim me for himself. To push that "rock star" out of the way.* She was reminded of a haunting old ballad by Bonnie Raitt which she loved, "I Can't Make You Love Me." The melody played in her head as she thought of the words. She sat up, wiped her wet face with the heels of hands, and opened the violin case that was resting in a corner of the room by the closet. She bowed each string a couple of times, twisted the tuning pegs and tuned it by ear. She moved the bow gently on the strings to play quietly. She had played her violin along with that song many times before while she listened to it. But this time, it was more than a beautiful song. The lyrics in her head spoke to her with words of truth. At least as she understood them at that moment.

She couldn't make him love her and now she couldn't stand to hear it anymore.

Liza was downstairs shelling green peas into a white ceramic bowl for dinner. She heard the soft and mournful sound of the violin playing. *Oh, no, what could she be dealing with now?* Liza knew her daughter well. She would keep it to herself and let her music speak for her until she was ready to speak of it herself.

The forlorn serenade stopped before she finished the song. Holly put the violin back in the corner of the room and laid back down on the bed resting her forearm over her forehead. *I'm ridiculous. He was gone for five years and he came back for a few days. How could that mean anything? There are no expectations. We each have our own lives and will continue to live them.* Holly sighed deeply. *But now everything has changed inside. And there's no turning back. I'm forever changed.* She gulped and held back tears that had flowed so easily. She remembered that the little box with the engagement ring was still in her shirt pocket. She took it out, opened it and looked at it, closed it and set it on her nightstand. She decided to go downstairs.

"Hey, Mom. Need any help?" Holly's voice was barely audible.

Liza looked up at Holly as she sauntered into the kitchen. Her eyes were swollen. "Why don't you finish shelling these peas while I peel potatoes?"

Holly robotically began to shell the peas. The room was silent except for the bubbling and gurgling sounds of boiling water in a large pot on the stove.

Then Holly spoke. "Mom...I don't want to marry Jared. I'm not going to. I can't."

"I know, honey. It was written all over your face."

"I don't know him well enough. It's only been about six months since we met. And I don't think that more time will change my feelings. He would be a catch for somebody. Just not me. Tano said I should think about it, but I don't need to." Liza stopped peeling a potato and turned to look at Holly's forlorn face.

"Tano matters a lot to you, doesn't he?"

"Yes, he does." The screen door slammed, followed by the sound of heavy footsteps.

"What the hell is the matter with you?" Garth roared at Holly. "Jared is perfect for you. Rich, got connections, nice lookin' guy. You'll be set for life. Why are you stringing him along like that?"

Liza spoke sharply. "Garth, why do you think it's your business anyway? Leave her alone!"

"Hey, it's my life. You tend to your family. If I screw up, it's on me." Even though her words were forceful, she mumbled them. Heartbreak had dampened her ability to defend herself.

"I think you need to go home, Garth. Bye." Liza emphatically pointed to the door.

"Do you think that rock star son of a bitch cares what you do? Cares about you like Jared? He's probably nailin' some groupie right now. Maybe a whole damn group of groupies." Garth sneered. Holly recoiled as if she had been struck.

"Watch your mouth, Garth! Go home now! Do I need to bring your dad in on this?" Liza's voice shook with anger.

"I'm outta here." Garth stomped to the screen door and slammed it again on his way out. Holly and Liza were silent as they continued with the task of making dinner.

"I'm heading back to Liberal tomorrow morning. I need to take care of something."

Liza knew what she meant.

"Are you sure?"

"I'm positive."

Two hours passed before Donna hopped down from the bar stool and finally left Tumbleweed. She wrote a note on a cocktail napkin and gave it to the bartender. "Give this to Tano from me."

Bye Tano. See you soon. Feel better.
xoxoxoxoxoxoxoxox DM

Tano had remained in his office checking mail and paying bills while Donna slowly sipped her drink. Holly hovered in his mind continuously as he tried to concentrate. He leaned back in his office chair, cowboy boots rested on the marble-topped walnut desk, his eyes scanned the room, not really seeing the Badge, Eric Clapton, Bruce Springsteen posters, and vintage guitars hanging on the walls. His mind volleyed from wanting to call or text her and then with letting her go. *I'll give her space. But I don't want to let her go.*

Matt, the bartender, called him and let him know that Donna was gone. When Tano emerged, he saw an old college friend and sat down to talk for a while.

"How the hell you been, Tano? You rock-and-roll Romeo," his old friend, Brett, said as he slapped him lightly on the back. Brett, who had played football, had lost his athletic build and his hairline was receding.

"Been doin' good. Hanging here at Tumbleweed when I'm in Boulder. And just playing with the band the rest of the time. How have you been?"

"You remember—I married Julia a couple of years ago. She was at CU when we were. An education major. We have a little two-year-old boy, Winston, now. In town visiting the grandparents. That free wheelin' life like we knew it is over. I'm in medical equipment sales. Travelin' some. What about you? Found the right girl yet?"

"Naw. Not looking. Been busy."

"Yeah, busy with the women." Brett laughed.

"Good to see ya, Brett. Tell Julia hello from me. Hey, hope to see ya at one of the Badge concerts one day. Your drink is on me."

"Will do. And thanks."

Tano stepped behind the bar and Matt handed him the napkin note. His face soured when he read it. He wadded it up and threw it away. "Matt, can you guys handle the bar for the rest of tonight? I'm bushed and I need to go home and get some sleep."

"Sure thing, Tano."

When Tano arrived at his house, he kicked his boots off, grabbed one of the Fender acoustic guitars from the stand and began to play unplugged. "Bell Bottom Blues," Derek and the Dominos, and

"Whiskey and You" by Chris Stapleton. But then the guitar playing gently evolved into "Faithfully," the Journey song about the hardship of a long-distance rock-and-roll romance. It could have been about them—Tano and Holly, if their affair had lasted. *I don't know if I can fix it. My words seemed so calculated and cold. She deserves better than that.*

He laid the guitar on the burgundy leather couch, opened a side table, pulled out a baggie of weed, and rolled a joint. He hadn't smoked weed for a couple of weeks. He felt bad about Holly. He missed her. He wanted the guilt he felt to go away. Maybe the weed would help him forget for a while. Maybe it would help him sleep. Maybe. One joint was enough. He laid down on the couch and promptly dozed off.

CHAPTER 27

For the next few days, the routine for Tano felt somewhat comfortable after the erratic recent days he spent in Texas and Oklahoma. He kept himself busy at Tumbleweed, reviewing the books, ordering inventory, meeting with liquor distributors and mingling with customers. His days were full, but the nights were long. His thoughts turned to Holly—the magical time together, before and now, his careless response to her when she mentioned Jared's proposal, her scent, her voice, her smile. He tossed and turned, got up and down, and resorted to a joint or a couple of shots of Jack Daniels every night to help him sleep. But then morning came too soon.

On Sunday afternoon, he brought mixed flowers of red, orange, yellow and pink to his mother; and for both parents, a gourmet pizza of black olives, mushrooms, artichokes, fresh tomato and sausage from Tumbleweed. His mother appeared to have lost some weight in the weeks that he was away, but her energy level was high and so were her spirits. His dad was content to play golf on occasion and to work on the model railroad that he was building in the basement. He was quiet and moving slowly.

"Hey, Dad, how about a round of golf next time I'm in town? Gotta work at Tumbleweed this week. Anthony's on vacation."

"Sure, son. You've been working too hard. Need to settle down."

"I'm good, Dad."

"Your father's right. The perfect little gal must be out there somewhere, and you know I could use a couple more grandkids," she teased. Thoughts of Holly surfaced in Tano's mind as his mother spoke and he wondered what they would have thought about her. *I think that they would have loved her.*

Two days before the Thursday concert in Denver, the Badge members and the manager, Rob, met Tano at Tumbleweed to go over the set list and to talk about the venue. They had never played at the outdoor amphitheater at Fiddler's Green before, but their roadies knew about the state-of-the-art sound equipment. The lighting tech had worked a few concerts there before. The band turned the sound and light systems over to them and would check out the venue on Thursday.

Rocky brought Janet to Tumbleweed for the meeting. Tano had not seen her since the shooting in Amarillo. Her left arm was in a sling still healing from the gunshot wound and subsequent surgery to her shoulder. She moved slowly, holding her right side with her left hand in the sling, still in pain. Otherwise, she looked the same and had the same biting, sarcastic attitude. She immediately approached Tano and tried to put her right arm around his neck and kissed his cheek. He felt obliged to give her a slight hug and said, "Good to know that you're going to be okay."

"Aw, it's nice to know you cared," she said, and winked at Tano. "It was just a scratch. Well, not really." She made a slight groaning sound. "Oh, and thank you for the flowers that you and uh, what's her name, you know, that flower child, sent to my room."

"Holly. Her name is Holly."

"Well, did she ever find her way home?"

Tano didn't reply. Rocky witnessed the awkward exchange between them and was annoyed at Janet's flirting. He grabbed her good arm and whispered to her, "I should have left you at home."

Janet pulled away and began to pout. When the group sat down at a big table, Janet scooted her chair back in the corner and behind Rocky but facing Tano, staring at him when she wasn't playing on her phone. Tano ignored her but was aware of her constant gaze. The bartender brought a round of margaritas and Coronas.

"So the concert's at seven. And since it's a new venue for us, we should get there at about four at the latest for a sound check and a light rehearsal," Randy suggested.

Quiet Jack said, "Yeah, at least. I want to hear how the sound bounces off my drums."

"I liked our setlist from Amarillo. We just wouldn't want to end with 'Luckenbach, Texas' this time around," Tano commented, continuing to avoid Janet's fixed gaze. "Any suggestions?"

"I think the same setlist is great. Remember we played Rick Roberts's 'Colorado' a couple of years back? You know from the Flying Burrito Brothers. Do you think we could revive it tomorrow night for the end?" It was unusual for Jack to speak about anything.

"Sounds great."

"I'll get this setlist to the light and sound techs," Rob said as he signaled to the bartender for another beer.

When discussion of plans for the concert was over, Tano asked Rocky, "Any news about the shooting in Amarillo?"

"Well, I think you knew that the detectives think that it might have been a woman for sure from the surveillance video. A person in a dark-brown hoodie and white tennis shoes. But there's no leads that we know of. It appears to be random."

"I told those dumb-ass cops that it was a woman who shot me. I heard her voice!" Janet blurted loudly.

"Yeah, and you were drunk on your ass so who knows," Rocky shot back. "I think we need to head out. Come on, Janet. You need your meds."

"Bye, Tano. Bye, guys. See you tomorrow." Janet waved with the fingers of the arm in the sling and winked at Tano again. As they walked on the sidewalk in front of the bar's windows, the band saw Rocky scolding her while Janet rolled her eyes at him.

"Jeez, the Rock sure has his hands full," Jack quipped. The band stayed for a couple more hours, drinking, eating nachos and taquitos. It was rare when they could be together without Badge as their focus. Randy and Jack left before the bar closed. Rob stayed until it closed at midnight.

When Tano got home, he took one of his guitars from the stand in the corner of the room, tuned it, and downed two shots of Jack Daniels but no grass, and headed to bed.

Wednesday morning arrived and was not unlike the previous days. Tano discovered that he liked the routine. No matter, he had to do it anyway. He felt emptiness from Holly's silence every day and he missed her. She clearly didn't want to talk to him anymore and it was his own fault. She could be engaged by now. Maybe he could message her in time. Maybe he should take a chance. He had never met a girl like her before. Sweet, genuine, loving, fun, a violinist, a dancer, a farm girl, sexy. Could he really let that go? There were the awesome memories of the past few days together. And there was a little baby once long ago. *I don't give a fuck about that hot-headed brother. Nothing and no one would keep me from her if I just knew how she felt about me.*

Early in the afternoon, after the lunch crowd had dwindled, one of the regular liquor distributors arrived armed with some new brands of tequila and mixers. Anthony had returned to Tumbleweed earlier in the day from his vacation and met with them. The three of them stood behind the bar looking at price lists, available shelf space, and delivery schedules. Someone walked in the door. Anthony looked up, nudged Tano, and nodded toward the door. Tano looked up. And there she was. Standing near the door, surrounded by a copper glow from sunlight on her hair, was Holly. She stood motionless and silent waiting for a signal of some kind from Tano. Stunned by her appearance, he was frozen for several seconds before he could speak. He felt an indescribable sensation in his chest when he saw her.

"Come here, baby," he quietly spoke.

Holly walked toward him and stood in the middle of the room. Tano stepped from behind the bar. He motioned to her to come closer. She took a few steps and stood face to face with him, arms at her sides, wanting so much to reach out and touch him.

She looked into his golden-brown eyes and in a hushed voice said, "I told him no."

CHAPTER 28

Early Saturday morning, Holly had left Sage, Oklahoma, carrying a blue and white china plate of homemade cinnamon rolls that Liza made for her, and drove home to Liberal, Kansas. A trip that took a little less than two hours. In her mind, she went over and over the events of the past week looking for clues about how Tano felt about her. On one hand, he had looked for her after five years apart. That must mean something. But on the other hand, when he found her, maybe she disappointed him. Maybe she was just a good time. Maybe pushing her toward Jared was his way out. Maybe he was testing her. Maybe. Maybe. Maybe. Only he had the answers that she may never know now.

She had slipped the engagement ring, still in its box, in the pocket of her tight faded jeans. It left a little bulge in her pocket. As she drove, she listened to the Badge playlist. Tears came to her eyes as she recalled playing the violin with him in the van, in the rain, when she heard him sing "Free." But tears fell when she heard him sing "The Girl from Yesterday," the song he wrote about her and dedicated to her in Amarillo. She couldn't take anymore and needed to regain her composure. She turned the music off and just listened to the hum of the tires on the highway. The scent of the warm cinnamon rolls wafted through the car.

When Holly reached her little white-frame Craftsman-style house in Liberal, before she left the car, she called Jared and asked him to come over when he had time. Then she checked the mailbox, went inside, and dropped her bag in the entryway. She filled a little pitcher with water and watered the tiny vegetable garden outside by the back door. She opened a window in the bedroom on the north side of the house to let fresh air in.

While she was in her bedroom, she remembered there was a small pink fabric-bound journal tucked away in the top dresser drawer among her T-shirts that she had not looked at for years. She opened it to the last page and saw the last words she had written: "A tiny miracle has given my life direction." A smiley face was drawn below the words. She remembered why those words were the last entry in the journal.

She opened a new page and began to scribble words that seemed to materialize from somewhere deep within.

> *I was a fool to fall in love before*
> *And then to let it happen again.*
> *Feelings for him have consumed my heart*
> *And my thoughts with what might have been.*

She read the words out loud to herself. She thought that the verse sounded like a corny greeting card, even though each word was true. She closed the journal and set it on her nightstand. Maybe she would write more. There was a light knock on the front door.

Jared stood on the front step looking at his phone when Holly opened the door.

"Hi, baby. You're finally home. You missed a great meal at the Cattlemen's Ranch Steak House last night. You would have loved the steak and trout."

"Hey, Jared. Come in. Want something to drink? I don't really know what I have. I've only been home for about a half hour."

"I'm good. I can only stay for a little while. Have a meeting with a banker at one. I'm so glad to see you back home." He hugged her quickly, took a few steps and sat down on the white leather couch.

Holly sat down next to him. She didn't know how to begin to say what she had to say. She took a breath and said, "Jared, I've been thinking about your proposal." Jared's face brightened in anticipation as he looked at her face. "I've been thinking…" She pulled the ring box out of her jeans' pocket and held it in her open hand. "I'm not ready. I'm sure I'm not ready. Please take it and keep it. I have to say no."

Jared looked down at the little box and wouldn't look up at Holly. "It was too soon. I knew it was. It was worth taking a chance. My timing wasn't good. That rock star showing up...." His voice began to quiver with resentment.

"No, Jared. It was just too soon. Tano's appearance just made it obvious to me. Take it," she said as she handed the little box to him. "You picked out a lovely ring for me. Thank you."

Jared finally looked up at her, stood, and said, "Okay, then. Well, I guess I'll see you around?"

It was apparent from his response to her that not only would there be no engagement, but the relationship was over. "Yes. You will. We both live in the same town." She reached over and attempted to hug him lightly. He pulled away. She felt bad for him. But she felt bad for herself too. Jared lost her. She believed that she lost Tano. The hasty marriage proposal had cost them both. He stood and walked to the door and turned to look at her before he left.

Holly, in a voice that was nearly a whisper said, "Bye." She followed behind him and closed the door. When she looked out the side window, he was sitting in his car, with his hands on the steering wheel staring straight ahead. He was gone when she looked again.

With the absence of the weight that Jared's proposal had laid on her, she believed that she could think clearly. She got out her laptop and looked online for the Badge tour schedule. She knew that Badge was scheduled to play in Denver on Thursday. Impulsively she bought a concert ticket online, contacted United Airlines and booked a flight to Denver on Wednesday morning. *I can't let this end without giving it one more chance. He's worth the risk of rejection. He's worth everything.*

On Wednesday afternoon, Holly's heart raced at a maddening pace as she approached the door to the Tumbleweed with excitement and apprehension to see him. *Here I go.* Her hand shook as she slowly pushed the door open.

Tano reached for her, gently placed a hand on each arm, and pulled her close. He didn't say a word and just held her. He could feel her heart beating hard against his chest. He smelled the fragrance of lilies of the valley as his chin rested near her hair. Anthony and the liquor distributor took in the scene for a few seconds, nudged each other, and resumed their previous conversation.

Still in a tight embrace, Holly looked up at Tano as he spoke. "I hoped you would say no."

"But you didn't say."

"It had to be your decision. It doesn't matter now." He continued to hold her as if he couldn't let go.

"I had to see you one more time. I had to know. I had to know if you were finished with me."

"No, I'm not finished. I'm so surprised that you're here. How long?" He hugged her tightly.

"I bought a ticket to see Badge tomorrow night. I fly home on Friday. I made a reservation at the Hilton on Pearl Street."

"You flew? You bought a ticket? You're not staying at a hotel. You're staying with me."

"I didn't know. I didn't know if you would want to see me. When we talked, it felt like it was over. Like with Donna."

"It's not. It's nothing like Donna." He didn't have the words to say how he felt about her. He would let his actions speak for him. They remained locked in an embrace in the middle of the bar, as if they couldn't let go. He firmly kissed her lips. A couple of college-aged men walked around them and stepped up to the bar. "I guess we should take this someplace else. Let's go into my office."

Holly followed him into his office. He shut the door and kissed her again and again.

"You know, if Anthony's gonna be here for the rest of the day, I want to take you home with me. Like soon." He smiled at her. "Call the hotel. Cancel your reservation. I'm gonna go talk to Anthony right now."

A few minutes later, he returned. "Let's go, sweet thing. I have the night off." He grabbed her hand and they headed for the door. "Thanks, Anthony. I owe you one." As Tano pushed the door open to leave, a squatty, chunky woman pushed her way into the doorway, dressed in a leopard print shirt, leopard print shoes, carrying an oversized leopard print purse, red hair in a curled matted mass. Donna.

"Oh, hi, Tano! Glad to catch you! You leaving?" Donna's eyes narrowed into slits, and her cheeks grew red when she saw Holly standing behind him. "Why is she here?" she sneered and turned to Holly. "I thought you went home. To Hicktown."

"It's none of your concern. See ya," Tano harshly said, and shoved the door open all the way, grabbed Holly's hand and pulled her along with him.

"But, Tano, you and I..." Whatever she said to him went unheard.

"She showed up here last Friday right after I talked to you. There's something wrong with that chick. It's beginning to be serious. One more episode from her and I go to the police." Holly was silent. The warm and fuzzy mood that preceded Donna's entrance was gone. She agreed with him. There was nothing more to be said about her.

They walked quickly to the parking garage across Pearl Street. Tano had driven his steel gray Porsche Cayenne, leaving the van at home since he wasn't on Badge business. When they got in, he kissed her again and again. "My house is close. Let's go."

He drove a few miles up Boulder Canyon and turned right on a short dirt road which was the entrance to his property. Holly nearly gasped when she saw the beautiful sprawling log home with the gleaming copper metal roof. "Tano? Is this your house? It's so beautiful."

"Yep, but I'll give you a tour later. First, let me show you the bedroom." They smiled at each other. He entered the garage with the opener, stepped through a door between the house and garage pulling Holly along. They walked quickly through the living room while Holly tried to take in as much of the ambience as she could. The wooden stairs to the master bedroom loft began in the center of the room. Tano was taking the stairs quickly, pulling Holly by the hand behind him. In the middle of the master bedroom with a vaulted ceiling was a four-poster bed with massive log pillars. The puffy comforter of maroon and forest green was thrown back, revealing stark white sheets. Four or five pillows rested against the pine headboard. Holly saw nothing else after Tano picked her up and laid her on the bed. She kicked off her boots. He unbuttoned her denim shirt, stripped it off her, and threw it aside. While he leaned over her, she unbuttoned his jeans and he unbuttoned hers. Within seconds, all their clothes were scattered around the bed on the floor. There was no time to arrange pillows or the comforter. They fell into each other so easily with an urgent and intense passion like never before. Tano's actions said more to Holly than he could ever put into words.

CHAPTER 29

When they rolled apart, Holly laid on her back. Tano laid next to her, on his side, with his arm across her stomach, and his face nuzzled against her neck. His moustache tickled and she felt his warm breath on her skin. A ceiling fan nestled in the vault of the ceiling whirred almost imperceptibly, circulating air that cooled their warm damp skin. Her eyes scanned the bedroom. Leaded glass French doors led to a small deck overlooking a grove of pine trees and illuminated the room with afternoon light. A small stained-glass window with a red, blue, green and purple design in the shape of a badge hung over the French doors showering a rainbow of light across the headboard of the bed.

Tano's breathing deepened and signaled to Holly that he was dozing, allowing her to quietly take it all into her memory. The time she had spent with him was no more than a tiny fragment of his young life which was already full of experience. *I would be foolish to overestimate my significance to him. My time with him could be measured in minutes. Earth shaking, unforgettable minutes to be sure. But could they ever compare to the sum of all his previous days? Would there be more? Could I fill his days? Would he fill mine? Yes.*

He stirred for a moment, kissed her neck lightly and pulled her closer to him. "Be my girl," he whispered in her ear.

At first, Holly thought she misunderstood the unexpected words. She turned. Their faces were nearly touching, and she whispered, "I am." Their lips touched with a kiss that sealed a bond that those simple words had created. They laid in silence with their bodies intertwined, still being cooled by the fan, with his hand lightly stroking the soft skin on her back.

The intimate silence ended abruptly when shots rang out. Pop! Pop! Pop! Pop! Pop! Pop! Glass shattered and the thud of bullets bounced off the log siding of the house.

"What the hell? Stay here!" Tano leaped out of bed and looked out of the balcony doors. He slid his black boxers on and ran downstairs, but suddenly stopped at the bottom of the stairs when he realized he could be in the line of fire and glass was scattered across the wood floor. "God damn it!" he hollered. "This again? God damn Donna! I know it's her!"

The shooting seemed to stop. Tano hunched down as he walked to the window to look for any sign of a shooter, carefully stepping over and around glass on the floor. He saw nothing and no one. Traffic was moving in both directions on the road unhindered at its usual speed. He waited and he watched for a minute or two. Seeing nothing suspicious, he ran upstairs, grabbed his phone, called the sheriff's department. Holly was still lying in bed, frozen, afraid to move.

"Tano, tell me! What's going on? What happened? Are you okay?"

"I know it was that fucking Donna! It was her! God damn it! She's nearby anytime there are shots fired! The downstairs is a mess. Glass everywhere! She got the leaded glass front door, too." He rubbed his hands across his face and through his hair.

Tano threw his clothes on. Holly sat up, grabbed her clothes from the floor and hurriedly got dressed. "Put your boots on."

Within a matter of minutes, the sound of multiple sirens echoed in the canyon as a string of sheriff's department vehicles approached Tano's house. Not knowing if the shooter was still active, the deputies emerged from their vehicles, service revolvers drawn, wearing bulletproof vests as they visually scanned the surrounding property. A police helicopter hovered over the house.

"What can you tell me about what happened here? Did you see

a shooter?" asked Sergeant Edison while the rest of them combed the area.

"I don't know. We were upstairs when we heard shots and glass shattering. The front of the house was targeted so she must have been down on the road directly in line with the house."

"You said, she. Do you know who the perpetrator is?"

"Well, I suspect it was a woman who has been stalking me. This isn't the first time there have been shots fired near me. Or maybe at me in the past few days." Tano proceeded to tell the deputy about the shooting in Amarillo, the shots fired in Sage, and Donna's suspicious appearances and behavior.

"I just saw her less than an hour ago at my bar, Tumbleweed, downtown. She was a bartender there a couple of years ago. I had to fire her. She's psycho, man. I'm guessing that when you find the bullets, they will be from a Winchester .300 Mag. The same bullets found in Sage."

"Tumbleweed, huh? Been there a few times. My wife loves tequila."

"Sergeant?" One of the deputies approached. "We haven't seen any sign of an active shooter nearby. But we found this by the side of the road." The deputy was holding a long nylon leopard print scarf.

"Christ. Donna was wearing a full get up of leopard print stuff when I saw her today!"

"I think we need to get her in and have her answer some questions. You said she worked at your business a while back. Do you have any identifying info about her?"

"I'll call my partner and have him look up her personnel file. She may be going by Donna Brown or Donna Smith. Lately, I heard she was using my name—Montano. Donna Montano." Tano stepped away and called Anthony. He was able to provide a birthdate and an old photo.

Tano showed the photo to Sergeant Edison. "This photo is a couple of years old, but she still looks like that. A mess."

Other deputies photographed the exterior of the house and

then went inside for interior photos. Sergeant Edison and Tano followed them inside. Holly stood by the door when they entered. Sergeant Edison approached her.

"Hello, I'm Sergeant Mac Edison. Can you provide me with any information about the bullet barrage? Your name?"

"I'm Holly Harris. I'm afraid that I don't know much of anything. We were just upstairs and heard the shots. "

"Mr. Montano here tells me that there have been some other recent incidents." Holly recapped almost verbatim what Tano had told them.

"Sergeant Edison? We have retrieved these bullets. Winchester .300 Mag." A deputy held up a plastic bag containing the bullets.

"I just knew it," Tano blurted. "The same bullets that were found in Sage." He turned to Holly. "And get this, Holly: They found a leopard print scarf out by the road in front of the house."

Holly's eyes widened as she gasped, "Donna!"

Sergeant Edison took a close look at the bag of bullets. "I guess I'll be contacting the sheriff down in Oklahoma to get the lowdown on their investigation."

Tano took Holly's arm and pulled her away from the deputies. "We can't stay here tonight. This place is a mess. And I don't know if that psycho is coming back or what. I'm going to get us a hotel room for a couple of nights."

He dialed a number that was preset in his phone and Holly overheard him speaking to someone. "Hey, Kelly. It's Tano. Ben Montano. Yeah, it's been a while. You been good? That's great. Hey, I need to get a hotel room for tonight and tomorrow night. Any chance that the hotel has an available room? No, it's two adults. Sure, I'll hold on." In a moment Holly heard him say, "No kidding! Awesome! My luck that they canceled. Hey, we won't be able to check in for a couple of hours. Maybe around seven or eight? Is that going to be a problem? Great. See you tonight."

"We are staying in Denver tonight. It made sense since I need to be there anyway tomorrow for the preconcert stuff that Badge does. That good with you?"

"Of course." Holly was just happy to spend the night with him again.

"I'm going to call the insurance agent, and I need to get somebody here to board up the broken windows until they can be replaced."

While Tano was busy making calls, Holly strolled through the house, looking past the chaos in the living room. The kitchen was separated from the living room by an island of ash cabinets with a black and dark brown granite countertop with copper flecks in it. The kitchen was L-shaped, opening on one end to a breakfast nook containing a small dark pine table with attached benches which resembled a picnic table. A rectangular stained-glass light fixture with inlaid blue columbines hung over the table. The centerpiece of the kitchen, however, was a Viking commercial stainless-steel gas range and double oven. The ventilation hood was copper to match the custom knobs on the stove and the copper flecks in the granite countertop. A powder room was in a short hallway past the breakfast nook. The cabinets were dark pine with a white marble countertop and white fixtures. A couple of sets of spurs and a Stetson cowboy hat hung on the wall as accents.

Holly wandered down a short hall where they had hurriedly come into the house from the garage just a short time before. When she opened the interior garage door, she saw what she had not noticed before. Parked in stalls next to the Porsche Cayenne were a classic dark blue Corvette and a yellow Ford Deuce Coupe.

"There you are. I thought maybe you were lost."

"I was just giving myself a tour and found myself out here. I didn't notice these classics before."

"Yep, the yellow coupe is a '32 Ford. A deuce coupe. I couldn't resist buying it when I saw it. See these are called 'suicide doors' because of the way they open. The door hinge is on the opposite side. It has a 327 engine with a Weiand tunnel ram manifold and a 780 dual pump carburetor. Does that mean anything to you? I can't say enough about this little beauty. Love the three windows."

"Well, yes, from what you just told me, it's hot little hotrod. The white tuck-and-roll interior is very classy. The shifter reminds me of the Badge shifter you gave me. I learned some from my brothers about classic cars and what it takes for high performance. What about the blue Corvette?"

"Well, that's a 1968 Corvette with a 327 engine, four-speed transmission, too. Come here and look at it. I prefer the Corvette body styles of the 1960s. My dad had a 1968 Corvette, and he sold it years ago and he always talked about that car, so I bought this one for him to drive once in a while. For old times' sake. He has only driven it once though. I think he's afraid of its power. But I take it out and drive it through the canyon when I get a chance. Who wouldn't want a Corvette?"

"The blue interior and bucket seats are so pretty."

"Want to take it to Denver tonight?"

"Sure! Let's do. But my rental car and my bag are down on Pearl Street in the parking garage. Do you want me to follow you to Denver? Or should I leave the car for now? I need my bag though."

"Let's turn the rental car in here in Boulder. Then that's out of the way. When do you return to Kansas?"

"Friday, I fly out in the afternoon."

"I fly to Jackson Hole on Friday afternoon, too. Badge plays there on Saturday night. We can hang out together there until we leave." He put his arm around her and pulled her close while his thoughts turned to the prospect of her leaving. *I hate to see her go again.*

"Mr. Montano? I found you." The insurance agent quietly stepped into the garage. "Okay, I'm pretty much done here. I guess you arranged for the windows to be boarded up this afternoon. And then when you can, call me and we can get a restoration company in here to clean up the mess. I'm glad that you're okay."

"Thanks. I'll contact a glass company soon."

Tano and Holly walked back into the house. Some of the sheriff vehicles had left and the police helicopter had returned to the airport. Sergeant Edison was still there. "Okay, Mr. Montano. We might come back to have a look around the scene. I've alerted law enforcement in this area to be on the lookout for Donna Smith or

Brown or Montano so that we may question her. We have circulated a photo of her. Please call me at this number if she makes any kind of contact with you." He handed Tano his business card. "You both are lucky you weren't in this room when those shots were fired. Those are some mighty bullets."

Holly followed Tano upstairs while he packed for the nights in Denver and the Jackson Hole concert. It was surreal that there was so much destruction downstairs and yet the bedroom one floor above was untouched, serene and peaceful. The imprints that their bodies made on the bedding a few hours before were still visible. He grabbed Holly around the waist and gently tossed her on the bed. She laughed and he laid down next to her. They were still and quiet, reflecting on the events that had transpired, until he whispered in her ear, "How do you feel about moving to Boulder? To be with me."

CHAPTER 30

Holly was stunned and inhaled deeply. Just hours before she believed that it was over between them. That all hope was gone. That she would have to convince Tano to give her another chance. Did he mean what he said? She turned and looked into his golden eyes and quietly asked, "Hey, are you serious about that?"

"I wouldn't have asked you if I didn't mean it. I wouldn't play with you like that. I don't want to have to search for you again." Tano watched her face as she pondered his question. Her eyes scanned the ceiling and she clasped her hands together and rested them under her chin.

Holly's heart had leaped into her throat. There was so much to be considered but she would make it work. She smiled at him and said, "Yes. I could move to Boulder."

"Could or will?"

"I'll move to Boulder and be with you." Tano pulled her close and hugged her tight. She had given him the answer he wanted to hear. He didn't want to risk losing her again. He wanted to share his life with her. He couldn't promise forever. The journey to forever is full of uncertainties. But he knew at that moment that he had found a girl unlike any other who made him happy just by stepping into the room or walking by his side. Honest and unpretentious. Pretty and fun. Smart and loving.

There were a million things to think about, to take care of, to arrange, to organize, to move. Holly couldn't tarnish the special moment with practical thoughts. She wanted to believe that it would be easy to relocate to Boulder, to find a job, a place to live, to be in a relationship with Tano who traveled much of the time. She would make it work. He meant everything to her and if he let her, she would show him.

"After the Jackson Hole concert, Badge will be in California and out west for another week. Can you pull it together and be here when I get back? Please?"

"I'll try. There will be a lot to do. Workwise and with my house and..." Holly stopped short of finishing the long list in her thoughts.

They were still lying face to face on the bed. She reached up and touched one of the dimples on his cheek with her finger. "I know. It will come together. It doesn't have to be done all at once. What matters is that you will be here." Tano kissed her deeply and held her tight. Knowing that if they laid there another minute, they wouldn't leave, he rolled on his back and said, "I guess we better head to Denver to the hotel. So grab your purse and let's get your stuff downtown and return the rental car."

The romantic bubble that had surrounded them in the master bedroom vanished at the sight of the destruction strewn across the living room when they went downstairs. Russell, a husky, tan carpenter friend of Tano's, arrived to board up the windows and the holes in the front of the house.

"Hey, Russ. Good to see you. I don't think you need to go in the house to cover the holes and broken windows. So I'm going to lock it up—well, I'll do the best I can."

"Man, somebody had it out for you. You take care there, buddy. And you, too." Russ nodded at Holly.

"Thanks. We'll be fine. Headed to Denver."

It was almost seven when they hit multi-lane US-36 in the Corvette on the way to Denver. The drive seemed to be much shorter and quicker than usual as they zipped in and out of the traffic with the iconic precision of a 'Vette. Tano chose Beach Boys music for the trip and said, "The Beach Boys always make me think of summer. And it's summer and here we are on the road." Holly looked at him while he drove. She loved the way his dark hair curled in back and rested on the collar of his shirt. She reached up and touched his hair.

But Holly's mind was still spinning with thoughts about the move to Boulder. She continued to keep them to herself and started to make a mental list. Suddenly, an unrelated thought struck her that had probably been spinning in the recesses of her mind since the leopard print scarf was found by the road.

"You know Anthony sent you a picture of Donna that you gave the police, right? Well, Garth told me that he encountered a dumpy woman driving on the road east of the house right after the shots were fired at us from that direction. He didn't really describe her. I wonder if it was Donna. Could you send me that photo of her and then I'll send it to Garth to see if it was her?"

"Yeah, remind me when we get to the hotel. Good thinking. Even though I feel sure it was that dumb chick who did this, it would be good for the sheriff to know that somebody saw her there in Sage right after the gunshots."

When they drove into downtown Denver, Tano turned into the Brown Palace Hotel drive.

"Are we staying here?" Holly was pleased and hopeful.

The classic, elegant Brown Palace, built in 1892, rested on the corner of 17th Street and Tremont, and was in the shape of a perfect triangle, inspired by the Italian Renaissance with an exterior constructed of red Colorado granite and Arizona sandstone.

"Yes, we are staying here tonight and tomorrow night. What do you think? That okay?"

"Yes, I'm excited! I ate lunch here at the Ship Tavern once. A burger, I think. Some friends and I from UCCS came to Denver one weekend and stopped here for lunch before we hit the clubs. It's so elegant. That atrium lobby—it goes up forever. I want to see more."

Valets opened each door of the Corvette for both Tano and Holly.

"Go easy with it," Tano said as he handed the keys to the valet. They opened the trunk and pulled out their bags.

They entered the lobby and just as Holly remembered, the atrium extended eight or nine floors up capped by a stained-glass ceiling. Each floor wrapped around and opened into the atrium with ornate wrought-iron rails outlining each long circular corridor and each staircase extending to the floor above. Holly continued to gaze at the ceiling while Tano checked in.

"Ben Montano checking in." The cute young clerk blushed when she looked up at him.

"Kelly? Mr. Montano has arrived," the clerk said to someone in an adjoining office. Kelly emerged from the concierge office. She was tall and brunette, around thirty years old, with big round brown eyes which crinkled when she smiled at Tano. She was dressed in a navy-blue suit wearing two strands of pearls and diamond stud earrings.

"Hey, Tano. It's been a while. How have you been?" Kelly leaned over the counter exposing her cleavage which spilled from the white shell she wore. She reached for his hand and touched it with her fingers.

Tano appeared to be oblivious to her flirtation, even though Kelly was completely transparent. There was apparently some kind of past that they shared which she was clearly hoping to remind him of. Tano pulled his hand away and reached for his wallet to give the clerk his driver's license and credit card for confirmation. He was actually well aware of her forward demeaner but continued to ignore it.

"So, Tano, I reserved that special room for you. Suite 840. Can I do anything else for you tonight?" Kelly continued to stare intensely at Tano.

"I'm good. Thanks. Come on, Holly." He took the room pass keys from the counter, put them in the back pocket of his jeans, picked up his bag, and grabbed Holly's hand and walked toward the elevator. Kelly's eyes narrowed as she watched them walk away. *That man has got the nicest ass.*

Holly was unphased by the obvious flirtation—this time. Handling the attention to Tano from other women would be something she would have to accept. In truth she knew that there was nothing she could do to prevent it. *Look at him. He's gorgeous.* It would be up to Tano not to act on it. She had to trust him and believe that he chose her with his heart, among all the women he knew, to be his girl.

The elevator stopped at the eighth floor. Holly looked down at the lobby and took a photo with her phone. They walked down the hallway to Suite 840. Holly gasped and put her hand to her mouth. "It's the Beatles' Suite! Oh, my God, I didn't know that such a room existed! This is awesome!" she gushed as they entered, still taking photos with her phone.

"Yeah, the Beatles stayed here in 1964 when they came to Denver. I thought you might like to stay here with me. It seemed like a good room for us." He was pleased by her excitement.

"It's amazing. Look at the posters on the wall—from the *Sgt. Pepper* and *Abbey Road* album covers! And more—live shots, too. So cool! Thank you for picking such a special place."

"Well, it just happened to be the suite that was available. Nothing but the best for my girl." He picked her up and laid her on the bed covered with a gold brocade comforter, and then laid next to her. She held her phone up and they looked at the photos that she had just taken.

"Let me get a shot of you by that poster over there," Holly said, pointing at the framed poster of the *Abbey Road* album cover. Tano slid off the bed and obliged. "And over there," she added, pointing to the window which framed the nearby skyline of Denver. She continued to take photos of the room. "Oh, that reminds me. I wanted to send that photo that you have of Donna to Garth. Can you send it to me?"

He pulled his phone out of his pocket and forwarded the photo of Donna to her. "Wow, that isn't a very flattering picture of her," Holly said as she sent the photo to Garth with a text message.

Hey, is this the woman you saw in the tan Buick on the road east of Mom and Dad's after those shots were fired?

"There could never be a flattering photo of her," he quipped. "There's a fine restaurant downstairs. The Palace Arms. Do you want to get some dinner?"

"That sounds great. Do we have to dressed up?"

"Not really. You can change if you want. I'm not."

"Well, I have a white silky shirt. I think I'll change into that." Holly grabbed her bag and pulled out the white shirt. She held it up and looked at it. It was slightly wrinkled. She went to the closet and took the hotel iron from the top shelf.

"You don't need to iron that. It looks great. No one will be looking at your shirt after they see your pretty face."

"Well maybe." She put the iron back on the closet shelf. She unbuttoned her denim shirt and slid it off, exposing a little white lacy bra and slipped the white silk shirt on over her head and tucked it into her tight jeans. Tano watched her as he waited on a red tapestry side chair. She brushed her long red hair, touched up her mascara, blush and lipstick.

"Beautiful," Tano said when she emerged. "Let's go." He lightly touched her hair with his hand and kissed her forehead.

As they walked to the elevator, Holly pulled her phone out of the back pocket of her jeans. "I just got a text from Garth. He says that it's her! It was Donna! She's the one he saw driving on the road east of our house where we think the shots came from! Tano, I think those shots were intended for me! I think she really tried to shoot me!"

CHAPTER 31

When they stepped out of the elevator, Holly followed Tano to a gold brocade upholstered loveseat in the lobby where they sat down. Tano took his phone out of his pocket. "I'm calling the sheriff. I don't want this to be hanging over us at dinner."

While he made the phone call, Holly stood and wandered through the lobby to check out the paintings on the onyx-covered walls and displays in the lighted glass cabinets built into wall alcoves. While he had been speaking to the sheriff's office, he had received a text from Anthony at Tumbleweed asking him to call him. Holly was still perusing the lobby when he called Anthony.

"Hey, Anthony. I'm glad you texted. I wanted to let you know that this afternoon my house was shot up. Holly and I were there—upstairs. But we think that crazy, sick bitch Donna did it. There was some evidence. A leopard print scarf on the road in front of the house like that getup she was wearing. So I want you to be on the lookout for her. You know she walked into the bar just as we were leaving. You saw her, didn't you? What did she do when we left?"

"Yeah, well, she stormed out right after you left," Anthony told Tano. "But I wanted to tell you that she came back again! About an hour later. Looking for you. And I said that you wouldn't be back tonight and that you were with your lady. She started screaming at me. 'That skinny red-headed slut! She needs to back off! She still doesn't get the message! He's mine, goddam it! He's mine!' Then she picked up one of the bottles on the bar and hurled it against the mirror back there and it shattered everywhere. I'm cleaning up the mess now, but Tano, she's nuts, man! You should have seen her—wearing purple yoga pants and a neon pink halter top! Geez, she looked like a potato stuffed into a spandex tortilla."

"Did you call the cops?"

"Yeah, they just left and said something about an APB for her in the works already. I guess that must be from the shots fired at your house, huh?"

"Yeah, they'll probably coordinate with the Boulder County Sheriff on that. Listen, I gotta go. I don't want Holly to know about this new deal at the bar. I don't want Donna to ruin our night. We are at the Brown Palace. I gotta go."

"Okay, but look out for yourselves."

Tano made a decision not to tell Holly about what happened at the bar, and although she noticed that he was on the phone longer than she expected, she didn't ask him what took him so long. He approached her standing near a display of historic artifacts, took her hand and they walked down a long hall to the Palace Arms restaurant.

"They said they circulated that photo to local police to be on the lookout for her and to bring her in for questioning. I don't know where she lives or the kind of car she drives. That photo is the only help that I can provide. Now that's done. Let's see if they have a table for us in the Palace Arms."

"A table for two, Mr. Montano?'

"Yes. Is there a wait?"

"No. Kelly told me that you might be joining us for dinner tonight. We have a table reserved for you."

"Nice, thanks." He looked at Holly and raised his eyebrows.

"Hmm, that Kelly is sure looking out for you." Holly gave him a sideways glance.

Tano winked at her. The hostess seated them at a booth in an intimate corner of the restaurant and handed them a wine list and menus. The seats were covered with red upholstery. The tables were elegantly set with white china on a white tablecloth. Holly read a short history of the restaurant which was printed on the menu when it was handed to her. The unique classic ambience of the Palace Arms had been enhanced by a collection of museum quality military prints and antique artifacts on the walls covered with silver and gold wallpaper and trimmed with a rich dark wainscoting made of terracotta.

"Look, this says that one of the artifacts here is a set of dueling pistols that belonged to Napoleon. I see them. There they are," Holly said as she pointed to them. She turned to view the entire room.

"I've been here before but never really paid attention to all that stuff. I mean, I know it's there but you're so observant. I just learned something new from you, sweet thing. So, do you want to start with wine tonight?'

"Oh, yes. This is a place where you drink wine. You pick one."

Tano smiled to himself, amused by her apparent excitement. When the waiter returned, he ordered a bottle of 2012 Drouhin-Laroze Grand Cru, a pinot noir from Burgundy, France. He returned, poured a little into the wine goblet for Tano to taste.

Tano swirled the wine in the goblet, held it to his nose, sniffed the fragrance and said, "Perfect. Thank you." The waiter poured glasses for them both. Holly took little sips of it, wanting the bottle to last through dinner.

"Well, what looks good?" Tano asked.

"I think I'll order the arugula and pear salad for the first course. And probably the *coq au vin*. And what do you think?"

"Lobster bisque and beef Wellington."

The waiter brought a basket of bread with butter. While they waited for the first course, Tano raised his wine glass and said, "Here's to my beautiful lady." Holly smiled at his handsome face with those dimples and sexy moustache and gently touched her glass to his and took a sip of wine.

Donna was wild with fury. Earlier she dressed up in her best co-ordinated leopard print outfit and had gone to Tumbleweed to talk to Tano about their future together and to ask him to stop playing games with her to make her jealous. She thought that she would surprise him with a grand entrance and instead found him rushing out the door with that "skinny redheaded slut."

"She is a stalker! He dumped her in Oklahoma and then she shows up here! This is my turf, bitch! Go away or I'll do ya in!" she screamed to the empty room as she recalled the earlier encounter. She noticed her reflection wearing the spandex outfit in a mirror on her living room wall in her apartment. She had gone back to Tumbleweed a second time to see Tano and he wasn't there again. This time she could no longer control her temper. She had grabbed a tequila bottle and threw it at Anthony but hit the mirror behind the bar instead.

"I wish you coulda seen me, Tano! I look good! Look at me! Look at me!" she continued to shout as she waved her arms, her eyes bulging with anger.

Suddenly she caught a glimpse of her face on the TV across the room as it reflected in the mirror. She whirled around to see a photo of her face accompanying a news story asking the public to call the police if she was seen. The anchor went on to say, "Due to evidence found at the scene, this woman is wanted for questioning involving a drive-by shooting this afternoon in Boulder Canyon. No one was injured. Law enforcement in Oklahoma wants to talk to her as well. She goes by Donna Brown, Donna Smith or Donna Montano. She is believed to be in the Boulder area."

Donna's heart began to beat violently, and she could feel it in her throat and in her temples. *That picture isn't even a good one of me!* she thought as she stared at her likeness. *I gotta get outta here! Police are bound to show up looking for me if they find out where I live. I had to do it! I had to! Tano! I had to! You can't keep this up! Avoiding me!*

She hurried to her bedroom, grabbed a hot-pink-and-purple print soft-sided suitcase from under her bed and began to throw some clothes in it. The leopard print clothing was still laying on the bed when she noticed that the leopard print scarf was missing from the pile. *Maybe it's in the car.* She threw them in the suitcase along with a random assortment of clothes. Then she got a text from her sister, Cathy.

Donna, WTF? Why is your photo on the news? What did you do? Call me now! Before Mom and Dad see it!

Donna rolled her eyes and ignored the text and stuffed her phone in the waistband of her spandex yoga pants. She grabbed a little pile of cash from her kitchen cabinet, the Badge concert ticket, her extra-large jeweled black purse, and the suitcase. She saw a big, floppy hot-pink hat hanging on a peg near the back door, snatched it and put it on her head.

I gotta go someplace.

She started her beige RAV4 and headed up the street without any real direction.

I gotta get out of Boulder.

She made a right turn on 30th Street, headed for the Baseline Road exit onto eastbound US-36.

I gotta keep moving. Denver—that's where I'll go. Need to be there anyway for the Badge concert tomorrow night!

In just a few short minutes, her mood had shifted from crazed anger to alarm and then to happy anticipation at seeing Tano in concert. She inserted a Badge CD into the CD player and began to sing along as if she didn't have a care in the world.

CHAPTER 32

Both wanted to talk about the events of the day, which began with Holly timidly entering the Tumbleweed Bar not knowing if Tano was there and what he would say if he was. And then his affectionate, warm welcome and then the love making at his house and his asking her to move to Boulder and her answer of "yes." And then the shots at the house. They sat at their table in the Palace Arms and sipped wine in odd awkward silence while the previous moments of the day tumbled through their minds until Tano finally made conversation.

"Hey, I don't think I mentioned to you before, but I'm probably going to build a rehearsal studio at the house sometime soon, and Rob is looking at getting Badge a tour bus. We've been performing all over the west, the roadies are driving separately, and the band is sometimes split up or we fly. It'll be easier to ride together and party if we want to, or sleep or whatever. And I've always wanted to build a rehearsal studio back behind the house."

"That's a lot to look forward to. A studio in the canyon. How cool will that be! Can't wait to see it built. And the bus makes so much sense. It will be easier for all of you."

"Damn, that reminds me. I should text Rob. Just tell him about Donna. You know she could show up tomorrow night—or anytime for that matter." He hesitated for a moment as he said her name because it created a negative vibe, but it was too late. "Remind me to do that later."

While they waited for the meals to be brought to their table and sipped the wine, Holly began to feel a little buzz from it. That little buzz diverted her practical thoughts to the stark realization that

Tano wanted to be with her. That he asked her to come to Boulder. That she was in love with him. Alcohol always narrowed her often fleeting thoughts to the present and she was glowing in the flickering candlelight. Tano saw it. He reached across the table to hold her hand. There was a long, silent gaze between them when their eyes locked on the other. Holly felt a surge of adrenalin as it rushed through her veins from the top of her head to her toes. *This is really happening. This is really happening to us.*

Now the silence between them was anything but uncomfortable and awkward. Tano could feel an electricity as he held her hand. *After I pushed her away, she came back. I messed up but she came back.* Of all the women he had known or used or left with a broken heart, there were none like Holly, whose presence consumed him with an intensity that he had never felt before. He was in love. Maybe it had happened when she took that fortuitous ride with him in his Chevy van five years ago. After all, he had held on so tightly to those memories of her.

The server brought the first courses and interrupted the romantic trance that they shared for a few moments. He poured the rest of the bottle of wine into their goblets. "More wine, sir?"

"Yes, another of the same." He took a spoonful of the bisque. "Here—you should taste this. Do you like lobster?' Holly picked up a spoon and dipped it into the soup.

"That's really good. I do like lobster but as you can guess, an Oklahoma girl eats beef, pork and lamb every day. Want some salad? This is probably more than I should eat before the *coq au vin* comes."

"No, I'm good. Eat what you can. So..." Tano paused while he took a bite of bread. "I have an idea for something special after dinner."

Holly looked up and smiled at him. "Is it a surprise?"

"Yeah, it will be. I just thought of it. I need to text somebody really quick. Sorry." Tano took his phone out and sent a text to someone. The server brought the main courses and removed the first course china plates.

"I'm curious now." She tilted her head and smiled at Tano. She took a bite of the *coq au vin* braised in Burgundy wine. "This is perfect. How is yours?"

"Beef Wellington—it's the bomb." Tano paused while he took a bite of mushrooms and then looked up at Holly. Her face was radiant in the candlelight. "So, sweet thing, tonight we are going to celebrate. Tonight is about you and me. What is and what will be."

They talked about the upcoming Fiddler's Green concert and the schedule for the next day. Holly took small bites but still couldn't finish all of her meal.

The server removed their plates. "Dessert for you tonight?"

Tano looked at Holly who shook her head. "No, none tonight. Thank you." He filled Holly's wine glass, looked at the time on his phone, and then leaned back in his chair. "So, we have a special event arriving in about ten minutes."

"Arriving? Interesting. I'm intrigued." Holly took a few more sips of wine. "I need to visit the restroom before we go."

When Holly left the booth, Tano made a phone call. "Hey, Kelly, one more favor. I don't have the number for the spa. Could you call them and make a reservation for me for a couple's massage tomorrow morning? Just text me the time when you get it. Yes, with her. And hey, thanks for the other favor. And making it happen at the last minute. Yeah, I guess I owe ya. I'll think of a way." *Not the way you think.*

Holly returned to the table and finished the glass of wine. "Ready, sweet thing?"

"Yep. I want to see the surprise." She held on to his arm as she walked next to him. As they exited the restaurant, some people turned to look at him. At them. Possibly recognizing him and smiling at the good-looking couple.

As they entered the hotel foyer, Holly could see a white carriage parked in front of the hotel doors being drawn by a majestic chestnut Clydesdale. His white mane and the white feather above his hooves were perfectly groomed and gleaming. She turned to look at Tano who grinned at her revealing his deep dimples.

"Is this the surprise? Is it? It's so elegant. Is it just for us?" The sun was setting and the bright blue sky was gradually darkening into streaks of pink and purple, but the carriage was outfitted with small white lights. The driver helped Holly into the carriage and Tano climbed in next to her and put his arm around her and pulled her close. The seat was upholstered in luxurious purple velvet and the white carriage was outlined with a gold pinstripe.

"Yep, it is. I pulled a few strings to make it happen so quickly. But here we are."

"I feel like Cinderella. It's so beautiful tonight."

When the carriage pulled away, a young girl standing on the sidewalk jumped up and down and hollered "Tano! Over here!" Tano waved at her. She turned, giggling to her friends. "It was him! I told you!"

The fancy carriage slowly made its way through the streets of downtown Denver—to Lo-Do, Union Station, Larimer Square, the Capitol building, the 16th Street Mall, the Denver Art Museum, the U.S. Mint and more landmarks. Despite being amid hordes of people and cars on this warm summer night, Holly felt like they were alone in the world, just the two of them riding in the carriage with the steady, clop, clop, clop of the horses's hooves to accompany them. Tano held her close. He could smell the fragrance in her hair as a light breeze lifted the copper strands. With his strong arms around her, Holly never felt safer. She was at peace. The churning inside that she felt for five years apart from him was gone.

The grand carriage returned the couple to the Brown Palace after a couple of hours. Tano hopped out, put his hands on Holly's waist and lifted her down. When she stood in front of him, he kissed her. "Thank you, Tano, for thinking of such an elegant surprise," Holly said as her cheek brushed his mustache.

"Well, the night is young. Let's check out that 70s disco bar up the block. What do you think?"

"That sounds like fun. That disco music is great workout music, too."

Tano took her hand as they sprinted to the bar. When they

opened the door, they were bathed in pink, blue and purple neon light from the ceiling and surrounding the bar. The dance floor was a series of transparent tiles, lit up from beneath in a checkerboard of orange, yellow and white illuminating couples on the dance floor. There were three sparkling, crystal, rotating disco balls—one over the bar, one over the dance floor, and one over the high-top metal tables. A DJ stood in the corner of the room spinning disco tunes from a table that stood on legs made of black lights. "September" by Earth, Wind & Fire, was spinning on the DJ turntable.

"Let's find a table. It's packed in here. Wait—there's two at the bar." The neon lighting surrounding the bar reflected on their faces, giving their skin a glowing lavender color. Holly's long copper hair looked like it was blue. Tano's smile gleamed in the light.

"What will it be?" asked the bartender, dressed in tight white flared pants and tight silky red shirt, reminiscent of the disco years.

"Holly? What do you think? Beers?"

"Yeah, that's good," she said, knowing she wouldn't drink too much since she had wine earlier.

"A couple of tall drafts. Got Sam Adams?"

"Yep, sure thing."

They turned on their metal bar stools to watch groups of dancers doing the hustle and the bump.

"Hey, you're a dancer. Show them your stuff. Come on, Holly. Let's dance."

Holly laughed. "Those aren't the dance moves I learned in college."

"Yeah, but you know how to move. Get your groove on, girl," he teased. They took a few sips of the beers that were set down in front of them. Holly grabbed his hand, pulled him off the bar stool and onto the dance floor just as the DJ began a Saturday Night Fever medley, beginning with "Night Fever."

The classic disco music filled the bar with rhythm and motion. A strobe light flickered over the dance floor. The longer they stayed on the dance floor, the more intense Holly's dancing became. Tano loved watching her as he swayed to the music, moving her torso, her arms overhead, her feet in step with the beat. She was an awesome beauty moving perfectly with the rhythm of the song. Holly looked at his handsome face in the flickering light as he danced in front of her. She was so proud to be his girl.

When the DJ played "How Deep Is Your Love," the strobe lights stopped and the colored lights in the dance floor began to pulse with the beat of the music. Tano took Holly's hand and did his best to remember and mimic the moves of John Travolta from the movie. Their dance was surprisingly smooth as he twirled her around and then leaned her back. When the song was over, he pulled her close and kissed her deeply. A couple near them clapped. Tano and Holly laughed and returned to their seats at the bar which were still empty.

"What a blast!" Holly said as she sipped her beer.

"Glad you're having a good time, sweetheart." He loved to see her so happy. He always wanted to see her that way, and he vowed at that moment to do just that.

While Tano and Holly were fine dining, touring Denver in a white carriage, and disco dancing, Donna was pacing. And pacing. Talking to herself. Making plans. She had found a rundown motel room in south Denver, a few miles from the Fiddler's Green. She felt safe from the law for the time being.

"I gotta get him away from her. I want him so bad. And I know he wants me!"

She was desperate. She wrung her hands. She threw pillows from the bed. She kicked the orange upholstered vinyl chair in the corner of the room. She was fully aware that the police were looking for her. It would limit her plans and her movement and created the need to be invisible. She looked at herself in the bathroom mirror.

"Why can't he see? Look at me! I'm perfect for you, Tano! Our two bodies belong together!" she hoarsely shouted, and then stopped for a moment to visualize their bodies as one. She licked her lips and squealed. Her phone chimed with a text message.

She continued to ignore multiple texts and phone calls from Cathy, who was frantic to find her and talk to her. Cathy was afraid that Donna's mind had crossed a threshold into insanity. She had ignored her recent extreme behavior, believing she was just being dramatic, looking for attention, but that she would never go that far. Their parents apparently had not seen the news carrying Donna's photo. They usually went to bed at seven. She would have heard from them by now if they knew.

Donna continued to look at herself in the bright light of the bathroom mirror. *I need to disguise myself so that I can go to the Badge concert. Maybe I can get close to him.* She went to her car and picked up the bright pink floppy hat that she brought with her from the back seat. *Maybe this hat will work. I could tuck my curls up in the hat. But what should I wear?* She began to rummage through her suitcase to look at the random assortment of clothes that she brought with her. *If I'm too stylish, everyone will notice me.* She laid all the clothes out on the bed. *Maybe I'll mix and match.*

At around midnight, Tano said, "Ready to call it a night?"

"Yeah, I think so. What a day this has been! Thank you so much for making tonight so special."

"Anything for you." He kissed her forehead as they walked arm in arm back to the Brown Palace. "Let's hit the sheets," he said when they returned to the Beatles' Room, which they promptly did. "Goodnight, sweet thing. I have a surprise for us in the morning."

Holly laughed. "You always have a morning surprise."

Tano snickered. "Not that. Well, maybe. But that's not what I was talking about."

"Goodnight, Tano." She pressed her body close to his, kissed his cheek, and they fell asleep.

CHAPTER 33

Streaks of pastel light began to fill the early morning sky as Holly woke up. She rolled over onto her back and stretched her long legs and raised her arms over her head. Her eyes surveyed the room, taking in all the framed Beatles posters and drawings on the walls. She could hear Tano's even breathing as he lay asleep on his side with his back to her. She wanted to touch his back but didn't want to wake him. She wanted to assure herself that she wasn't dreaming. In a few moments, her eyelids felt heavy and she drifted into a light sleep.

The morning light woke Donna, too, in her shabby motel room. She had gone to sleep under the comforter strewn with various pieces of clothing that she had laid out in order to choose what to wear to the concert. Some of the clothes had fallen on the floor where they continued to lay. Clothing wasn't on her mind, but hunger was. There was a little diner across the street from the motel. Its neon "Open" sign emitted a dim orange light which permeated the frayed curtains in the room. *I can't think on an empty stomach.* On the floor she found a pair of white leggings and an XXL pink T-shirt with a brown kitten wearing a purple bow on it, threw them on, and walked across the street for breakfast as the sun continued to rise.

"Hello," the heavily made-up woman with a husky voice, probably in her 60s, said as she handed Donna a sticky laminated menu. "My name is Bobbi and I'll be your server. Can I get you coffee? Juice? Tea?"

"Yes, coffee and a large orange juice."

"I'll be back to take your order."

She perused the menu. It was hard to decide between the breakfast specials and the a la carte items. The server, who Donna noticed limped when she walked, returned with the coffee and juice.

"I'll have two eggs over easy, bacon, hash browns, an order of corned beef hash, two of the biscuits with country sausage gravy. And then could I get a cinnamon roll to go?"

"Sure thing. It'll be right up."

Donna needed to sort through her ideas to get close to Tano, even though she was aware that she was on law enforcement radar. She knew that Tano wanted to sing to her at the concert. He surely wanted to introduce her as "The Girl from Yesterday." He wanted her to be there and she had to dress for the part, too. *He must stop playing these cat and mouse games with me. It's time, dear Tano, for you to commit to me like I know you wanted to when you gave me this ring.* She turned the fake engagement ring round and round on the ring finger of her left hand.

The waitress brought two full plates of food and set them down on the table in front of Donna. "Can I get you anything else?"

"No, I'll let you know. Don't forget the cinnamon roll."

"I'm bringing you one fresh from the oven in a few minutes."

"Thanks." Donna dug deep into the corned beef hash with a fork in one hand and held a biscuit dripping with gravy in the other. She alternated bites between each hand, barely pausing to chew. When she finished the biscuits, she picked up the bacon and dipped it into the egg yolks, took a bite, and then shoveled in a fork full of hash browns. She paused in her eager eating to pick up the saltshaker and sprinkled salt lavishly over what remained on her plate which she swirled together in a messy slurry of egg, potatoes, gravy and hash browns.

"Here's your cinnamon roll, ma'am." The waitress brought a white paper bag containing an extra-large iced cinnamon roll. "What else can I get for you?"

"A little more coffee and juice, and how about just a short stack of chocolate chip pancakes—heavy on the whipped cream."

"Yes, ma'am." Although Bobbi, the server, was happy to know that the meal ticket would probably generate a good tip, she was stunned by the amount of food Donna had put away.

While Donna waited for the pancakes, she began to focus on her plan to go to the concert, undetected, and to get close enough to Tano so she could put her arms around him and the whole world would see that she was his girl. The server brought the plate of pancakes heaped with swirled whipped cream. Donna dug her fork deeply into the center of the stack. With the first massive bite, syrup and whipped cream dripped onto the brown kitten printed on her T-shirt. She took a napkin and wiped it off. With the next bite, it happened again. *Good thing I didn't wear my fashion stuff here.* The feasting paused momentarily as her eye caught the fake engagement ring on her left hand. She held it up and looked at it as it sparkled from the fluorescent diner lights above her.

"Who's the lucky guy?" the server said as she brought the meal ticket.

"Oh, he's in a rock band. You ever heard of Badge? My guy is Tano. He sings and plays the guitar. He wrote a song about me."

"No, can't say as I have. I guess I would say I'm kind of a bluegrass fan."

"Well, here, take a look at him." Donna googled a photo of Tano and showed it to the waitress. "That's my Tano."

The waitress held Donna's phone in her hand for a moment. *Could this guy really be her boyfriend? I don't get it.*

"Wow. You got yourself a good looker. When's the big day?"

"Yes, I do. Um....we haven't decided yet. He's on tour a lot." Donna smiled as she took a spoon and scooped up the last of the melted whipped cream mixed with syrup on her plate. She left a five-dollar bill on the table as a tip, grabbed the paper bag with the cinnamon roll and paid the cashier.

As she left the diner, she noticed that there was a Goodwill store across the street in a shabby rundown strip mall. *It looks like that place just opened up. Maybe there's something in there that could be a disguise.*

She waddled across the street and was the first morning Goodwill customer. She stood in the doorway while her eyes scanned the store. She immediately caught sight of a curly black Afro wig resting on the head of a mannequin wearing a purple-and-red embroidered sarong. She scurried over to look at it. It was marked with a twenty-dollar price tag.

That's it! I have to cover up this gorgeous red hair of mine—it will give me away. She took the wig off the mannequin, walked over to a mirror on the far wall of the store and tried it on. *Hey, I look good like this. Tano will like it, too.* Carrying the wig, she browsed the rest of the store and found a pair of XL shiny brown spandex pants. She held them up to see if they might fit and decided to buy them too. Eight dollars. She dug into her purse. She was carrying a thousand dollars cash. It was all the money she had left from her savings that she had been using since she was fired from her job at the call center several weeks before.

"Thank you. Come again," the clerk quietly said as she handed the change from the fifty-dollar bill Donna gave her.

"Thanks, but I won't need to. I'm marrying a rock star," she said, and held her left hand up to show the clerk the fake engagement ring.

"Congratulations," the clerk said. But Donna was already walking out the door.

"Are you awake, pretty girl?"

"Yeah, I am now," Holly whispered as she stretched again.

Tano reached over and put his hand around her waist and pulled her close to him. "I like waking up next to you." He moved her tousled hair away from her face.

"Me, too." Holly looked up at him, gently kissed his cheek and smiled.

"Well, in about an hour I scheduled a couple's massage for us down in the spa."

"Is that the morning surprise?"

"Yep. Have you had a couple's massage before?"

"No. I've never had a massage before."

"Let's see—what time is it?" Tano grabbed his phone to look at the time. "Okay, it's seven thirty. Our massage is scheduled for nine and then we can catch breakfast at Ellyngton's."

"That sounds great but is there time for that? I mean, when do you have to meet the band at Fiddler's Green?"

"Around three for a sound check and a light rehearsal. The setlist isn't much different than the last concert except for 'Colorado' at the end."

"So, do you think there would be a little time for me to hit the gym before the massage?"

"Yeah, sure. I'll join you."

Holly sat up. "So, do we shower before the massage or after or what?" Tano put his hand on her back.

"Let's go to the gym, come back, rinse off and put the fluffy white robes on and go down to the spa for the massage. "

Holly splashed water on her face, brushed her teeth, smoothed her hair, and dressed in a Badge T-shirt and shorts. Tano threw on a white V-neck T-shirt and some gray sweats. He took Holly's hand.

There were a few people in the Brown Palace Fitness Center when they entered through the elegant onyx-encased entrance. Holly headed toward one of the treadmills. Tano went for the free weights and began repetitions with various weights and dumbbells. When his workout was finished, he stepped onto a treadmill next to Holly, who continued to alternately walk and then run.

"I think I'll do a little bit of spinning, too," Holly said when she stepped off the treadmill, her face glowing from exercise. *It feels so natural to be with her*, Tano thought to himself as he watched her.

At around eight thirty a.m., Tano once again took her hand and they went back to the Beatles room, showered quickly, and put on white fluffy terry cloth robes before the massage. "So, what do I do? Strip down to undies or what?"

"Yeah. Whatever you want. Some of it will have to come off for the massage anyway."

"Okay," Holly mumbled. She felt quiet apprehension about a

total stranger touching her body as she slipped on the robe and tied the belt around her waist.

"Let's go."

The elegant spa entrance was flanked by marble columns and the same distinct elegance seen throughout the hotel. They walked to the reception area.

"Yes, Mr. Montano. You have reserved the VIP Couples Suite. Go on in and make yourselves comfortable." A tiny Asian receptionist with delicate features pointed the way toward the suite. Two massage beds covered with white sheets were positioned next to each other. The room was dimly lit and highlighted with delicately scented candles of floral and spice. The walls were covered with a wainscoting of terracotta tile in brown shades which matched the wainscoting throughout the hotel. Holly and Tano sat on two gold brocade side chairs to wait. Soft sounds of nondescript instrumental music softly played in the background. She nervously smiled at Tano who winked at her.

Two masseuses—a muscular Latino man and a tall pale blonde woman—entered the room. "My name is Willow and this is Mario. I understand that you both would like a Swedish massage today. Am I right?'

"Yeah." Tano said, and Holly nodded not really knowing the answer to the question.

"We'll step out while you get yourselves arranged on the massage table. Please help yourself to a glass of our complimentary Brown Palace house champagne while you wait." Willow and Mario left the room.

"Okay, sweet thing. Here you go. You will like it. I know you will." Tano poured two fluted champagne glasses to half full. A plate of gold-wrapped chocolates was arranged on a silver tray next to the champagne. "Want one?"

"No, I'm good." Holly sipped the champagne. "Give me a little more before they come back." Tano smiled at her, his dimples framing each side of his moustache. She was so transparent.

Willow and Mario returned just as Holly and Tano each laid

down on their stomachs on the massage tables with the crisp white flat sheet covering them from the waist down. Willow poured small amounts of lemongrass and sage essential oils on Holly's back and began to rub her back in long, slow gliding strokes. Mario simultaneously massaged Mario's back as if the masseuses had choreographed the massages. A light buzz from the champagne and the scent of the combined oils relaxed Holly. The firm motions loosened muscles she didn't know she had. She closed her eyes and let herself be mindful of the moment. Tano, who had had many massages in his life, closed his eyes as Mario pressed firmly into his muscular back, loosening tension and tightness that had developed within the past few days.

The massages continued for nearly an hour. Holly and Tano were silent. When Willow and Mario finished, Willow said, "Thank you for visiting the spa this morning. Please be sure to rehydrate. You may take a shower here if you wish. The showers are through that door."

Tano and Holly sat up and wrapped themselves in the flat sheets that had covered them. "Well, want to shower? I have a better idea."

Holly smiled at him. "I choose the better idea." They both walked into the shower area and wiped away the excess oil on their bodies with pristine white towels and wrapped themselves in the fluffy robes. Holly's body felt loose and at the same time energized. They walked quickly to their room.

"Well, we've got time for another surprise this morning." Tano pulled Holly close as they opened the door to the room and hugged her tightly and buried his nose in her neck. An electric sensation radiated through her body as she felt his warm breath on her skin and his hard body pressed against hers.

Holly chuckled. "I knew it."

Tano slipped his warm hands inside her robe and around her waist, opened her robe and kissed her deeply. He felt her breathing begin to intensify. They fell onto the bed. She rolled on top of him and a passionate give and take began. Their oiled bodies slid onto and into each other. Pillows and sheets fell from the bed. After a long, breathless episode of lovemaking, Holly reached down and pulled a sheet over them. The evaporating sweat gave her a chill. Tano turned her on her left side and pulled her close to him to spoon and then he whispered, "I think I could fall in love with you."

Tano's voice was so quiet that Holly wasn't sure if she heard him correctly, but she didn't want to say, "What?" She was already certain that she was in love with him. But hearing him use the words "I think" caused her to pause from telling him that she affirmatively loved him.

"I think I could fall in love with you, too." She repeated his words. She scooted her body even closer into his. They laid still and quiet for a few moments. He began to lightly rub his hand along her side, moving from her hip to her waist. Holly heard her phone ping with a text message. But she didn't move, and she didn't care. She wanted to lay there and feel his touch forever.

CHAPTER 34

Donna's mind had split into two separate halves of consciousness, with her thoughts drifting between them. The chunk with a semblance of reality reminded her that she had stalked Tano through three states, shot Janet, fired a gun at Holly, blasted the front of Tano's house with bullets, was on the run from the law, and cautioned herself that she would need a disguise in order to slink unrecognized into the upcoming Badge concert. But the deranged part continued to block all reason and reinforced her belief that she was indeed engaged to Tano, that he had always wanted to be with her, and that Holly was standing in her way.

Donna ambled back to the motel carrying a rumpled white plastic Goodwill bag containing the brown spandex leggings and the curly black wig, and the paper bag with the cinnamon roll in it. Before she completed the short distance to her motel room door, she couldn't resist the scent of the fresh-baked cinnamon roll and reached into the bag, pinched off a hunk, and gobbled it down. Her fingers were sticky with white icing when she reached into her purse to find the room key. She went inside, dropped the bags on the bed, washed her hands, and couldn't wait to put the Afro wig on her head. She looked at her reflection in the dresser mirror across the room and smiled. *No one will know it's me. But deep down Tano will know. When he sees me there, his loyal fan, his one true love...* She continued to study her reflection as she pulled the cinnamon roll out of the bag, tore it apart and devoured it. White frosting glaze smeared on her chin.

When she finished off the cinnamon roll, she turned and began to gather the clothing she had scattered across the bed and on the floor the night before.

"What will go good with these sexy spandex pants?" she muttered aloud to herself.

She sorted through the various tops she had randomly gathered when she left her house. There was the leopard one, the puffy red ruffled one, a sheer white button-down shirt, an XL black-and-white CU T-shirt, a blue smock top spattered with tiny white flowers. She removed her clothes and stretched and tugged on the shiny brown spandex pants and began to pair them up with the various tops. She thought that the leopard one looked best but Tano had already seen that one. She eventually settled on the black-and-white CU T-shirt, tied it at her waist, exposing her ample midriff which overhung the waist of the spandex pants but was unnoticed by her. She finished off the outfit with a pair of red rubber flip-flops decorated with turquoise and yellow plastic flowers on the tops.

She knew that the extra-large black jeweled purse would be disallowed at the Fiddler's Green because of its size. She fished around in it and pulled out a pink plastic makeup bag to use at the concert instead. But first she needed to apply fresh makeup. She discovered that the inside of the makeup bag and all its contents were dusted with a pink powder from something that spilled inside it. She would use it anyway and wiped out the inside of it with a tissue. She walked into the bathroom, turned on the light which gave her skin a yellowish cast. She dumped the contents of the makeup bag onto the bathroom counter and after cleaning the white icing off her face, she began to apply makeup.

She smeared on two heavy coats of beige liquid foundation, a distinct circle of pink rouge on each cheek, thick crooked lines of black eyeliner, thick bright blue eye shadow, and coral lip gloss. No mascara even though her lashes were blonde. She looked at herself, ready to go, ready to see Tano, to finally hear him say the words she wanted to hear: "You're the girl for me. You're truly the 'Girl from Yesterday.' I love you and can't resist it any longer." She closed her eyes and sighed deeply, imagining what it would be like when that happened. She began to fill the makeup bag with her room key, lip gloss, a wad of the cash, and a printed ticket for a seat on the lawn at Fiddler's Green. Before she slipped her phone into the makeup bag, she took a selfie. "Damn I look hot," she said to herself.

The doors to the venue would not open for at least another six hours but she was ready to go. She decided to pick up all the clothes she had scattered around the hotel room and shoved them into her suitcase. She laid back on the bed, turned the TV on and began to watch *Star Trek* reruns until she would summon a Lyft to drive her the few miles to Fiddler's Green.

"I guess we better get up. The Ellyngton serves breakfast until about eleven, I think." Tano sat up. Holly sat up beside him holding the white sheet to her chest, her bare back still exposed.

"Okay, you shower first. We're still so oily," Holly said.

Tano looked at her, smiled, and raised his eyebrows. "Hey, that was a slip and slide ride."

Holly laughed. "That is a good description of what just happened." Tano stood, totally nude, pulled clean clothes out of his leather bag, laid them on the bed, and walked toward the bathroom. Holly, admiring his back side, reached for her phone on the nightstand next to the bed. The ping had been a text from Garth. There were also two missed calls from him.

> Where the hell are you? Stopped by your place this morning. House was all shut up. Called your office. They said you was out of town. What the hell you doing? Are you with that Tano jerk?

Holly put the phone in her lap and pondered whether she should respond or not. It was none of his business, but she knew he was going to flip out when he found out that she would be moving to Boulder. She heard the shower water running in the bathroom. She decided to take care of it while Tano was out of the room.

> I'm in Boulder. Yes, I'm with Tano. No need to worry.

Garth quickly responded.

You're gonna lose your job and everything over this worth-less guy.

Holly texted back to put an end to the exchange and tossed her phone on to the nightstand:

Talk later.

Tano emerged from the bathroom with a towel wrapped around his waist, his tanned skin glistening from the wetness, his long wavy hair in dripping curls. "Your turn."

Holly slid out of bed with the sheet wrapped around her, looked in her bag for toiletries and clothes, and made her way toward the bathroom. As she walked past Tano, he tugged on the sheet and it fell away from Holly, exposing her little rear end. She laughed and gently pulled the sheet away from him, leaned into him and kissed him lightly on the cheek.

While Holly showered, Tano remembered that he planned to warn Rob that Donna might appear at Fiddler's Green for the concert so that the venue security could watch for her. He didn't really want to discuss Donna in front of Holly again.

"Yeah, she's crazy, man. She shot up my house. I'm gonna send you the photo I have of her. Show the security guys. She's dangerous and wanted by the sheriff in Boulder County and maybe in Oklahoma, too. Yeah, there were some shots fired when I was in Oklahoma with my girl, too. We think she's been stalking me. Remember? She was at the concert in Amarillo. Yeah, see ya later."

Holly emerged from the bathroom, dressed in light blue skinny jeans and a maroon V-neck T-shirt, with a minimal amount of make-up on. She towel dried her hair as much as she could and combed it with her fingers, separating the long copper strands, and then blew it dry while Tano sat in a side chair and watched her. When she was satisfied with her hair, she walked over to Tano, took his hand and they headed to Ellyngton's for breakfast.

When they stepped into the entrance of the restaurant, Kelly, the hotel concierge, was walking out the door. "Hey, Tano, did those surprises work out okay?" She refused to acknowledge Holly.

Tano put his arm around Holly, pulled her close and said, "We had a great time. Thanks for making it happen." Holly saw his eyes drop for a second to look at Kelly's ample cleavage which was spilling out of a low-cut royal-blue satin shirt.

Kelly touched his arm and said, "I would never let you down. Come see me again soon. Will ya?" Then she reached into the black leather portfolio she was carrying and handed him her business card. "In case you don't already have one of these—my direct line and cell number are on this."

Holly couldn't resist rolling her eyes and didn't care if they saw her.

"Gonna be on tour. We'll be back."

When Tano used the word "we," Kelly finally looked at Holly, her eyes narrowed to slits as she backed away and walked out the door.

"Your table is this way, Mr. Montano." The young, petite, blonde hostess was clearly star struck by Tano, but she tried to remain cool. Her hand shook as she handed them the menus.

"Well, what do you think?" Tano said as he opened the menu. "I worked up an appetite a while ago."

Holly smiled at him and crinkled her nose. "Me, too. I think I'll have a Belgian waffle, fruit, and a side of bacon. A mimosa too."

"Huevos rancheros and a Bloody Mary."

After they placed their order, Tano finally decided it would be a good time to ask Holly about her plans to move to Boulder. He knew she had been sorting it out.

"So...I have to ask...what are your plans when you return to Liberal? You know, about moving to Boulder?"

When Holly spoke, the words poured out quickly. "I've been thinking about it. I first need to take a leave from my job while I look for one here—hopefully, with the subsidiary energy company in

Broomfield. I plan to leave my house vacant for now, until I get settled here and then I can decide what to do with it and the furniture and stuff. So I'll bring clothes and things I need for now. But I need to find a place to live here and so I'll probably stay at a Residence Inn until I find a place—"

Tano interrupted her. "I want you to live with me. When I asked you to be with me, I meant to live with me. Listen, I looked for you. I had to find you and now I don't want you to go away again. Don't worry about a job. Something will work out." He winked at her.

The thought of living with him hadn't occurred to Holly. It didn't seem clear that was what he meant when he asked her and it would have seemed presumptuous to assume that he did.. She stared wide-eyed at him.

"Seriously. I'm gone on tour some and that big house is empty. And you know, when I come home, I want to come home to you there. Will you change your mind now?"

A dark, handsome young server dressed in black pants, white shirt and black vest and bow tie brought their drinks to the table. Holly paused to speak while he stood there. "No, I wouldn't change my mind. But I wouldn't want to impose on you." She sipped the mimosa.

"I wouldn't have asked you if it was that way. Let's drink a toast to it. You coming to live with me." Tano raised his Bloody Mary glass and Holly touched her glass to his. "So, it's settled. Maybe you want to teach ballet. Hell, even open a ballet school of your own." But then he felt he had to ask her, "You know I'll be gone. Sometimes for a couple of weeks at a time. How do you feel about that?"

"Well...I know that. I know you'll come back home. I'll be there. I want to be there."

The exquisite plates of food were delivered to their table. Tano changed the subject.

"So, you fly to Kansas on Friday. And I'm flying to Jackson, Wyoming, on Friday, too. The guys are leaving on Friday morning to drive up in the van. What time is your flight? Mine's at one thirty. United.

"My flight is at one. Southwest."

"That's great—we can wait together until you board."

"Another mimosa, ma'am? And you sir? Another Bloody Mary?"

"Yes, bring us another round."

After about three hours of *Star Trek*, Donna was getting antsy. She thought that she already looked good and was ready to go, but she was hungry again. She walked back across the street to the diner for lunch. Donna was pleased that the waitress who had served her breakfast didn't recognize her with her disguise.

"I'll have a large Diet Mountain Dew, a BLT. Does it come with fries? Okay, yeah, fries, side of mashed potatoes and gravy, and a salad with fat free ranch dressing." While Donna waited for her lunch, her thoughts drifted to the Winchester .300 Mag in the trunk of her car. She imagined sneaking it into the Fiddler's Green, finding Holly in its scope, aiming for her red head, and pulling its trigger. *Boom! You're gone, hippie bitch!* She was so preoccupied with her thoughts of murder, staring into space, that she didn't notice when the waitress brought the plates of food until she smelled the bacon. *It'll happen if he doesn't quit fooling around with her. It's my turn.*

CHAPTER 35

In the middle of the afternoon, Tano and Holly drove the blue Corvette to the outdoor Fiddler's Green Amphitheatre to meet with the sound, lighting, and guitar techs and rehearse a little, especially "Colorado" which Badge had added to the set list just two days before.

When they walked into the staging area, Janet, who had been standing next to Rocky wearing a hot-and-heavy dark-brown wool poncho to hide her arm that was still in a sling, immediately rushed up to Tano and attempted to hug him, even though his arm was resting around Holly's waist. "Good to see you, Tano," she said while she continued her awkward grip around his neck, pressing her tall bulky body into his.

He took a step back, looked directly at her and said, "Jesus, Janet." He glanced at Rocky who was directly in front of them, glaring at them with disgust. "Hey, Rocky's checking you out. He must need you or something."

"Him? Okay, catch ya later," Janet whispered in his ear, and then looked at Holly with contempt.

"Why does Rocky keep her around?" he mumbled to Holly. He waved his hand in front of him to deflect the intense floral scent of her perfume. He rubbed his nose and then he realized some of the obnoxious scent was now on his clothes.

He took Holly's hand. "Come on," and they walked toward the instruments set up on the stage. The guitars, amplifiers, drums, and other instruments had been set up by the roadies and guitar techs. One tech, Pete, was tuning one of Tano's Fender electric guitars. "How's it going there, Pete?"

"Good, just finishing up this bass and you're good to go."

The band members began to congregate on stage, plucking guitar strings, listening to the acoustics, adjusting the amps.

A caterer was setting up a buffet of gourmet pizzas and salads and metal tubs of ice speckled with tall brown bottles of beer and Cokes for the band. A fifth of Jack Daniels and four shot glasses were placed at the end of the buffet table. Holly kissed Tano on the cheek under Janet's watchful eye and said, "I'm going down to the front row to watch." Janet followed her and sat down a few seats away from her.

The band members came together with a cacophony of musical sounds while they simultaneously plucked and played a few random rifts of songs on the set list. When the noise settled, they began to play and sing "Colorado," starting and stopping a few times before they completed the song once. Tano began to play the guitar riff from the beginning of "We Gotta Get Out of This Place" and the band picked up on it and played it all the way through while the sound and light techs made adjustments on the stage.

The music stopped momentarily, and while the band members were talking, Janet turned to look at Holly and said, "So...really... how long do you plan to hang on him anyway?"

Holly felt her face redden with anger and her blood pressure rise, but in an even, cool voice, she said, "I plan to hang around for a long while. He asked me to move to Boulder." She stopped short of telling her that she was going to live with him.

Janet stiffened and inhaled deeply. Her eyes bulged with shock. For a few moments she was speechless until she said, "Oh, really. Well, don't bother to unpack. You're not his type."

"That's for him to decide. I'll take my chances." Holly could feel her heart pounding. *What a rude bitch!*

"You'll be gone in a few weeks. Better not burn your bridges back there in Hicktown." Janet smirked, stood, and walked onto the stage and began to speak to Rocky, motioning with her unslinged arm toward Holly. They both turned to look at her. When Rocky apparently motioned to Janet to move offstage, she stormed away, taking giant deliberate steps with her big heavy black suede boots.

While the band continued to rehearse and jam for another hour, Holly received another text from Garth insisting that she call him. She decided to get the call over with and walked up to the lawn seating area of the venue where it was less noisy.

"So what's the deal, Garth? What do you want?" She was obviously annoyed.

"I want to know what the hell you're doing!" Garth shouted into the phone.

"It's none of your business. I don't need your approval for the stuff I do. But if you must know, yes, I'm with Tano. He's rehearsing right now for a concert tonight. In Denver. Can't you hear them?"

"That guy is bad news! I can see he's a player and will play around on you! He's gonna cheat! Mark my word! And I don't wanna see it again! You need to get back to Liberal and get over this fantasy! Jared ain't gonna wait forever!" Garth continued to shout.

"Well, I'm flying back to Liberal tomorrow and packing up some stuff and moving to Boulder."

Garth was silent. Holly thought that he might have hung up, but she continued to listen for his response. "Mom and Dad ain't gonna like that one bit!"

"That's bullshit, Garth! They aren't concerned. They raised us to take care of ourselves. If I mess up, it's on me. You don't even know him! If you can't trust me, then there's nothing left to say. I'm done!" and she disconnected. *What the hell? This day began so beautifully.*

After about an hour, Tano stepped off the stage and sat down next to Holly. "That took a little longer than I thought it would. How's my girl?"

"I'm good," and she smiled and leaned against him to cover her cross mood.

"We gotta go back to the hotel. I need to change. I can still smell Janet's perfume on my shirt and it's annoying. I saw her down here talking to you. What did she have to say?"

"Nothing but rude remarks about you and me. I guess she's just one of those girls who is always pissed off and nasty."

"Yep—you got it." He took Holly's hand, waved to Rob and said, "Be back in about an hour."

Donna's stomach was full, and the next bite of food was no longer her focus. She went to the motel, applied more heavy makeup, grabbed her phone, took another selfie, and called for a Lyft. The gates to the amphitheater wouldn't open for an hour but she could wait on its fringes, listen to the "Donna" songs and the Badge albums on her playlist. Maybe even catch a glimpse of Tano when he arrived.

The Lyft driver dropped her at Marjorie Park north of the venue on Greenwood Plaza Boulevard. "Come back later for me? Ya hear?" She stuck her chest out trying to flirt with him.

The driver didn't look at her and mumbled, "Just use the app. Somebody will come for ya."

She plopped down on a park bench and began to play with her phone when her sister called her again. She declined the call. It rang again. And then a text came.

Please call, sis. I know you're in big trouble. Please tell me what's going on. Where are you? Please call. You need help. Did you really shoot at some people?

"Yep, I did, and I'll do it again," she said to herself. Fans began to saunter by on the sidewalk in front of her, occasionally snickering at her bizarre appearance even though she thought they were admiring her sense of style. She followed a group of about a dozen college-age girls and stood in line behind them. For a moment, she felt apprehension and adrenaline knowing that she might be apprehended at the gate if someone figured out who she was. The line began to move slowly, one step at a time, until she reached the security check point, laid her makeup bag in a white plastic tub to be scanned. She held her breath as she walked through the body scanner, wincing, waiting for the hammer to fall.

"Okay, enjoy the concert." A man with security waved her on through.

Oh, my God! I made it through! Donna had purchased a ticket for the general seating on the lawn in the back of the venue but first she walked down to the stage to see if Tano was there. Her heart raced with the anticipation of seeing him. As the venue became more crowded, she decided she had better stake out a space on the lawn.

Tano and Holly returned to the Brown Palace, hurried to their room, and changed their clothes. Tano wore a black leather vest with no shirt, exposing his muscular tan arms and chest, faded jeans, a dark brown tooled leather band on his left wrist and brown cowboy boots. He looked hot and she knew that the women in the audience were going to love him. Holly wore the faded skinny jeans and a deep purple satin tank top with pearl buttons, and brown suede cowboy boots with white stitching on the toe and heel. Tano walked over and unbuttoned two of the buttons to expose her cleavage. "There—that's better."

They returned to the venue at around six. The pizza was still fresh and warm and they each took a slice to eat and grabbed two longneck beers and sat down on a low black leather sofa in the hospitality room. Janet and Rocky, reeking of marijuana smoke, strolled through the room, ignoring both of them. Randy and Jack were sitting at a table with Rob, eating pizza.

"Hey, Rob? Did you distribute that photo of that psycho Donna to security?"

"Yep, I did. I haven't heard that she's been spotted around here yet. They know to watch out for her."

"Holly, I want you sit or stand on the side of the stage where I can see you."

The crowd noise reached a crescendo as the amphitheater filled. Randy, Jack, Rocky and Tano each downed the traditional three shots of Jack Daniels and walked out onto the stage to hordes of screaming fans. Tano carried a red plastic cup filled with Jack and Coke. They picked up their guitars and their drumsticks and launched into "Badge," their signature song.

The August evening was warm as the sun began to lower in the sky and shadows lengthened. But even with the remaining light of the day, the colors of the lighting effects on stage were vibrant and ever changing with the beat of the music. The lighting techs had added a black and white slide show, spanning the width of the stage behind them, of photos of the band throughout the years, beginning in the garage band days through the last concert in Amarillo. Holly was thrilled to see the early photos of Tano—always so good looking.

The lights dimmed and a spotlight emerged. The first set of hard driving songs was over. Tano took a drink of the Jack/Coke mixture. The Badge members stepped back into the shadows as Tano stepped forward with his acoustic guitar and sat on a darkened stage under a single white spotlight on a tall wooden three-legged stool.

"And now, here's a song for my lady." He strummed an introduction on his Fender acoustic guitar and began to sing "The Girl from Yesterday."

The crowd was silent. Donna, who had been content to watch him on the Jumbotron, jumped up and frantically began to push her way from the back of the venue, through crowded seated areas, to the front. "Excuse me, I gotta get up there. Oh, sorry, let me through. I need to be up front. Sorry, again," she blurted as she shoved her body through rows and rows of people who were annoyed that she was interrupting the mood created by Tano's beautiful song. "Please! He's singing that song for me."

A large hairy man wearing baggy overalls with no shirt was pushing his way through the crowd toward Donna when he bumped her hard, stepped on her foot, and she fell into a young man's lap.

"Hey, get off me! What's your problem?"

Donna heard him say to the woman next to him, "What kind of costume was that supposed to be?"

"Sorry, so sorry," Donna breathlessly mumbled.

As she pushed herself up with the forceful shove of the man, her foot began to throb from being stepped on. She ignored it and continued to desperately push.

Tano sang the final lines of the song: "For the little while we were together, she held my heart in her hands. The girl from yesterday."

Donna, breathing heavily, finally reached the front of the venue where hordes of fans were standing, shouting and applauding. Tano was finished with his solo. The stage lights became vibrant and electric with color again when Jack began an intense drumbeat and the rest of the band members joined him to cover the Lynyrd Skynyrd song, "What's Your Name?" Donna squeezed through the crowd, sidestepping one foot at a time until she reached the edge of the stage. No one noticed or cared when she hoisted herself onto the stage on her stomach and grunted while she pushed herself to standing. For a second, her eyes scanned the crowded lawn behind her, and then she bolted toward Tano.

"Tano! Here I am! Your girl from yesterday!"

No one could hear her words which were drowned by the music. Tano saw her shuffling toward him out of the corner of his eye and promptly side stepped a couple of times.

"Tano, I love you! Here I am! I'm here now!"

When she grabbed his right arm and pulled on it, he looked at her face and recognized that it was Donna. A wave of fear washed over him for a moment, not knowing what she would do, but he continued to sing, intending not to let her disrupt the concert, pulling away while the frantic insane scene unfolded. He looked toward Holly, who was wide eyed with shock. It had happened so fast.

Immediately, two security guards, stationed on the side stage, bolted to Donna, each of them yanking her by an arm and dragging her. She opened the fingers on her left hand wide, held it up and screamed, straining her voice, "Everybody! He gave me this! Everyone look! He gave me this ring! I'm engaged to him!" as she displayed the fake engagement ring. She continued to scream and then began to kick wildly, thrashing her head from side to side. The guards struggled but hastened her to the back of the venue and pushed her out of the gate, shouting at the guard at the entrance, "DO NOT let her back in! If she doesn't leave, call the police!"

Donna stood alone, outside the gate, shaking and screaming,

"You'll be sorry! Tano's gonna sue you!" until her throat hurt from shouting and tears began to stream down her face, causing the heavy makeup to drip on to her white CU shirt. With her head down, sobbing, she slowly limped to the park bench where she had sat before the concert and continued to sob, whispering to herself, "Why does he keep running from me? Is it a test? Why doesn't he give in to me? I know he wants it."

But suddenly, as if a switch had been turned off, her mood changed from despair to relief. *I know what to do. I'm going to go to the next concert—no matter where it is. I feel it in my bones. He's ready to commit to me. I saw it on his face.* She pulled her phone out of the dusty makeup bag and began to Google the Badge tour schedule. *Jackson Hole, Wyoming, on Saturday. I'll be there.* Even though she could still hear the music playing, she called for a Lyft to return her to the motel. Her somewhat rational, sane side spoke to her and told her that she may have been recognized and better take off.

When the Lynyrd Skynyrd song was finished, the band approached Tano who spoke with them for minute. Janet came running out on stage and tried to hug him. "Did she hurt you, hon? I would hate it if something happened to you." Rocky grabbed her arm and pulled her off stage. Tano didn't respond and walked to the side stage momentarily to see Holly, whose eyes were wide with shock. Her hands were clasped at her chest. She hugged him around his neck and said, "Are you okay?"

"Yep, but it was that crazy Donna! It was her! I couldn't say or do anything during the song. She's out of here now. Can you believe she would do that?"

"No. She's seriously unhinged. Go tell Rob."

Tano gestured to Rob on the other side of the stage. "Damn, Rob! That nut case was Donna! She had some kind of lame disguise on, but I saw that porky face. It was her. How the hell did she get in here?"

"Can't say. I'm gonna talk to the entrance personnel. She's gone now. They tossed her out. Security's gonna have to be beefed up for the next few weeks if she's following your tour."

Tano's full attention turned to Holly and he kissed her deeply. He could see that the incident had scared her. "Okay, Holly, do you think you could play the violin for us in 'Free'? Like we did five years ago? In the Chevy van? It's coming up. The final song before a break. I can't hold up the show any longer. What do you say? I want to tell Rocky that you're stepping in for it. Holly?"

"Yes, I guess so." She smiled at him, but her hands began to sweat. What if she couldn't find the key? Or the rhythm? She didn't even listen to the next song they played as in her in her mind, she went over the movement of her fingers on the strings to the accompaniment to "Free."

"Come on out here," Tano waved to her and jarred her from her intense thoughts. Rocky moved to the back of the set and picked up one of the guitars. She walked out on stage and picked up Rocky's violin. Her hands were shaking. She moved the bow over the strings a few times to get a feel for the instrument. Then she smiled and nodded at Tano who began to play the introduction of the song. For five years, every time either one of them had heard that song, it took them back to the summer thunderstorm and the steamy Chevy van on the road to Sage, the first day they met. Holly closed her eyes while she played and remembered again.

CHAPTER 36

Unexpected tears welled to her closed eyes, as Holly replayed the past roller-coaster weeks in her mind like a slideshow during the four-minute song. With the perfect, smooth strokes of the bow leading to a crescendo near the end, silent tears flowed down her cheeks. When the song was over, Tano raised his arm in her direction and shouted, "Holly Harris on the fiddle!" while the audience applauded and screamed.

He had been standing just a few feet away from her. She couldn't see him smiling at her as she played. When she opened her eyes, he stepped toward her. She was smiling slightly, and her cheeks were wet with tears. He could see that she had been moved by strong feelings. He knew that no matter what she said or didn't say, she was in love with him. And he with her. He kissed her on her wet cheek.

"Why the tears, sweetness?"

"I don't know. I just got so emotional."

Holly was still holding the violin in one hand while she pulled Tano closer with the other and hugged him tightly, stood on her tip-toes and whispered, "I...uh...thank you." She wanted to say more.

She handed the violin to Rocky, who uncharacteristically grinned at her and patted her on the back. "Great job, Holly." Over his shoulder, she could see Janet shifting her weight from one foot to the other, scowling at them.

"We're gonna take a short break now! Be back!" Randy shouted and waved to the audience. The band members set their instruments into their stands and Jack stepped down from the drums. They gradually made their way back to the hospitality room. Rob had arranged for an appetizer spread to be brought in—guaca-mole, hummus, chips, spring rolls, bacon-wrapped jalapenos, and fruit and cheese platters—in case the band was hungry after the first set. Tano grabbed a water bottle and downed it quickly. Then he picked out a longneck bottle of beer from the tub of ice and grabbed a spring roll.

"Help yourself to something, Holly, if you want."

Holly perused the long table of food, took a small plastic plate and added some guacamole, chips, and fruit to it. She sat on a long blue upholstered couch with Tano and nibbled at her plate. When she looked up, Janet was staring at them, not blinking, with no expression, as if she was catatonic. Holly leaned her head on Tano's arm while he talked with Rob, who pulled up a chair next to him.

"They didn't find her after they threw her out, Tano. No one realized it was Donna. She's out of here now, but man, she's really a strange and dangerous chick. And what's this about an engagement ring? They said that she was shouting something about it, man."

"I don't know, man. She's messed up. She needs to be put away somewhere."

The break ended after about twenty minutes. Tano stood and stretched his arms over his head. "Here I go, sweetheart." When he lowered his arms, he hugged her tightly and let his hands drop to her butt. "Stand where I can see you while I play." Holly smiled and nodded and followed him out to the stage.

When the Lyft dropped Donna back at the motel, she hurried inside to make the final arrangements to get the tickets for the Badge show and flight to Jackson Hole. She had one credit card that she kept for emergencies. This flight to Jackson Hole would qualify. She felt very self-satisfied when she was successful on both counts. "Yippee, here I come, lover boy! Tomorrow!" she said out loud to herself.

The sun had nearly set when she walked across the street to a convenience store and bought a six-pack of beer and a large bag of pork rinds to celebrate her good fortune. She had completely wiped from her psyche the unpleasant scene at the concert just a short time before and was humming a Donna song to herself.

She noticed a man standing outside of the motel room next to hers smoking when she returned to her door. He was mid-thirties, seedy, paunchy, overweight, wearing a white tank top with grimy greyish handprints smeared across the front of it, a Rockies baseball hat with fringes of his hair sticking out beneath it, and black-and-white basketball shorts. He was barefoot. He watched Donna as she approached, blowing smoke into the air in her direction.

"Hi," Donna said when she saw him leering at her as she fished for her room key in her little bag.

"Hey," the man said. *What kind of get up is that?* he thought to himself as he got a good look at her outfit.

"Nice night."

"Yeah." More smoke was blown in her direction.

Then spontaneously, without a single forethought Donna, pointed to the green plastic lawn chairs by the door and said, "Wanna join me for a beer? That's probably what these chairs are for."

The man took another drag on his cigarette and looked toward the sky as he exhaled a stream of smoke before he answered. "Sure, why not?" He picked up a chair and moved it closer to the chair that Donna had plopped down on.

"What's your name?" Donna asked as she handed him a bottle of beer.

"Trouble. What's yers?"

She didn't care to know his real name anyway. "D...D...Debbie. So, Trouble, what brings you to Denver?"

"Oh, just headin' to Nevada to meet up with my brother fer a job."

"What kind of work do you do?" Donna ripped the bag of pork rinds open with her teeth.

"A little of this. A little of that." Trouble reached into the bag and took a handful of pork rinds.

"Where are you from?"

"Man, you sure ask a lot of questions." Trouble lit another cigarette. "Arkansas."

"So that's your sedan out there with the Arkansas plates?" Donna asked, pointing to a battered and patched 1990s model Chevrolet sedan.

"Yep. What about you?"

"What about me?" Donna coyly asked with her mouth full of rinds.

"What's yer story?" Trouble swatted a mosquito on his shoulder.

"Oh, I'm from around here." She waved her hand as a mosquito hovered near her face. "These mosquitoes are getting worse. Wanna come in for a while and finish your beer?" Donna opened the door and invited him inside. "No smoking in here, Trouble."

Trouble stood up and stretched his arms over his head. His shirt rose exposing an ample puffy stomach. He took another long drag of his cigarette and flicked it onto the pavement. As he entered the room, he expelled a long and loud belch.

"Jeez, Trouble. Need some Rolaids or something?" Donna sat on the bed.

"Hey, what ya see is what ya get and everything that goes along with it." Trouble flopped down on the bed next to her. The mattress sagged nearly to the floor where they both sat. When they scooted themselves toward the center of the mattress, Donna fell on her back and before she could sit up, Trouble took it as a sign that she wanted to play. He leaned over her and kissed her, inserting his tongue deep into her mouth, untied the CU T-shirt, and shoved his clumsy rough hand under it.

At first Donna was repulsed and tried to squirm away. He reeked of pungent smoke. His skin was sticky and dripping with sweat. His unwashed hair carried a sour smell. He emitted a loud grunt when he hoisted himself on top of her. But then she decided that she liked it and responded eagerly to his advances. It had been months since anyone had touched her that way. She tugged and twisted to remove the spandex pants. Then one piece of clothing came off, and then another, and within minutes, the mattress was bouncing and swaying with the weight of their bulky bodies as they clumsily satisfied their carnal needs. Trouble, still wearing his baseball hat but nothing else, rolled off Donna and onto his back.

Donna sighed and pulled the covers up to her chin. She reached for her phone on the nightstand and raised it above her and took a photo of their faces as they lay together on the flattened pillows.

"What the hell you doin'? Taking selfies? Not of me, you don't." Trouble sat up and shouted.

"Too late," Donna laughed loudly.

"What ya need that for?"

"I'm going to make my fiancé jealous. He's gonna be so pissed. In case you didn't notice, I'm wearing a diamond ring." She was still lying on her back. She lifted her left hand and held it a few inches from his face.

"Man, you're a sick bitch. I'm going outside for a smoke." Trouble slipped on his shorts and grimy shirt.

"You coming back? I still have beer," she said cheerily, complete-ly oblivious to Trouble's obvious anger with her. The door slammed shut.

For several minutes, Donna lay in bed, playing with her phone, waiting for Trouble to return. *I wonder if he's still out there smok-ing. He better not try to ditch me. Not after I gave him what he wanted.* She scooted out of bed and slipped on the CU T-shirt and her hot pink panties and opened the motel room door. He was no-where in sight. There wasn't even a lingering plume of smoke. His car was still parked in front. *That son of a bitch! He's probably in his room. He could have at least said thanks.*

Donna slipped on the pink flip-flops, grabbed her keys, marched out to her car and opened the trunk. She shoved things aside with both hands until she found the pistol she had been carrying since she shot Janet weeks before. She turned and looked in both direc-tions to see if anyone was around to see her and walked toward Trouble's door with a pistol in her right hand. Tap, tap, tap. There was no answer. Tap, tap, tap. Still no answer.

"I know you're in there, you son of a bitch, and if you don't answer, I'm going to file rape charges against you. Now open up!" Donna empathically but quietly said to the crack in the door.

In a minute, Donna heard the doorknob rattle as Trouble opened the door. When he stood in front of her, Donna raised the pistol and pointed it at his puffy midsection.

"You're that crazy chick they're looking for! I just seen ya on the news! Cops are looking for ya." And in one yank, he pulled the Afro wig off of her head, exposing her matted hair underneath and tossed it to the ground. "I knew it!"

Donna pushed the pistol barrel into his stomach and yelled, "That was a dumbass thing to do. Now let's talk, you fat bastard."

Trouble raised both hands as if to surrender. With the pistol barrel, she shoved Trouble into his room and slammed the door behind her.

"Whatcha gonna do with that?" Trouble said weakly. His heart was racing, and he thought he might pass out from adrenaline and fear.

"Not sure yet. That depends on you." She laughed loudly. Her eyes were bulging with excitement. Her heart racing with anticipation.

"What do ya want anyway? I got a little bit of money. Is that what you want?"

"Shut up!" Suddenly there was a knock on the door.

"Everything okay in there? The motel office had reports of loud voices." A woman's muffled voice interrupted them.

Donna buried the pistol barrel deeper into Trouble's big stomach and whispered,

"Answer her, prick."

"Uh, yeah, we're okay. I think the volume was up on the TV."

"Okay, enjoy your evening."

"I plan to." Donna laughed to herself, amused by the shaking hulk who stood before her. "Yep, I'm that crazy chick from the news. What do you plan to do about it?"

CHAPTER 37

"Why are you so pissed off...uh..Debbie? What do ya want?" Trouble threw his hands up in exasperation and then slapped them on the side of his thighs.

"You disrespected me! I just want to teach you a lesson. You don't waltz into my room, have your way with this." She swept her hand from top to bottom over her stodgy body. "And then you sneak out of the room, pretending to smoke, and never come back. You disrespected me, prick!"

"Hey, yeah, I did smoke and then you were snapping selfies of us for some boyfriend. I don't want no trouble from some guy. What the hell?"

"And then you throw some crap at me about me being wanted by police or something. You don't know what you're talking about." Donna snarled through gritted teeth.

"Where is this guy anyway? What are ya doin' in a motel room?"

"He's a rock star. In concert right now. Not that it's any of your business." Donna continued to point the gun at the filthy shirt covering his big bloated belly. Her voice began to get hoarse as she spoke.

"Why aren't you with him?"

"Shut up. None of your business."

"Come on—just tell me what ya want. I told ya—I got money."

"I don't want your money. I want an apology from you. And then I want you to keep your ugly mouth shut for the rest of the night and for you to stay put until I leave in the morning. Don't get any ideas about calling police or I'll be back."

Trouble had no problem with her request not to call police since he was wanted on several arrest warrants for a series of offenses in Arkansas and Missouri. "Okay, okay. Sorry. I'm sorry. Put the gun away. I'll stay put."

"You're goddamn right you will." She pushed the gun into his stomach one more time to emphasize her point and then shoved him on to the bed.

"Okay. Okay. Can ya quit pointin' that gun at me? I said sorry."

Donna continued to point the pistol at him and backed toward the door. "Now, I said stay. Got it? By the way—how was it?"

"How was what?"

"Your time on and in this body?"

"Uh...it was great. Uh...the best. Yeah...it was."

"Good answer, son of a bitch." Donna opened the door and left. She caught a glimpse of Trouble's car in the parking area with the Arkansas plates, and impulsively and discreetly proceeded to let the air out of all the tires. "You aren't going anywhere soon," she said, laughing to herself. When she went back to her room, she took a shower to wash Trouble off of her, drank the rest of the beer, and finished the bag of pork rinds. "Damn, I shoulda got some Twinkies too."

The concert ended at around 10:00 p.m. when Badge performed "Colorado" as planned. Holly had stood in the wings and watched Tano the entire second half, taking it all in: the music, his talent, his sexy good looks, and the crowd's enthusiastic response to him.

"Good night! Drive safe! We'll be back!" He waved to the Badge fans as the band walked off the stage single file.

The applause and shouting continued, and then in unison, they heard the voices yelling, "More! More! Encore! Encore! Badge! Badge! Badge!" The band members assembled quickly, and Holly saw each of them shake their heads affirmatively. They walked out onto the stage again, to the pleasure of the jubilant crowd.

Holly heard Tano turn and shout to the band members, "Okay, let's give it a shot!" And they began to play the iconic beginning guitar riffs of "Rocky Mountain Way." They hadn't rehearsed it but if there were mistakes, no one would have heard it. The audience was shouting and singing along. When the song finished, Tano and the rest of Badge put their instruments down; Jack stepped down from the drums, they waved to the audience, and it was done. Tano approached Holly immediately and wrapped his arms around her and kissed her. He was hot and sweaty, and she tasted the salty perspiration on his lips from his moustache.

"Wow—Tano! It was awesome! The audience was really into the band tonight."

"Yeah, I think they like Colorado bands best here, but I like to think that it was you being here with me that made it so good."

Holly smiled. "You really think so?" They walked back to the hospitality area and Tano grabbed a bottle of water and drank the entire bottle with one swig. Then he grabbed a second bottle and drank about half of it.

"Do you want anything to eat? I'm just thirsty right now." Holly shook her head no. "Well, what do you think we should do now?"

"Well, since we are both leaving tomorrow, I think I would like to go back to the hotel and just spend some time alone. Does that work for you? I know you have to unwind though."

"Yes, I want some alone time with you. I need to talk to the guys and Rob first before we go. Hey, Rob, got a sec?" Rob and Tano walked toward each other, while Holly waited near the table of food. Janet immediately pounced when she saw Holly standing alone.

"So, when are you leaving? You don't think that you're going to tag along with Tano, do you? Don't you have to go back to Hicktown and do whatever hick stuff you do there?" said Janet with malice through gritted teeth.

Holly unexpectedly laughed at Janet's melodramatic comments and said, "You crack me up," to which Janet became enraged, her face red and she clenched the fist of her hand in the sling.

"Tano's just playing with you. That's what he always does and when he's sick of you, he'll come back to me. He always does. Wait and see, white trash!"

"Janet, you're a first-class bitch! Look at yourself. You're a joke to those guys." Holly could feel her blood pressure rise. Janet was getting to her.

"You better watch out. You never know when Tano will pick up another hillbilly chick along the road and shove you out the door and onto the road."

While Tano was talking to Rob, he turned and saw the two women engaged in what appeared to be a heated conversation, and he hurriedly approached them.

"Hey, Janet, why don't you take off? I saw Rocky carrying your broomstick," he firmly said, narrowing his eyes as he looked at her while he put his arm around Holly.

"Mark my words. He'll be back with me, won't you, baby?" Janet snarled at Holly and winked at Tano who quickly looked away. She threw her head back and stormed away from them.

"Hey, are you okay? What did she say?" Tano put a hand on each of her shoulders and looked directly at her face.

"I'm okay. She hates me that's all. She calls me names and implies that you two have something going on." Holly wouldn't look at him.

"No way! I have no interest in her. I can't stand her. She's negative and nasty and just plain ugly to me. Let's go."

Holly didn't want to admit it, but she was tired. The last few days had been a blur and a rollercoaster ride. She just wanted to be alone and in a quiet place with Tano as her sole focus. And with her as his.

They cautiously walked out to the parking lot, both scanning the area for any sign of Donna, disguised or not lurking among the cars. The Corvette was only a short distance away. Tano revved it up when he started it. Holly smiled. She liked the sound of the pipes on the car.

They zipped through Denver and returned to the Brown Palace within minutes. They both flopped on the bed on their backs side by side and lay silently, looking at the ceiling, reliving the concert and the past few days. The concert music was still playing in both of their heads. Tano grabbed his phone, synced it to the television and began to play music from one of his playlists to clear the heavy guitar from their ears. It was an untypical mix for Tano of soft rock from the 80s to current music. "Gravity" by Sara Bareilles was the first song. So soft and soothing. Holly turned on her side, laid her arm across his chest, and her left leg over his. She buried her nose in his neck. She could smell the manly scent of his warm skin. A scent that only belonged to him. It was a rare moment when she was totally present—not thinking about anything other than the moment.

Tano squeezed her tightly and turned to her and whispered, "I have to tell you. You need to know. I love you. I think I've always been in love with you." He gently moved her hair from her face.

Holly's heart leaped. She looked at his face, so close to hers. "I'm in love with you, too. I think I always was. I couldn't move forward."

"We will now." And he pulled Holly on top of him.

CHAPTER 38

Tano's eyes remained closed when he felt the very slight movement of the bed as Holly got up at sunrise. When he opened his eyes, he saw her, wearing the black Badge T-shirt that she slept in, standing near the window. She held the Badge pendant in her hand and was sliding it back and forth on its chain staring out the window. She was deep in thought.

"Hey, sweet thing. We don't have to be at the airport until around eleven. We got a few hours. Come back to bed with me." Tano yawned and stretched his arms over his head.

When he spoke, he saw her shake herself from her thoughts. She stepped away from the window and began to pick up clothes and assorted items scattered throughout the room. "I would just feel better if my things weren't spread all over the place since I need to pack soon."

"Come here." Holly couldn't resist his beckoning her. Her sub-conscious had awakened her early. Just two days before she had shakily walked into Tumbleweed, not knowing if Tano was there, not knowing what to expect or what he would say to her if he was. Those quiet moments by the window at dawn helped her to absorb it all. It had been a blur and she needed to organize it in her memory. Him wanting her, the gunshots sprayed at his house, the horse-drawn carriage ride, the massage, the concert, the violin, and Donna.

She stretched out under the sheets next to Tano and cuddled around him. "What's going on in that pretty little head? It's awful early to be locked so deep in thought."

"I was just thinking. About the past couple of days. About the past couple of weeks since you found me in Sage. So much has happened."

"Is it all good?"

"Yes. Very good." She drew a heart on his stomach with her index finger.

"There's more to come." Tano kissed her on her cheek and pulled her closer. Her face rested against his, and she could feel his eyelashes tickle her cheek when he blinked. Both began to doze for a few minutes. The room filled with the yellow of daylight arousing them from their momentary nap.

"Let's just order room service. I want you to be my only focus for the next few hours." Tano sat up, grabbed the room service menu from the drawer in the nightstand. "Here, take a look," he said as he handed the menu to Holly. He laid back down and rested his arm around her waist while she perused the menu.

"Do you know what you want already? Should we order soon?"

"Yeah, I know. Let's order. Eat breakfast and then shower and get ready to go to the airport."

"Okay, a small orange juice, a bagel, and fruit."

Tano phoned room service and placed the order. They laid back down to wait for the food to arrive. Holly finally picked up her phone. More messages and missed calls from Garth. She rolled her eyes and laid her phone down.

"What's up, sweetheart? That brother of yours?"

"Yeah, I'm so tired of it. When I get home, I have to put a stop to it."

"Holly, I guess he just cares so much. But he doesn't need to worry about me. I'm not gonna break this heart." He rested his hand on her heart—his touch aroused Holly.

Tap, tap, tap. "Room service."

Their breakfast was wheeled in and interrupted the beginning of what might have been early morning foreplay. On the cart was a small bouquet of wildflowers and a small complimentary bottle of sparkling wine for mimosas with a card that read, "Come visit us (me) soon. Your hotel concierge."

"I'm guessing Kelly had something to do with that."

"I hope it's not poisoned," Holly laughed. Tano poured the orange juice into two glasses and topped them with the sparkling wine. He held it up to toast Holly. "To us and what lies ahead of us." They tapped their glasses and took a sip.

Donna slept restlessly all night. She woke up with a jolt several times imagining that police were at the motel room door. Each time she was awakened, she walked to the motel window, moved the curtain aside and saw Trouble's car still parked there with four flat tires. She got up at dawn and took another shower to wash Trouble off her. While she dressed in a huge pair of elastic waist beige shorts, a lime green crop top, and the flowered flip-flops, she looked at her phone laying on the bed. Cathy had texted several times pleading for Donna to contact her or someone in the family.

"Whatever." Donna spoke out loud to herself. Then she remembered the selfie she had taken of herself with Trouble. She opened the photo on her phone and studied it for a few minutes, and then snickered to herself. Tano had blocked her on Facebook, Messenger, and by text, but she knew the e-mail address at Tumbleweed and decided to send the photo to his business. Someone there would see it and show it to Tano. *He's gonna be so furious when he sees me with that guy. But he won't run away anymore. He'll keep me close so that it doesn't happen again. I'm brilliant. But now, I'm hungry.*

It was about seven in the morning when she sneaked across the street to the convenience store and bought assorted snacks for "breakfast" and the plane trip. She picked up two packages of Twinkies that she had been craving since the night before, a one liter Mountain Dew (not Diet as a special treat), a small can of Vienna sausages, a can of sardines in mustard sauce, a small box of saltine crackers, a bag of snack-size Snickers, and ten dollars' worth of scratch lottery tickets. She scratched the coating off the numbers. One of them generated a two-dollar payout. *My lucky day.*

She hustled back to her motel room, not wanting Trouble to notice her. She quickly ate both packages of Twinkies and gulped about half of the bottle of Mountain Dew. She threw her clothes in her bag and noticed that the leopard print nylon scarf was still missing. She looked around the room and under the bed. *Where could it be? I really liked that look on me.* She hurried to her car. It was her luck that Trouble had not made trouble for her.

She drove to Denver International Airport. It seemed too early to check-in—the flight was scheduled for takeoff at one thirty p.m., but she was suddenly nervous about getting through security anyway with her name and face plastered all over the news media and potentially to airport security. There was a McDonald's at the airport. She would camp out there for a while. *They have those breakfast burritos.*

Trouble had seen her waddling across the street on tiptoes as if he would hear her footsteps. *That bitch is bad news.* Then he noticed that his car seemed to be resting on its rims—close to the ground. *Oh, man, look what she done! No piece of ass was worth that much trouble.* His face was red with fury when he shuffled out to look at the damage done. Right then and there, he decided to call Denver police and anonymously report that he had seen her.

"Yeah, I seen that gal you been lookin' for. The one I seen on the news. That Donna? She said her name was Debbie. But I seen her. She had a gun. She pointed it at me too. She was stayin' at the Turnpike Motel and I just seen her leave. Yeah—it was a beige kind of car. No, she didn't say where she was goin'. No, I don't want to say my name." Trouble quickly disconnected. *I done my good deed for the day. Now I gotta fill them tires up. Maybe they have somethin' in the motel office. A pump or compressor or somethin'. I wanna get out of here.*

Tano and Holly finished their breakfast and laid back down on the bed. "We won't have this kind of alone time again for a week. It's been great having you with me for the past couple of days. I guess we moved forward, didn't we?"

Holly turned toward him and ran her hand through his thick

wavy hair and lightly kissed him on the neck. "I couldn't be happier than I am right now. I'm finally at peace."

Tano lightly rubbed his hand up and down her back. He slid his hand under the Badge T-shirt and continued to lightly touch the soft skin on her back with his fingertips. Holly closed her eyes to focus on the sensation of his touch. When they kissed, it was deep and long and he slid her shirt up to her shoulders. She quickly slipped it over her head and threw it on the floor. She laid on top of him. She heard his breathing deepen while her ear rested near his face. He rolled her off him and laid on top of her. She felt the weight of his hard, lean body. The heated passionate lovemaking that ensued was intensified by the recent revelation of their mutual love for each other and the stark realization that they would be separated for several days.

They rolled apart, damp, sweaty and breathless. Tano laid his head on Holly's chest and listened to her heartbeat. "Your heart— it's beating fast," he said.

Holly touched his damp hair with her hand and smiled. "What do you expect after that marathon session?"

Tano continued to rest his head on her chest, peacefully listening to her heart beat. When it began to slow to a normal pace he sat up and said, "Well, it's ten. We need to get going, I guess. I'll shower first, if that's okay?"

"I don't mind. I want to make sure that I have everything packed anyway."

Donna arrived at DIA around nine thirty a.m., found the McDonald's and ordered two breakfast burritos, a hash brown, and Diet Coke. She didn't have to check in for her flight to Jackson Hole, Wyoming, for a couple of hours. Although she wanted to wander through the shops and kiosks, she decided to stay in one place hoping not to be recognized. She didn't bring an iPad or laptop, so she played on her phone while she waited. She checked her e-mail to see if anyone at Tumbleweed had responded to the selfie she had sent earlier of Trouble and her. Nothing yet. Her phone vibrated in her hand. Cathy was calling again. Donna declined the call but decided to text her and ask her to stop.

Quit texting and calling. I'm fine. I'm traveling. Tell mom and dad not to worry. Please stop.

At around eleven a.m., Donna saw a silhouette that she thought she recognized enter the sliding doors at the end of a long corridor from where she sat. She knew his gait and couldn't believe her eyes. As the silhouette got closer, her intuition was confirmed. Tano, pulling a carry-on bag, was holding Holly's hand as they entered the security check-in lines. *He must be flying on the same plane with me to Jackson Hole! What is SHE doing with him?*

When Tano and Holly exited the security area, Donna stepped into the long security line forgetting about Tano and Holly momentarily while she anxiously waited to be checked in and scanned. She held her breath and her heart thumped loudly when she handed the boarding pass and her driver's license to the security agent. The agent looked above her half glasses resting on her nostrils and squinted at Donna's face, and then looked at the driver's license again while Donna attempted to mask her fear of being recognized and wanted by police. She handed the license and boarding pass back to Donna and motioned her on through. She set her bag on the scanner belt and walked through the metal detector without pause and was home free. She swallowed hard as she gathered her bag and walked to the concourse and gate assigned to the airline flying to Jackson Hole. Her head felt light from the adrenalin rush and she stopped at a chocolate shop and bought a bag of chocolate-covered peanuts.

When she entered the gate in Concourse B, she looked for Tano seated in the waiting area. He wasn't there. She wanted to stay hidden from him if he was flying on the same plane. She planned to surprise him after they were in the air. She sat huddled near a group of elderly ladies with a travel agent to tour the Grand Tetons. She listened to them chatter among themselves and snickered while she watched each of them take a Dramamine tablet and chase it with bottled water.

"I'm staying with you until you board. By then it will be time for me to board at my gate." Tano held Holly's hand while they sat on stiff royal-blue upholstered chairs in the waiting area. "How about a coffee or something to drink? There's a coffee bar kind of place over there."

"Yes, a hot chocolate if they have it. I know it's warm out, but it sounds good today." Tano left and returned within a couple of minutes.

"Okay, now I'll be in Jackson tonight and tomorrow, and then Santa Barbara on Monday, Seattle on Wednesday and fly home on Friday. Will be home for a week. When do you think you will arrive?"

"Well, I don't want to be there until you're back. I don't want to stay there by myself yet. Besides I don't have a key or know how to get it in. So, I think I should plan on next Friday or Saturday. Does that sound okay? I'll call and text you with what's going on." She sipped the hot chocolate.

"The sooner the better. I'm going to miss you. I love having you there with me at the concerts."

"Janet can keep you occupied," Holly teased.

"Fuck no! I don't know if Rocky's bringing her along or not, but she's his problem. I'm hands off with that chick. Everything about her is fake."

"I'll miss you, too. I have so much to do to make the move to Boulder. Liberal, Kansas, is like another planet to me now."

The airline attendant announced that boarding would begin.

"Okay, baby. I love you. Think about me, sweetheart."

"I will. I love you. Give the audience what they want! See you in a week?" Tano walked with her until she boarded. He handed her carry-on bag to her. He patted her little bottom and she turned and hugged him around his neck again. He saw that her eyes were teary.

"Hey, it won't be long."

"I know. Bye. Can we talk tonight?" She reluctantly let go of him and held on to his hand, and finally took a few steps to board the plane.

"Sure, baby."

Holly was still dragging her feet. She turned and blew him a kiss. He pretended to catch it. She found her seat on the aisle next to a portly middle-aged, probably married, couple. She took her iPod and earbuds out of her purse to listen to music while the rest of the passengers boarded. She missed him so much already.

Tano hustled down the long corridor to his gate. Boarding had probably begun.

Donna watched and waited for Tano to show up. Boarding of the Jackson Hole plane had begun. As she waited in line, she continued to scan for him. Just before she stepped onto the plane, she saw his familiar silhouette approaching quickly. He was by himself. *Yay!* She saw him pause for a moment and take his phone out of his shirt pocket and put it to his ear and continue walking toward the gate. *Maybe he just saw the selfie of me and Trouble!* Donna snickered as she found her seat in the back. She stretched her thick short neck, trying to see over and around the entering passengers. *When this plane is off the ground, I'm gonna find him. He will be so surprised and happy to see me.* She continued to watch and wait for him. When the plane began to taxi, she suddenly realized that Tano must have been seated in first class. *That's okay. I'll find him. The chase is over.*

CHAPTER 39

Holly could feel the vibrating whir of the plane's engines and felt the slight jerk and then movement as the plane began to taxi. She realized that everything that had happened in the few days and even the last few moments were no longer in the present and had swiftly been transformed into memories. When the plane lifted into the air, she quietly said to herself, "I'm coming back. Bye, Tano."

The portly middle-aged man seated next to her said, "Did you say something, young lady?"

Holly nervously turned the silver bracelets on her left wrist. "No...well...yeah, just thinking out loud."

"Where ya headed?" The man had obviously lavished himself with a heavy splash of Old Spice.

"Liberal, Kansas. What about you?'

"Chicago. My son and three grandsons live there. He's a stockbroker...my son is. But what I really want to do is sample some of that deep-dish Chicago pizza that he brags about all the time." The man's wife, who was busy knitting something with blue and green yarn, smiled and nodded.

"Yeah, food is always his focus," the wife said, and she reached over and patted his round stomach. She was small with very short dark brown hair and large round black plastic rimmed glasses that gave her an owl-like expression.

"Hey, Darlene, you're gonna give this little lady a bad impression of me," he joked. "So Liberal, Kansas? What do you do there?"

"Well, I'm an energy analyst and I teach some ballet classes at the community college there. But I'm actually moving to Boulder very soon. Next week to be exact." She leaned forward to look out the side window next to the man's wife. The plane was surrounded by light blue sky above scattered white fluffs of clouds.

"Changing jobs?'

"No, my boyfriend is there." Holly had never really referred to Tano as her boyfriend before and was surprised to hear those words come out of her mouth. "But yes, I'll just change jobs or transfer within my company, if I can. Or if not, I may just try something new. Maybe open a ballet school."

The flight lasted a little over an hour. It had been a smooth flight. It seemed that they had just taken off when they began the descent to the Liberal Mid-American Regional Airport. "It was nice meeting you. Enjoy the Chicago pizza."

"Yes, now you take care there, young lady." The woman continued to knit but looked up for a second and smiled at Holly." Holly gave them a little wave as she grabbed her carry-on bag and disembarked from the plane.

The airport was small, and within minutes Holly had reached her car in the parking lot. She felt like she was on another planet. Just a few hours before she was kissing Tano at the Denver International Airport and now here she was in quiet Liberal, Kansas. She remembered that her gas gauge had showed that she needed to fill up when she had hurriedly left for Denver just a few days before. She stopped at a gas station a few blocks from home. While the tank was filling, she went inside to grab a bag of chips and a soda. While she was paying for the snacks, she happened to look up at a TV mounted high on the wall behind the store clerk. The sound was turned low, but the broadcast was close captioned and she read the words as they scrolled across the bottom of the screen.

"A passenger plane bound for Jackson Hole, Wyoming, from Denver, Colorado, has crashed about 60 miles north of Denver just a short time ago. Details are not yet available. Emergency crews have responded."

Holly's stomach lurched. Her heart sank and the blood rushed from her head. She felt like she would faint. She had to concentrate as she took each step to her car as she tried not to stumble. She gripped the steering wheel with numb hands to stop them from shaking. She tried to focus. She felt her chest heaving as she struggled to catch her breath. She tried to figure out what to do next. She couldn't think. She was suddenly nauseous and took a sip of the soda. *Maybe it was a mistake. Maybe there were two flights to Jackson Hole.* There was only one thing she could do. She tried to call him. His phone went directly to voice mail. She left a message.

"Tano, please call me! I've heard there was a plane crash! Please call me and let me know you're okay. Please! Please! As soon as you can!"

When she disconnected, she held the phone in both of her hands. It was her sole connection to him now and she couldn't make it ring. She suddenly realized that she was still sitting next to the gas pumps and somehow started the car and headed to her house, praying as she drove. *Please, God. Please, God. Don't let him be hurt or gone. Please, God. Help him if he needs it. Please save him. Please.*

She robotically walked to her front door, unlocked it, left it wide open, went into her bedroom, fell on the bed, still holding her phone. She turned on the TV in her bedroom, searched for a news station and googled "Denver plane crash" on her phone. The news feed on her phone indicated that there were some fatalities. *This is a bad dream. This isn't happening.* She laid her head on her pillow and covered her eyes with her forearm. Tears trickled from her eyes at first, and then in a steady stream. She dialed his phone number again. She listened to his voice message, just to hear his voice, but didn't leave another message.

It was nearly five p.m. when the television news station carried a story about the plane crash during its regular early evening broadcast.

"A passenger plane bound for Jackson Hole, Wyoming, from Denver, Colorado, crashed about sixty miles north of Denver, northwest of Fort Collins, about two hours ago. Initial reports confirm that there are fatalities. Survivors have been taken to the nearby hospital. Some are reported to be in critical condition, others with non-life-threatening injuries. It is reported that the plane experienced engine failure shortly after takeoff, and the pilot was attempting an emergency landing. There are conflicting reports that indicate that there may have been an unruly passenger on the plane but there is no indication that the behavior of the erratic passenger contributed to the crash."

Holly began to feel like there was a shred of hope. There were survivors. She had to believe that he was one of them. She dialed his number again. Still no answer. Maybe he was okay. Maybe he just couldn't answer. *Please, Tano. Hear me. Call me. I'm so afraid. Fate wouldn't allow us to find each other again and then separate us so quickly. I love you so much.* She sat up and her stomach began to wretch. She staggered into the bathroom and threw up although there was nothing in her stomach but the couple of sips of Dr Pepper she had drank at the gas station. She laid back down on the bed. She would be paralyzed until she heard news about him. A half hour later, the same news story repeated. She didn't even look at the TV, just listened to the words. Waiting and waiting.

At six p.m., her telephone rang. She jumped and her heart began to beat wildly. But when she looked at her phone, she saw that it was just her coworker Alexis. She probably just wanted to talk. She didn't answer. As soon as she put her phone down, it pinged. There was a text message. *Oh, jeez. Garth again.* In frustration, she tossed her phone to the end of bed with the unread text from Garth. Her heart was still racing and her hands shaking. She took deep breaths and tried to calm herself.

The phone rang again. She reached down toward the end of the bed and slowly picked it up. It was Tano! At least it was his phone!

"Hey, baby." Holly began to sob when she heard his voice. "I heard about the crash. I got your message. I'm okay. I'm here. I didn't get on the plane."

CHAPTER 40

"**B**aby, why are you crying? I'm fine."

"Tano—I don't know—I'm so relieved. Why did you wait so long to call me? Didn't you know that the plane had crashed? Didn't you think I would be worried and upset?"

"Oh, jeez. I guess I didn't think about that. Yeah, I heard it crashed on the TV in the waiting room. Sorry, Holly. What happened is that after you boarded your plane and I was walking back to my gate to board, I got a call from my brother, Jason, and he told me that my mom had just been rushed to Boulder Community Hospital because she was having chest pains and couldn't breathe. So I picked up my bag and left the airport and went straight to the hospital. I've been there all afternoon."

"Your phone. Didn't you have it? Didn't you see that I called and left a message?"

"Yeah, I had it but there was no signal in the hospital. I was waiting for news about Mom and I didn't know about the plane. I guess I wasn't thinking about you...well, that didn't sound right. You know what I mean."

Holly grimaced when she heard his last sentences and then paused to take a breath. *That was revealing. Let it go.*

"Holly? You still there?"

"Yes." Another long pause. "So what happened to your mom? Is she going to be all right?"

"She had a severe allergy attack and she couldn't breathe. Maybe from one of her medications. She's staying overnight at the hospital. She's feeling better."

"Oh, Tano," she hesitated for a moment trying to decide whether she should say it or not. "I love you and I was afraid I lost you. I just didn't know."

"I love you, too. It's okay, Holly. I'm here. I'm safe and I'm in one piece. But now I have to figure how to get to Jackson Hole by tomorrow."

"I wonder what happened on that flight. Have you heard anything?"

"No, only that there was a fatality, some injuries. The plane broke in half."

"Oh my God. It sounds like it could have been worse."

"Holly, I want you to come back. I want you to come with me to Jackson Hole."

Holly's heart leaped when she heard those words. "How would that happen so quickly?"

"I don't know yet. I'm going to talk to Rob about it now. I'll call you later. Everything is okay. Bye, baby."

"Okay, bye." Holly laid back down on the bed, looked at the ceiling, taking deep breaths. *Thank you, God.* It had been unlike her to lay in bed all afternoon. It was time to get up. She walked out to the mailbox, collected the mail, brought it in and sorted it into piles: bills, letters, and junk. She opened her back door to check on her tiny garden. It was looking droopy so she filled her black metal watering can that was hand-painted with purple and yellow pansies and gave her tomatoes and peppers a hefty drink of water. She picked some of the vegetables that were ready and laid them on the kitchen counter when she went into the house. She walked from room to room, not doing anything until she settled on emptying her carry-on bag.

The television had been on all afternoon. While she stood in her bedroom, putting things away, she heard a news broadcast. "Live from the scene of a plane crash near Fort Collins, this is Mary Shepard. A plane bound for Jackson Hole, Wyoming, from Denver crashed here early this afternoon. As you can see behind me, the plane broke in two. Miraculously, there has been one confirmed fatality thus far. Early reports are that the plane began to experience engine issues and the pilot attempted to return to DIA or to the closer Fort Collins airport when the plane went down in this meadow you see behind me. We interviewed a passenger as he left the hospital with his arm in a sling, who told us that the plane began to shudder, and a woman passenger became hysterical and screaming that her boyfriend was on the plane and she had to find him. She assaulted the flight attendants and an air marshal and refused to remain seated and belted. The plane landed hard on its wheels but broke apart. We will continue to follow this story as details emerge."

Holly washed the tomatoes and peppers and put them in her refrigerator. Her phone pinged. It was Garth again. *Might as well get this over with*. The day had already been stressful enough.

Holly, call me damn it. What do you think you're doing?

She dialed Garth's number. "Hey, Garth. So, what is it this time?" she said with evident annoyance.

"Damn it! Are you giving up everything for that low life? He's gonna hurt ya! He's gonna cheat! What about your future? Your job? What about Jared?"

"We've been over this already. What business is it of yours? Jared and I are through. It's time that I take a chance. Yeah, maybe risk it all. I don't care. He is worth it to me."

"What are Mom and Dad gonna say?"

"Nothing that could change my mind. I know in my heart that this is right. You have to stop. I know you think you're helping. Trust me and stop! Now!"

"It's no use talking to you. Don't come crying to me. Whatever! I'm done!" Garth hung up.

"Just be happy for me," Holly whispered out loud to no one. She knew that he was probably storming around his house, throwing things, cursing. He was always ready for a fight with that short temper. Their parents were so stoic and even tempered. She wondered how Garth became so high strung.

Two hours passed and night was falling. Holly sat on her couch waiting for Tano to call her when she leaned her head back and fell asleep. The emotional turmoil of the day had taken its toll. She was emotionally drained and physically exhausted. At around ten, Tano called her.

"Hey, Holly. Were you sleeping?"

Her voice was muffled and quiet. "Yeah, I must have dozed off."

"Well, good news! Rob chartered a private plane to get me to Jackson Hole by tomorrow afternoon. The guys are already there. But for you…" Tano paused before he continued. "Okay, get ready… he chartered a helicopter out of Kansas somewhere to fly you to Jefferson County Airport in Broomfield. Then we can fly together to Jackson Hole. So what do you think?"

"Really? A helicopter? Well, like when…where?" Holly's voice was shaking from surprise and apprehension.

"Okay, the helicopter is scheduled to land at Liberal airport tomorrow morning at nine. My flight to Jackson Hole is at noon. Out of Jeffco too. Can you make it? I'm counting on it."

Holly could hear in his voice that he was excited that he had found a way to be with her again. Of course, she would. A helicopter? Definitely, a new adventure.

"Yes, of course, I'll be there. Like…what do I pack?"

"Just a few things. You can fly home after Jackson or you can come with me for the next leg of this tour—out west. Get used to it, Holly. I'm going to want you to come with me sometimes."

Holly was thrilled to hear him speak a little about the future. Maybe he didn't expect their romance to be short lived. Their future was full of uncertainties. Their relationship was so new, yet so comfortable. She began to fold clothes for the trip and laid them in her carry-on bag. She walked into the bathroom and looked at her face in the mirror. Her cheeks were smeared with black mascara. Her eyes were red from crying and her complexion was colorless in the glare of the bathroom light. Fear had seized her for most of the afternoon and gripped her physically. She undressed, stepped into the shower. She stood under the stream of warm water, closed her eyes, and let the water wash over her head and trickle down in rivulets over her body. It tingled as it streamed over places where Tano had touched her. Her thoughts turned to him and to Jackson Hole. *He's okay. He's still here. Let the despair that I felt wash away.*

She emerged from the shower and wrapped herself in a fluffy pink bathrobe. She felt clean, brand new, energized. Now she could focus on getting ready to meet Tano the next day. She began to truly comprehend what he had said. A helicopter. Yep, a helicopter was going to fly her to Denver. She felt a twinge of apprehension and at the same time gratitude to Tano for making it happen. *I love him so much.*

CHAPTER 41

"Hi, Mom. Whatcha doing?"

Holly decided that it was time to have a conversation with her mom about the move to Boulder. Who knows what Garth had told her? She would be leaving for the airport soon to fly to Colorado to meet Tano. She could hear Reba McEntire ballads playing in the background in her mother's kitchen as she answered the call. When Liza listened to Reba, it meant that she was troubled about something.

"Oh, I just set some whole wheat bread dough to rise. I'm heading out to pick raspberries for jam in a little while. I think I'll throw some strawberries in with it this time. And you know, Dad and I are planning on building that chicken coop that we've talked about for years and you know I love those Araucana chickens—you know, with the light blue eggs..."

Holly interrupted her. "Mom, that's great but I know that Garth must have told you that I'm moving to Boulder. I want to be with Tano, Mom. And he wants me there. I can't say no to that."

"Well, honey, yes he did. What about your job? Your career? The house? Isn't it kind of soon?" Holly could hear her mother's apprehension as the pitch of her voice became higher with each word.

"I'll work those things out. I haven't had time to think about them. I'm flying in a helicopter, no less, from the airport here in Liberal in about an hour to meet him in Colorado, and then we are flying in a private plane to Jackson Hole, Wyoming, for Badge's next concert."

"A helicopter? A little plane? This is so unlike you, honey, to act so impulsively. You know how I worry."

"Yes, but I'm not worried at all. I know in my heart that it's right. I would regret it for the rest of my life if we drifted apart. I can't risk that."

"So, when is this move supposed to happen?"

"Next week. At least initially. I'll be back and forth for a while."

"What about your dad? Will you talk to him about it?"

"You tell him to trust me. I'll talk to him about it when I'm settled. And the same goes for Garth. He has to stop pestering me."

"You have a safe trip, honey, in that whirly bird. You know we love you and we worry. Let us know when you land." Liza's voice was even higher.

Holly walked through her house, checked all the windows to see that they were latched, watered her little garden again, picked up her bag, and locked the door behind her. The airport was a few minutes away but there was enough time to listen to Jason Aldean twice as he sang "Fly Over States." She turned the volume up and sang along until she arrived at the airport at eight thirty a.m. A navy blue and silver helicopter was parked on the tarmac—not a common site at Liberal Mid-American Regional Airport. She parked, grabbed her brown soft leather carry-on bag and walked into the terminal. She wasn't sure what or who to look for but immediately, a dark haired, very tan young man dressed in khaki clothes wearing aviator sunglasses, approached her and said, "Are you Holly Harris?"

"Yes." She expected he was the helicopter pilot but was cautious.

"You match the description I was given. I'm Roger Newman, your pilot to Broomfield this morning." He reached out and shook her hand. "I think the plan was for us to depart at nine a.m. but since you're here and you're my only passenger, are you ready to go?"

"Yes, let's do it."

She followed a step or two behind him as they walked toward the helicopter. He opened the cockpit door, set her bag on the floor and she climbed in. The step onto the foot plate was tall and Roger stood behind her with his hands held below her little behind in case she needed a boost. She seated herself in the front next to the pilot's seat.

"Here, you wear these." Roger handed a head set to Holly. "This bird is pretty noisy. We can communicate with these."

"Should I put them on now?"

"Yep, I'm going to start up momentarily." Holly slipped the headset on. In a moment she could feel vibration in the cab and hear a muffled whir from the helicopter blades turning over their heads. Roger asked air traffic control for clearance for takeoff. They continued to wait while the rotors developed sufficient speed for takeoff.

Suddenly, she felt the helicopter lift and the ground below them seemed to be instantly sucked away. Holly's stomach was in her throat and her hands gripped the armrests tightly. Watching the lift made her feel like they were being pulled from earth, and for a moment she felt a little vertigo and motion sickness. After the helicopter began a level-forward progression, Holly's nerves settled and she released her grip.

"Are you okay over there?"

"Yeah, it just happened so fast."

The view through the glass that surrounded them was panoramic. The altitude of the helicopter was only a few thousand feet and when she first dared to look down, she could see pivot sprinklers, crops, livestock, swing sets in yards, vegetable gardens and treetops. She thought she saw people waving at them.

"We're flying into Colorado now. See the herd of antelope below?"

Holly looked through the side window and below them she saw the antelope sprint away from the sound above them. She held the Badge pendant that she wore in her right hand and moved it from side to side on the silver chain. The sun was shining on Holly's hair through the glass that enclosed them and it emitted a slight fragrance from her shampoo that didn't go unnoticed by Roger. The sky was clear vibrant crystal blue. A few billows of white clouds streamed above them like balls of cotton. Standing tall in the distance, Holly could see the Rocky Mountains beginning to appear. *I'm getting closer to him. I feel it.*

While Holly was in flight, Tano arrived at the Jefferson County Airport to wait for her. He had some time and thought he should check in with Anthony at Tumbleweed.

"Hey, Anthony. How's it going there?"

"Man, Tano, you dodged a bullet. That plane going down? "

"Yeah, I was damn lucky. I haven't heard much about what happened. You know, my mom gave us a scare, so I didn't fly and now I'm at Jeffco getting ready to fly to Jackson after Holly gets here. Rob sent a helicopter for her. She was pretty shook up when she heard about the crash."

"Well, you wouldn't believe it. You know there was one fatality in that crash? You just wouldn't believe who it was." Anthony paused before he continued. "It was Donna! That crazy ass Donna! Did you know she was flying?"

"No, man, I never boarded. I waited with Holly and then got the call about my mom and left. I didn't see her. Are you sure?"

"Oh, yeah, and that's not all. TV news got ahold of a video that a passenger took of Donna on the plane, just going ape shit. Kicking, hitting and screaming while they tried to get her to sit in her seat while the plane was in trouble. You could probably go to the news station website and see it."

"Man, that chick was going to self-destruct. Jesus, I don't know if I want to see that. Well, that stalking is over with."

"Yesterday, she sent an email to Tumbleweed with a photo of her and some guy in bed. Evidently for you. To make you jealous."

"She was at the Fiddler's concert and tried to jump on stage with me, too." He paused while he processed the news of Donna's death. "How's it going there?"

"It's good. Been steady. That new tequila that we brought in for the Cactus Moon cocktail has been real popular."

"Hey, I'll be gone until the end of this week. California. Then home for a while and spend some time at the bar."

"Okay, man, take it easy."

Tano held his phone checking messages and Facebook. Curiosity got the best of him and he opened the Tumbleweed e-mail to see the message from Donna. He squinted as he looked at the photo she had sent, as if it hurt his eyes. There she was laying on a pillow next to a sloppy looking guy, still wearing that black curly wig with that heinous grin on her face. Under the photo, she had written, "Don't be mad! I saved some for you. XOXOXOX DM"

"Oh, man. So out there. Demented," he muttered under his breath. He heard the doors to the terminal open and saw the shape of Holly walking toward him, her long copper spiral locks bouncing slightly with each step. She wore a black tank top, black jeans, a belt with a turquoise buckle, a teal-colored handkerchief around her neck and tan boots. He whispered to himself, "Here Comes My Girl," the title of a Tom Petty song in their setlist. He stood and took a few steps toward her.

When she saw him, she walked a little faster, and shoved the carry-on bag that hung on her shoulder behind her and threw her arms around his neck. He buried his nose in her hair as they embraced. He smelled the familiar lily of the valley scent. Holly clung tightly to his neck and wouldn't let go. Tano managed to pry her away from his chest to say hello with a kiss. She kissed him with an intensity that he didn't expect. She had tears in her eyes when he looked at her face.

"Hey, I'm here. I'm not going anywhere. Except with you."

Holly managed to smile. Seeing him again was overwhelming after the agony she experienced the day before when she thought he was gone forever.

"Come on. Let's check in. You been to Jackson Hole before, sweetie?"

"No, but I am now. I know that it's beautiful there."

"Are you nervous about flying there?"

"No, I'm with you. I'm not afraid."

They boarded the private plane to Jackson Hole. The flight was unremarkable except for a slight turbulence as the plane flew over the Continental Divide. Holly held Tano's hand for the entire flight and would not let go. Tano consciously decided not to mention Donna's demise yet and let her savor their reunion. The flight was relatively short – about an hour and a half.

Rob had arranged for a shuttle at Jackson Hole Airport to bring them to Hotel Jackson, where the band would stay. When she saw them, Holly was in awe of the Grand Tetons that seemed to spontaneously spring up from the earth. Tano smiled as he heard her gasp at her first view of the them. There was a light dusting of snow on the mountain tops. A little hint of winter that would soon return.

Within minutes they arrived at Hotel Jackson. It was a big, elegant and rustic stone building within walking distance to historic Town Square that they passed through on the way. Tano pointed to the Pink Garter Theatre where the Badge concert would take place. Holly was quiet, taking in the ambience of the place.

When they arrived, Tano went to the hospitality desk to check them in. Rob had booked suites for each of the Badge members..

"Tano, I have to head to the restroom," Holly said. "I didn't want to go on the plane. I'll be right back. Wait here?"

"Of course, baby," he said, as he continued the check in. The hotel clerk gave him two key cards. He turned to sit on one of the buff-colored leather chairs by the two-story river rock fireplace in the expansive lobby when someone came up behind him and tugged at his arm. He wriggled out of the grasp and turned to see Janet standing there. She reached up with the arm that wasn't in a sling, hugged him around his waist, and awkwardly wrapped her leg around him and tried to kiss him. He twisted his torso squirming away from the grip of her leg.

"Oh, it's you, Janet. So...what's the deal?"

"Oh, Tano. I'm so glad to see you. I'm so happy that you're here. You know—that plane crash and everything. You would have been with us in the van, if it wasn't for that Hicktown hillbilly. But it's okay. You're here. In one piece. And alone. Tano, I have to say that I'm getting tired of Rocky." She continued to blurt everything. "I want us to get back together again. What do ya say, Tano? You and me?

We were good together, right?" She pulled herself close to him with her one good arm and tried to kiss him again. Tano smelled strong alcohol on her breath and her intense perfume which stung his nose. Neither of them noticed that Holly was quickly approaching.

"Hey, we only went out a couple of times. There is no 'us.' Get over it."

Holly approached and yanked on Janet's high ponytail. "Hello, Janet." Holly's eyes narrowed as she spoke to her. "Do you need help finding your room or something?" Holly was angry when she saw Janet hanging on Tano but wasn't surprised and kept her cool.

"Let go, bitch! Tano! Why is she here? I thought you were done with that homeless Okie hitchhiker!" She turned to Holly. "Don't you have to round up some cattle or slop some hogs or something?"

Holly laughed which infuriated Janet even more. "You're the only hog around here." Janet opened her mouth but before she could speak, Tano said, "Holly's moving in with me. She's my girl. We're heading up to our suite now. Get on back to your room with Rocky."

"Well, if you just need a house sitter, it sounds like a good situation for a homeless hitchhiker." Janet was enraged that Tano had rejected her again, that Holly was there, and that she was still stuck with Rocky. She stormed through the lobby to the lounge and seated herself on a tall bar stool to sulk. "Give me a shot of Patron." After a few minutes, "Another shot please." After the second shot, she began to convince herself that she still had a chance with Tano. "He will positively be mine," she spoke out loud to herself.

The bartender heard her speak and said, "I'm sorry. Were you talking to me?"

"No, just thinking out loud. But could I get a couple of limes and another shot?" "Silver Springs" by Fleetwood Mac played quietly in the bar.

CHAPTER 42

"**S**o, let's say you and I go get reacquainted," Tano said with a smile.

"I've only been gone for a day." Holly laughed.

"Too long."

The Jackson suite had been reserved for them. It was spacious, with leather furnishings and sleek, clean modern lines, yet the Old West ambience was retained with weathered gray barnwood on select walls. The carpets were cream colored. A horizontal gas fireplace that had been installed in the wall was silently burning. A black marble two-top bar stood in the corner of the room with a mini fridge that was stocked with various liquors. The pristine white and tan bathroom suite contained a deep soaking tub. The paintings on the wall were an eclectic collection of western and modern art. Rustic elegance would be the best words to describe the suite. When Tano entered the room, he dropped their bags and headed straight for the carefully made bed and flopped down on his back.

"Come here, sweet stuff." He kicked off his brown and white cowboy boots. Holly kicked off her boots and lay down next to him, throwing her leg over his and resting her head on his hard-muscular shoulder. He reached across her and tugged at her waist and pulled her on top of him. Long strands of her copper hair fell over his face. He took his hand and moved the tresses behind her back. The kisses began lightly but quickly developed into full-blown foreplay. Shirts slid off over their heads, next the jeans, and they wriggled out of the rest of the clothes. Daylight filtered through the sheer layer of curtains, casting a foggy afterglow on the afternoon interlude.

"So, I think we reconnected?" Tano whispered to Holly as she rolled off of him.

Holly laughed. "I guess that's one way to put it." She laid on her back with her arm resting on her forehead. Her gaze moved across the ceiling. "Tano, you have to know that I made myself sick with worry about you and the plane crash. My thoughts just ran all over the place. I didn't know what happened...."

"Hey," Tano interrupted her. "Hey, I'm right here. No need to relive yesterday." He held her tightly and then inhaled deeply and sighed. "I do have to tell you something though. I wanted to spend some time with you alone before I mentioned this kind of news."

Holly turned to look at him and immediately furrowed her brow with concern. "Okay?"

"Well, you know that there was one fatality in the plane crash."

"Yeah?"

"Well, Anthony told me today that it was on the news that it was Donna. Seriously. Donna. She was on that plane."

Holly gasped. "Really? How?"

"I don't really know, but I guess she created a big ruckus when the plane started to have problems. Someone videoed the scene. Anthony saw it on TV. She was kicking and screaming and wouldn't strap into her seat. He says that it's probably on one of the news sites. Do you want to see it?"

"No. I can only imagine. I don't want that image to even enter my brain. Did you know she was on that plane? So, she's gone. It feels surreal."

"No, I left while the plane was boarding, and I didn't see her. She was such a mess. She was heading toward destruction anyway. I don't know if she could be helped. She was a threat to both of us and the band." Tano couldn't decide whether he should show her the photo of Donna and the scruffy guy in bed that she sent to Tumbleweed. He decided to let it go. Maybe someday. She wouldn't want to let that image into her brain either.

Holly lay silent for a minute thinking about the news. "I guess I don't know what to say. It's such a shock and a relief at the same time. I'm sure she was responsible for that random shooting that went on. It was only a matter of time before somebody got hurt—well, other than Janet." Holly lay silent for a minute thinking about the news. "So, I guess you have a sound check and rehearsal this afternoon?"

"Yeah, at the Pink Garter at around three. Oh, jeez." Tano looked at his phone. "It's two now. Are you hungry? Want to order room service?" He handed Holly a menu from the nightstand.

"I'm good. Rob will have stuff to eat at the venue, right? I'll just snack there."

Tano jumped into the shower and beckoned Holly to join him, which she eagerly did.

"Come closer, sweet stuff, and let me clean you up." Tano laughed and rubbed shower gel between his hands and proceeded to rub suds all over her body, and she proceeded to do the same to Tano with slow rotating movements of her hands.

"Turn around. Let me rub your back," Holly said.

"No, I like the front-to-front contact best." They stood under the rain showerhead and embraced while the water trickled over them like a tropical stream sensually rinsing the lightly fragranced shower gel away.

"This is the best shower I've had in a long time. It must be the rain showerhead." Tano laughed. "But we gotta book it soon." Tano got out of the shower while Holly rinsed her long hair. Tano dressed in a black western shirt, rolled up the sleeves, faded blue jeans and the brown and white cowboy boots, and waited for Holly.

"This long red hair takes a while to dry. Oh, Tano, you're gonna knock the ladies dead tonight. You look so good."

"Your hair looks great that way. Natural." He humbly didn't respond to her compliment.

Holly and Tano met Rob in the lobby. The roadies and sound techs were already at the venue setting up with the Pink Garter production crew. It was a block away from the hotel and they decided to walk. Janet was missing from the entourage. Tano didn't ask about her, but he overheard Rocky sigh and say to Rob, "Janet will probably come later. She got hammered in the lounge already and I had to come down and get her. She's sleeping it off now."

No one responded but they wanted to say, "Man, you need to break up with that chick or get her some help or something." They didn't think he wanted to hear what he already knew.

The Pink Garter Theatre was a former movie theater converted into a small intimate venue with seating for 420 people. Much smaller than the venues that big name bands like Badge were used to playing but it was on the way to California and Rob was a friend of the owners of the Hotel Jackson who asked if Badge would perform in Jackson Hole.

Tano held Holly's hand as they walked. "Tano, we need to come back here again and spend some time in the Tetons. They are so majestic and beautiful. We could hike. Get some great photos, too." Holly was reminded to take photos and pulled her phone out of her purse and took some of the buildings in the Town Square and of the Tetons in the background.

"Sure, we will. Sorry this is a quick trip this time. Yep, we will be back."

When they entered the theater, Holly was enchanted by its charm. It reminded her of something out of a black and white 1940s movie. The raised curved stage wrapped around the front of the venue. The lighting techs were already experimenting with the colored flood, wash and back lights. Greens, reds, blues, purples, and pure white. The sound equipment and drums were in place and the guitar techs were finishing tuning the guitars.

Tano and Holly sat down in front row seats. "Jeez, I don't usually get to see the stage from this perspective. Looks great."

For the rest of the afternoon, Holly watched the rehearsal. The setlist would be the same as the Denver concert, but Grand Funk Railroad's "We're an American Band" would end the set. Before the doors opened and the band leaped onto the stage, Rob had arranged for some light catering and Macallan scotch to be delivered. Grilled steelhead trout, Panzanella salad, and meats and cheeses prepared by a local caterer. The band had complained that the food he had ordered recently was too heavy before the performances and it didn't sit well with the traditional shots of scotch. Holly and Tano each grabbed plates of food and bottles of water.

The band members downed the three shots of the scotch and trotted out onstage. The concert began at seven. The songs performed were much the same as the Denver concert. There hadn't been time to change the setlist. The crowd was on their feet all night, really getting into the music which was performed so closely to them. The stage lighting was phenomenal and gave every song some color. Janet never made an appearance, much to Holly's relief.

"This is a great little venue. Badge should make it a regular stop," Tano said as he emerged from the stage. His hair was damp and curly, and Holly could see perspiration glistening on his chest. While he hugged her, she reached up to touch the wavy hair that rested on the back of his collar. The roadies loaded the equipment. The entourage would be leaving for California early in the morning. And Tano was riding with them.

Tano and Holly walked back to the hotel in the crisp fall air. "I'm leaving early. I'll arrange for the shuttle to take you to the airport. I won't be there to tell you goodbye. What time is your flight to Denver?"

"It's at nine thirty. Then I catch the plane to Liberal at noon. And I'll be flying. You'll be driving."

It had already been a long day. A helicopter flight, a charter plane flight, the encounter with Janet, the concert, the news about Donna. Tano and Holly snuggled for a few minutes before quickly falling asleep. It was morning too soon. They showered, packed, and Holly walked Tano to the van. Janet was sitting in the front seat of the van holding her head.

"Bye, baby. I'll call and text every day. I'll be home on Friday.." Tano put his arms around Holly's waist and pulled her close. "When do you think you'll be in Boulder?"

"I think I can time it so that I arrive on Friday, too. When you get there."

"Awesome."

"Travel safe, Tano. Love and prayers."

"You, too, baby."

Holly watched while they drove away. Tano reached his arm out of the window to wave to her.

CHAPTER 43

"Hi, baby, they just dropped me off at Jeffco a few seconds ago to pick up the Porsche. I'm heading to Boulder now. Just passed the windmills by Rocky Flats. Should be home in about a half hour."

"I'm just exiting on to US 36 from the Interstate so I'm probably fifteen to twenty minutes behind you. I'm excited to see you," Holly gushed. *Jeez, I sound like a twelve-year-old.*

"Me, too. See you soon. Hey, drive safe."

Several days had passed since Holly and Tano departed Jackson Hole. While Badge was performing at various venues in California, Holly began to pack things. She took a leave from her job, asked a neighbor to check on her house and to pick the few vegetables left in her garden. With great optimism and hope she began to load her Jeep. Before she left, she walked through the house once more when she heard a light *tap, tap* on her front door.

"Jared? What...what are you doing here?" Holly gasped when she saw him. Jared stood at the door with his hands in his pockets, looking at the ground until he heard her voice.

"Hey, Holly. Garth told me that you're moving to Boulder. I guess I caught you just in time. I didn't know it would be this soon."

"Yes, I'm leaving real soon. Today."

"To be with him?" Jared mumbled the words.

"Yes. He asked me."

"Well, I had to come by. I have to ask you. I need to ask you one more time. I hoped you had that rock star out of your system by now and let go of whatever happened between you. I know that I could give you a happy, secure life. I know that we belong together. Can you picture a life with me? Will you consider marrying me?" He reached into the pocket of his button-down shirt and held the unopened box containing the engagement ring in his hand.

Holly was stunned that he came to propose to her again. She looked at his sagging blue eyes and sad face. He seemed like he was shrinking before her eyes and suddenly she felt sympathy for him. She was breaking his heart as he stood there, and there was nothing she could do to stop it. No matter what he offered her or how much he loved her, she could never let go of her feelings for Tano. Never. There was no substitute.

"Jared. You know what my answer is. Tano wants to be with me and me with him. I don't know what the future holds for us. I know this sounds corny, but the right girl is out there for you. Someone who would be grateful for everything you have to offer her and for the man you are. It's just not me. I'm sorry. My answer is no."

This time Jared didn't abruptly leave and pretend that her answer didn't matter. He reached for her and gently hugged her close like he would never let her go. Holly could feel the heat from his flushed cheek against hers. Finally, he pulled away and while he fought to keep his eyes from welling with tears, he quietly said, "Okay. I know. Go be with him. Maybe we can keep in touch?"

"Yes, maybe." Holly knew that wouldn't be a good idea. The break from him had to be clean and final. She didn't want to let him think he had a chance with her. "Bye, Jared."

Jared walked to the door, turned and looked at her one more time, raised his right hand and bid her goodbye. Holly stood by the door and watched him drive away. She sighed deeply. But now it was time to go.

As Tano drove up Boulder Canyon, he felt relief that he would be home to relax for a while with his lady. At the same time, he was troubled by something he had done in Santa Barbara. When the concert at the Santa Barbara Bowl was over, Tano began to drink shots of whiskey. One right after the other. Like he didn't know what else to do without Holly there. He sat on a low couch in the corner of the hospitality room drinking as he felt the alcohol gradually dull his senses. A local radio station had awarded a couple of backstage passes to its listeners. One of the two young women winners immediately homed in on Tano and sat down beside him on the couch. She was in her twenties, wearing a red spandex dress that accented her curves, with long dark hair and heavily made-up brown eyes.

"Hi, Tano. I'm Krystal—with a K. I won tickets to come back here and meet you guys."

Tano, who was already feeling a strong buzz, squinted at her through his heavy eyelids. "Yeah, well nice to meet ya."

Krystal moved close enough to him that her breast was touching his left arm and placed her hand on his thigh inches from his crotch, teasing him. Her face was inches from his. She leaned close to his ear and whispered, "I'm your biggest fan. And I have a way to let you know that I mean it."

Tano pulled his face away and looked directly at her. "Ya do, huh?"

Krystal leaned in closer. Her hand moved up his leg even further convincing him that she was a serious fan. Tano could feel her breath on his mouth when she slowly and gently touched her tongue on his lips. He knew that his resistance, if any, was fading. "How about you and me go someplace else?" she softly said.

"Yeah, how about it? Let's go. Where to?"

"I'm staying at the Hotel California."

"Well, ain't that a coincidence. Me, too." Krystal already knew that Badge was staying there.

Janet had been standing in the corner of the room, witnessing the intense exchange between Tano and Krystal, scowling and growling under her breath, "Not again. When do I get you back?" When they left the room, arms around each other, Janet was fuming and in her usual nasty way, turned on Rocky. "Let's go. I'm tired of this place. I mean it—I want to go. Now!"

What happened in the room at the Hotel California was a blur to Tano. He was thoroughly drunk. He remembered that she felt unfamiliar but good, and that she had smoke on her breath, usually a turnoff to him, that he ignored. He remembered her name but her face, which had been so close to his, was fuzzy. He remembered waking to see the tatoo of a peacock on her back that spanned between her shoulder blades as she slept. Him hooking up with someone, anyone, was part of his pattern and he freely admitted it. But for the first time, he was in love. With Holly. At least he thought so. And for the first time, he felt some guilt and regret. How did he allow himself to do it again? It meant nothing. It was just momentary physical pleasure. Could he change? He would have to let it go. Holly must never find out. He didn't ever want to hurt or disappoint her. She was so genuine.

As he drove, he was listening to a Sirius country station. A song played that he had never heard before, "Craving You" sung by Thomas Rhett, with lyrics Tano could have written himself. When he approached his house, he saw that the windows Donna had shot out had been replaced but the bullet holes in the siding still needed to be patched. Contractors had installed an unattractive temporary aluminum front door while the custom door was on order. He clicked the garage door opener and drove inside. Before he got out, he sat in the car checking text and phone messages. Just as he clicked the remote to close the garage door, he saw in his peripheral vision the shadow of a person standing there in the garage next to his car door!

When he turned to look, he couldn't believe his eyes. Janet was looming there, her arm still in a sling, puffy faced, reeking of perfume and alcohol when he rolled the window down a crack.

"Janet, what the fuck!"

"Hi, Tano, I Ubered here to surprise you when you got home. I've been waiting for you. You know, I came home a couple of days ago." She spoke cheerily and was totally unphased by Tano's negative reaction.

"Rocky told you to leave in Santa Barbara. And I want you to leave here now, too! Move, Janet, so I can open my car door, damn it." Janet stepped back. When Tano got out of the car, she followed him into the house.

"Okay, I'm getting an Uber to pick you up right away! Holly's on her way here. She doesn't want you here and neither do I." He checked his phone for the Uber app and then began to input the information for a pickup.

"Oh, Tano, but if you just needed a house sitter, you could have asked me."

"Janet. Don't you get it? I don't want you. I want you to leave! I don't want to see you again!"

Janet's eyes bulged with anger. "Well, maybe this will change your mind." She pulled a pistol out of the sling she was wearing and pointed it at Tano, who was standing about five feet away from her.

Tano was stunned and felt a surge of adrenalin, but at the same time he had to keep his wits about him before she did something stupid. Instead of backing away from her, he stepped up closer to her. Her eyes grew bigger with surprise, but she continued to point the gun.

"Okay, Janet, maybe I should reconsider."

When he was standing about a foot away from her, he smiled at her. And then in one swift movement, he lifted his arm and knocked the gun out of her hand. It slid across the wood floor and under a side table. He shoved her and she fell hard into a cushiony chair behind her.

"Don't you ever show your face near me again. I should call the police and have your ass thrown in jail. But I don't want to deal with you anymore. Now, get up. Go out on the front porch and wait for the Uber." He looked at his phone. "They just messaged me that they are on their way to pick your sorry ass up."

Janet recoiled in horror. "You can't mean it! You and I...we had a good thing. I wasn't really going to shoot you. I was just playing around." She began to sob uncontrollably. "I'm so sorry. Tano, please. Forgive me."

Tano grabbed her by the slingless arm, tugged her hulking body out of the chair, and swiftly walked her to the front door, opened it, and shoved her out on to the front porch.

"You wait for Uber here, and then you get the hell off of my property!" He slammed the door, sat down on the leather couch that faced the door, his head pounding from blood rushing to his head and his heart racing with anger. *What if she had shot me! What if Holly had walked in on this! Why does this stuff keep happening?*

After about five minutes, he stood and looked out the window to see that Janet was gone. Another episode with a crazy stalker was over. Holly was on her way and she would make it all better. He reached under the end table and retrieved the gun that had slid under it and stuffed it in a drawer in a sofa table under some papers.

A half hour had passed since Janet left. Tano thought Holly would have been there sooner. He turned on some music, carried his bag upstairs, no longer paralyzed by the events that had just transpired. Within minutes, he heard Holly at the front door, and he rushed down the stairs. There she was, standing there. A beautiful girl with a big smile. She dropped her bag and they embraced. He lifted her off her feet, kissed her on her neck, and then carried her over the threshold and into the house.

"That was so unexpected!" she said. "I'm so happy to be here. With you."

"Me, too." He carried her over to the couch and sat down next to her and kissed her deeply. She pulled away for a second to speak.

"I would have been here sooner, but there was some kind of an accident down the canyon about a half mile away. Police had the road blocked. It looked like somebody was hit by a car. Like a pedestrian. I only got a glimpse cuz I really didn't want to look, but whoever it was, it looked like Janet. Big girl laying on the ground. Blond ponytail. Arms waving wildly. Weird, huh?"

Tano didn't respond. His blood ran cold for a second, but it wouldn't last with that copper-haired beauty sitting just inches away. "All that matters is that you're here with me now. Girl from yesterday, I think I have a bottle of champagne. Let's celebrate." Tano hugged her quickly and walked into the kitchen and selected two fluted champagne glasses and pulled the champagne out of the wine cooler. *Pop!* The champagne cork popped just as Holly's phone pinged with a message.

"Probably Garth again." Holly pulled her phone out of the back pocket of her jeans. She scrolled through her messages, stood up and tried to take a step, but all of the blood had left her face, and then just as quickly reversed and surged to the top of her head leaving her face at first ghostly white and then flushed. Tano, unaware that something was happening, began to walk toward her carrying a champagne glass in each hand.

"What? What happened? Holly? What is it?" he said when he saw her face and that she was shaking slightly.

Holly couldn't take her eyes off of the phone. "Janet." Her soft voice quivered. "Janet messaged me. Two photos of you and a woman. Kissing. And walking together. Arm and arm. What is this? Who is this?"

"Let me see. She's just playing games as usual." Tano, in his drunken state, had been unaware that Janet had seen him with Krystal with a K and taken photos, too. Janet must have messaged Holly with those photos as revenge when he shoved her out the door. *Oh, shit*, he thought.

Holly held up her phone. Yes, it was Krystal with a K and him in the hospitality room. Her eyes were fixed on his face as he looked at the photos. She unconsciously held the badge pendant in her left hand. He was still holding the glasses of champagne.

"It looks worse than it was." His stomach turned. He set the glasses down and tried to reach for Holly. She stepped back.

"Oh, really? So how was it then?" Her voice was still quiet but shaking with anger and fear.

"Look, Holly. I'm sorry. I didn't mean for it to happen. I had too much to drink. I was really hammered. I know it sounds like excuses. I love you. I wasn't thinking. Just acting like I used to. If you had never found out, nothing about today would have changed." After he said that, he realized that the more he spoke, the worse it had become.

"No, nothing would have changed. I would still be a fool but just not know it yet. A joke. A plaything, nothing more than an Oklahoma country girl that you left on a dirt road main street five years ago. A dumb believer in a fairy tale." She didn't raise her voice but the emotions she was feeling were obvious in her words.

Tano reached for her again. She pushed him away and walked toward the door.

"What are you doing? You can't leave. Stay. We can work this out. It was nothing," Tano pleaded.

Holly's hand was on the handle of the aluminum storm door. She turned to look at Tano. She still loved him just as much as she had when he carried her through the doorway just minutes before. She was so hurt. She had trusted him. And she couldn't bear the thought of being without him.

"Holly, I came to Oklahoma to find you. Don't you think that you mean anything to me?"

"Maybe I meant something, but I guess not enough. You must have been disappointed." Holly didn't want to say anything more. She opened the door and stood on the front porch looking out at the beautiful mountainscape in front of her. Taking it in—maybe for the last time.

"Holly? Come in, please. Don't throw it all away."

Holly had shut down. She sat on the front step and quietly sobbed with her head in her hands. Tano sat on the couch that faced the door and watched her and waited. He knew that she needed for him not to hover. After a few minutes, she simply stood, wiped the tears from her cheeks with both hands. She didn't take a step, just turned and looked toward the house. Tano took it as a sign that she was coming back. He opened the door and stood on the front porch and waited. She took a few slow steps toward him. When she was standing inches from him, Tano was stunned when she squinted her eyes, pushed her hand hard into his chest and shouted, "You're nothing but a no-good cheating bastard and I'm out of here!" She grabbed the bag that she had left on the porch and stormed off to her car. Tano was frozen momentarily, standing there, watching her, stunned by the outburst from the gentle girl he thought he knew.

Holly opened the car door, threw her bag in the back seat. Before she got in and slammed the door, she reached up to her neck and tore the Badge necklace from her neck and threw it on the ground and started the car. Tano hurried after her, shouting, "Holly? Hey! What are you doing, man?" He had never felt so helpless before. When he reached her car, he put his hand on the door handle to open it just as she slammed the car in reverse, throwing him to the ground. The tires squealed as the car lurched forward when she pulled away. She could see him getting up from the hard ground in her rearview mirror. She had no idea where she was going, except away from him. She felt like she had been turned inside out. Her hands were shaking. Her throat ached. Despite the rage that was consuming her, she could feel her heart breaking, its pieces lodging in her aching throat.

The country station she was tuned into quietly played, "Strawberry Wine," a favorite of hers. It reminded her of her roots and the memory of the dirt road main street where they had said goodbye five years ago. Tano was no longer visible in her rearview mirror. No matter—a river of tears blurred her vision. She already missed him, but it was time to focus on the road ahead, away from him, wherever it would lead. Her trusting heart was broken.

CHAPTER 44

Tano pushed himself up from the ground. "Holly! Don't!" He began to shout but his voice trailed off. He knew she couldn't hear him. He brushed the gritty dirt off of the heel of his hand and the back of his jeans as he watched her drive away until he could no longer see her car. He ran his right hand through his dark wavy hair and rested it on his chin and closed his eyes reliving the last few minutes that had destroyed a good thing. *How will I ever be able to fix this? Should I even try?*

He began to walk down the sloping driveway to the canyon road and then he ran. He didn't know why. Maybe she changed her mind and would be waiting for him there. When he reached the highway and looked toward the east, he could see brake lights from a line of cars and the rotating red lights from emergency vehicles from the accident that Holly had told him about. He didn't care if it was that fucking Janet laying in the road down there. She had wrecked everything with her interference. With those damn photos. But he knew deep inside that he ruined it. He had messed up. Messed up badly. He knew that her car was there in that traffic jam. He couldn't reach her. Even if he could, he knew that she didn't want to see him. He turned and began a slow walk up the sloping driveway to his house, hands in his pockets looking at the ground. When he reached the top of the driveway in front of the house, he noticed a shimmering object on the ground. He stooped to pick it up. It was the necklace with the silver Badge pendant that he had custom made for Holly. The chain was broken. He held the shiny silver strand in his hand for a moment and blinked hard and put it in his pocket. He had found her somehow and he lost her already.

When Tano reached the house, he locked the front door, opened the garage door and started the blue 1968 Corvette convertible, put the top down, and shot down the driveway. He turned west on Boulder Canyon Drive. He had a destination in mind and hit the accelerator. The canyon road was winding with sharp hairpin curves. Tano didn't slow for any of them, not giving a thought to his own safety. He zipped in and out of traffic, passing cars, giving it the gas all the way as the mountain road climbed. He needed to drive. He needed to move. He needed to be aggressive. He was pissed off and at the same time, he was sad and full of regret. New and unsettling emotions for him.

A little dive bar, the Canyon Hideaway, on the outskirts of the small trendy mountain town of Nederland, fifteen miles from Boulder, was his destination. He stood in the doorway of the bar for a moment, letting his eyes adjust to the darkness inside. He approached the bar which was lit only by the soft blue neon light of a Budweiser sign. Just like he wanted it to be. The entire bar, tables, chairs, and walls were a nondescript dark brown—probably from years of smoking customers before the statewide smoking ban. The bar top was sticky from several layers of smoke and varnish. There were several tables of college-age men and women drinking beer. One young couple was closely dancing in a corner of the room barely visible in the darkness. Four bearded mountain men were playing pool and cursing at each other.

"Hey, how are ya? What can I get for ya?" asked a skinny college-age bartender in a nasally voice. He had a scraggly bearded face and a tatoo of a pirate on his scrawny forearm.

Tano looked up at the neon Budweiser sign. "Bud, I guess. A tall one."

"Sure thing." He turned and filled a pilsner glass with beer from a tap and included a hefty layer of foam on the top. No matter to Tano. He had chosen the Canyon Hideaway because it was exactly that—a hideaway. He needed to think. Even with all of the success and excitement that had filled his life—the music-award nominations, the concerts, the songs, Tumbleweed—none of that mattered tonight. There was only one thought on his mind. Holly. And as much as he wanted to revel in the awesome time they had together and how he had fallen in love with her, he could only think of the last few moments he had had with her. Her excitement to have arrived in Boulder to be with him dissolved into sudden shock and pain on her face right before his eyes. And the tears. Her leaving him in the dust when she drove off. The broken necklace on the ground. He could still feel the thump on his chest when she had shoved him away. Country music played softly in the bar. "Between an Old Memory and Me," huskily sung by Travis Tritt, taunted Tano with the lyrics.

"Tano? Ben Montano?" said a raspy voice next to him. When Tano turned, he saw a woman standing there. She looked familiar but he wasn't sure who she was.

"Yeah?" His handsome face looked puzzled. He simply didn't recognize her. She was in her early thirties with chin-length blonde hair, one side clipped back behind her ear with a glittery gold barrette. Even in the darkness of the bar, Tano could see she wore heavy face makeup because it reflected in the dim Budweiser lighting and gave her a harsh look. She was wearing a red T-shirt tied at her waist, which hung over the top of her tight jean shorts. She wore gaudy rings with fake colored jewels on several of her fingers.

"It's me. Remember? Scarlet. Scarlet Patton. From Boulder High. I was on the cheerleader squad when you played football. Remember? We had a date once. Well, kind of." She snickered to herself. The "date" was actually a romp in his black Ford pickup after a football game.

"Oh, yeah." He suddenly remembered why she seemed familiar. A blurry memory of being with her once began to return in his mind. It appeared that life had been hard on her already. "What have you been doing?"

"I could ask you the same thing. What are you doing in this dive when you're a rock star and you own that fancy ass bar in Boulder?" As much as she tried, she couldn't get him to smile.

"I wanted a beer in a place where I could be alone tonight. So, what are you doing here?"

"Sounds heavy," she said, referring to Tano's response. "Well, I got married to a guy from up here. Jonathan Hamilton. We had a couple of kids. We got a divorce two years ago. I work at a dental office a little way from here. My kids are with their dad for the night. So, I stop by here and kick back a couple of beers when they leave. I didn't expect to run into you here tonight."

Tano was finished talking to her. "Well, good to see you." He turned and took a gulp of the beer. Scarlet continued to stand by him, moving closer until her chest brushed the top of his right arm. She was coming on to him. He could smell her overwhelming perfume.

"How about you and I have another 'date' tonight? You remember that time we were together?" She reached up and touched his cheek with the back of her hand. The disgusting memory of being with her before was becoming more vivid and he was repulsed by her.

"No. I really just want to sit here alone tonight."

"Well, that's no fun." Scarlett was still rubbing her breast on his arm.

"Hey, Scarlett. Good to catch up. But I have a girl. So it isn't happening with you."

Tano surprised himself. He used to have a girl. A special girl. A unique one-of-a-kind girl. Not anymore.

Scarlet took a step back and put her hands on her ample hips and said, "Well, okay then, I guess. See ya around. Maybe at the BHS reunion?"

"Maybe." Tano would not look at her and finished off the beer. "Another beer here?" he said to the bartender. Out of the corner of his eye, he saw her wander away and start to hang on one of the mountain man pool players. *That's one desperate chick.*

While Tano finished the second beer, the lyrics of the country music continued to speak to him. Thomas Rhett's cover of "When I Was Your Man" quietly mocked him. He laid some cash on the bar and walked out to the Corvette and raised the convertible top for the drive home. He saw Scarlet standing near the doorway of the bar smoking and watching him.

He drove slowly down the canyon toward home. White moonlight reflected off the hood of the car. *What do I do about Holly? I don't deserve her. I want her back. Maybe this is how it was supposed to be. Maybe it was supposed to end on that dirt road main street five years ago. How will I ever know?*

The End

LIST OF SONGS

INTRODUCTION

- "Chevy Van" by Sammy Johns. GRC, 1973.

CHAPTER 1

- "Badge" by Cream. Atco, 1969.

CHAPTER 2

- "Free" by Zac Brown Band. Atlantic Nashville, 2010.

CHAPTER 4

- "Purple Rain" by Prince and the Revolution. Warner Bros., 1984.
- Nocturne no. 20 in C-sharp Minor by Frederic Chopin, 1870.

CHAPTER 5

- "Turn the Page" by Bob Seger. Capitol, 1973.
- "Running on Empty" by Jackson Browne. Asylum Records, 1978.
- "Pink Cadillac" by Bruce Springsteen. Columbia, 1984.
- "Moves Like Jagger" by Maroon 5, feat. Christina Aguilera. A&M Octone, 2011.
- "Harder to Breathe" by Maroon 5. J. Octone, 2002.

Chapter 7

- "Midnight Rider" by Allman Brothers Band. Capricorn, 1971.

Chapter 8

- "Sangria" by Blake Shelton. Warner Bros. Nashville, 2015.

Chapter 10

- "Girl Like You" by Jason Aldean. Broken Bow, 2018.
- "Blue Ain't Your Color" by Keith Urban. Capitol Nashville, 2016.
- "Simple Man" by Lynyrd Skynyrd. Sounds of the South, 1973.
- "Saturday Night Special" by Lynyrd Skynyrd. MCA, 1975.

Chapter 13

- "Under Pressure" by Queen and David Bowie. EMI Elektra, 1981.

Chapter 15

- "Cadillac Ranch" by Bruce Springsteen. Columbia, 1981.

Chapter 16

- "The Devil Went Down to Georgia" by Charlie Daniels Band. Epic, 1979.
- "Dust in the Wind" by Kansas. Kirshner, 1978.
- "Hallelujah" by Jeff Buckley. Columbia, 1994.

Chapter 18

- "What's Your Name?" by Lynyrd Skynyrd. MCA, 1977.
- "Smoke on the Water" by Deep Purple. Warner Bros., 1973.
- "Heart of Stone" by Rolling Stones. London Records, 1964.

- "We Gotta Get Out of This Place" by The Animals. MGM, 1965.
- "Lucky Man" by Emerson, Lake & Palmer. Cotillion, 1971.
- "Kashmir" by Led Zeppelin. Swan Song, 1975.
- "Lukenbach, Texas (Back to the Basics of Love)" by Waylon Jennings. RCA Records, 1977.

Chapter 19

- "Trust Me" by Janis Joplin. Columbia, 1971.
- "A Woman Left Lonely" by Janis Joplin. Columbia, 1971.
- "Maybe" by Janis Joplin. Columbia, 1969.
- "Gunpowder & Lead" by Miranda Lambert. Columbia Nashville, 2008.

Chapter 21

- "Donna the Prima Donna" by Dion. Columbia, 1963.
- "Donna" by Ritchie Valens. Del-Fi, 1958.

Chapter 23

- "Drive" by The Cars. Elektra, 1984.

Chapter 26

- "I Can't Make You Love Me" by Bonnie Raitt. Capitol, 1991.
- "Bell Bottom Blues" by Derek and the Dominos. Atco, 1971.
- "Whiskey and You" by Chris Stapleton. Mercury Nashville, 2015.
- "Faithfully" by Journey. Columbia, 1983.

Chapter 27

- "Colorado" by Flying Burrito Brothers. A & M, 1971.

CHAPTER 32

- "September" by Earth, Wind & Fire. Columbia, 1978.
- "Night Fever" by Bee Gees. RSO, 1978.
- "How Deep is Your Love" by Bee Gees. RSO, 1977.

CHAPTER 37

- "Rocky Mountain Way" by Joe Walsh and Barnstorm. AMC-Dunhill, 1973.
- "Gravity" by Sara Bareilles. Epic, 2009.

CHAPTER 41

- "Fly Over States" by Jason Aldean. Broken Bow, 2012.
- "Here Comes My Girl" by Tom Petty and the Heartbreakers. Backstreet, 1980.
- "Silver Springs" by Fleetwood Mac. Warner Bros./Reprise, 1976.

CHAPTER 42

- "We're an American Band" by Grand Funk Railroad. Capitol, 1973.

CHAPTER 43

- "Craving You" by Thomas Rhett, feat. Maren Morris. Valory, 2017.
- "Strawberry Wine" by Deana Carter. Capitol Nashville, 1996.

CHAPTER 44

- "Between an Old Memory and Me" by Travis Tritt. Warner Bros., 1994.
- "When I Was Your Man" by Thomas Rhett. Valory, 2015.

ACKNOWLEDGEMENTS

I would like to extend my gratitude to Taylor Morris for her valuable suggestions and outstanding copyediting. Deep gratitude goes to #33 for solid support and collaboration. And a heartfelt thank you goes to my family and friends who have so enthusiastically embraced my new writing passion.

CPSIA information can be obtained
at www.ICGtesting.com
Printed in the USA
FSHW012221031120
75419FS

9 781977 234506